Death
and the
Icebox

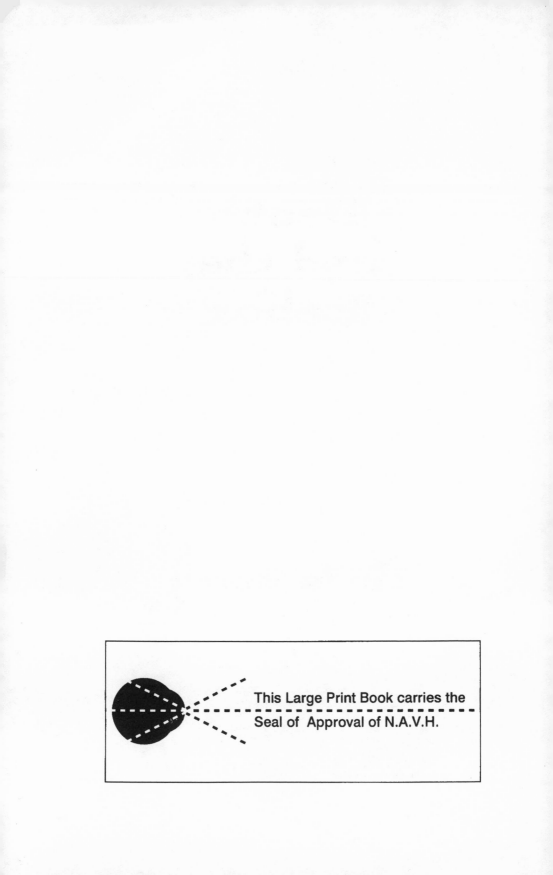

This Large Print Book carries the
Seal of Approval of N.A.V.H.

Death and the Icebox

A Trudy Roundtree Mystery

Linda Berry

WHEELER
PUBLISHING

Published in 2004 by arrangement with Tekno Books and Ed Gorman.

Wheeler Large Print Cozy Mystery.

The text of this Large Print edition is unabridged.
Other aspects of the book may vary from the original edition.

Set in 16 pt. Plantin by Christina S. Huff.

Printed in the United States on permanent paper.

Library of Congress Control Number: 2003115453
ISBN 1-58724-616-3 (lg. print : sc : alk. paper)

Death
and the
Icebox

As the Founder/CEO of NAVH, the only national health agency solely devoted to those who, although not totally blind, have an eye disease which could lead to serious visual impairment, I am pleased to recognize Thorndike Press★ as one of the leading publishers in the large print field.

Founded in 1954 in San Francisco to prepare large print textbooks for partially seeing children, NAVH became the pioneer and standard setting agency in the preparation of large type.

Today, those publishers who meet our standards carry the prestigious "Seal of Approval" indicating high quality large print. We are delighted that Thorndike Press is one of the publishers whose titles meet these standards. We are also pleased to recognize the significant contribution Thorndike Press is making in this important and growing field.

Lorraine H. Marchi, L.H.D.
Founder/CEO
NAVH

★ Thorndike Press encompasses the following imprints: Thorndike, Wheeler, Walker and Large Print Press.

Acknowledgements

There's no way for me to thank by name all the people who have encouraged and helped me with my writing, but there are some broad categories: my family, whose inveterate story-telling made me love stories and want to try to capture some of them on paper; the Denver Woman's Press Club, whose members are so versatile and talented that I've tried to deserve their esteem; my friends, who've read my stories and laughed over them.

There are, however, some individuals: my cousin, Johnny Shuman, Chief of Police in Swainsboro, Georgia, whose fund of stories about police work is unending, and who can tell 'em like nobody else; my husband, Jerry Berry, whose unfailing patience and support are priceless gifts; the Reverend Marshall K. Singletary of the Reidsville (Georgia) United Methodist Church, who helped me imagine a memorial service for a long-dead person; Russell J. Rhoden, of *The Tattnall Journal*, who let me browse through years and years of past issues; my sister, Dr. Jackie Swensson, for meticulous proofreading; Bonnie McCune and Suzanne Young, critiquers and encouragers.

Occasionally a reader will identify what I thought was one of my more eccentric creations and say, "I know that woman!" That prompts the reminder that my stories are, after all, fiction and the characters do not have living counterparts.

Chapter 1

On the day that was to launch a murder investigation and take us on a jerky trip down Ogeechee's memory lane, I was still trying to make the most of a recent on-the-job injury. Several weeks earlier I had taken a fall while following a hastily exiting patron of the Jive Joint who had gotten overstimulated and done some damage to the premises, which caused the proprietor to speed dial the Ogeechee Police Department, which brought me to the scene. When I took a tumble because of a carelessly discarded beer bottle, I heard a crack that had nothing to do with the flimsy construction of the door at the Jive Joint and, after the hospital's emergency room attendant cheerfully categorized it as a break caused by a FOOSH (Fall On Out-Stretched Hand), my left wrist and most of my hand were trapped in a cast. Since I'm left-handed, this is a real handicap, although, as I tell Hen, not as bad as it could be. Having spent my thirty-plus years accommodating to life as a left-hander in a right-handed world, I'm not as helpless as the average right-hander would be with a broken right wrist. I can brush my teeth with the wrong hand, for instance, and it helps that I'm pretty low maintenance. I usually don't wear much makeup, and I figure if I keep my naturally wavy brown hair short and clean I'll look as good as I need to.

My name is Trudy Roundtree and so far I'm the only female police officer the town of Ogeechee, Georgia (pop. 3412) has ever had. This situation is both good and bad.

The good part is that I have a perverse streak that thrives on being moderately rebellious, and moderate rebellion passes for flaming rebellion in this conservative little place.

The bad part is that the Chief of Police is my cousin, Henry Huckabee. Hen is in a constant turmoil over what he must see as the conflicting demands it puts on him to be my divinely ordained protector (since he's my nearest male relative and a few years older than I am) and also my boss in the dangerous field of police work. It is true, as he told me at the get-go, that the Ogeechee Police Department spends more time answering service calls than tracking down criminals and preventing crime, but that only means that when there is real danger it may take us by surprise.

Come to think of it, maybe Hen's turmoil is also one of the good parts of my job, since I consider it part of my life's work to raise his consciousness where the role of women in modern-day life is concerned. I know he'll be a better person for it. At any rate, since our grandmother and his mother (my Aunt Lulu) ganged up on him and made him hire me in the first place a few years ago, I think we both think he's stuck with me as long as I want the job and as long as I don't actually commit murder — or something worse, like maybe deciding to shack up with a twelve-year-old neo-Nazi drug dealer. I had come back home from Atlanta with a broken heart and I was slow to find my way back to what would pass for a reasonable life for a single thirty-something female. To everybody's surprise (and to Hen's disgust) it turned out that I like being a police officer.

Besides the fact that it gets on Hen's nerves, one of the things I like about my job is that I'm supposed to spend a lot of time out and around, being a visible reminder of law and order. Hen figures if a patrol car doesn't register sixty to seventy miles a day (a hundred or more on a night shift) the officer on patrol isn't doing the job right, the job being to keep in circulation and keep your eyes open. I have no trouble living with that rule. I grew up in Ogeechee, so it means I can legitimately do a lot of visiting with friends and acquaintances while I'm on the clock and creating a wholesome sense of a police presence in the community.

Lately my injury was causing a new and innocent kind of conflict for Hen. For him to admit I was coping well — better than he himself might have — would have been to give me credit for being more than a helplessly dependent female relative. On the other hand, since my injury was

11

unquestionably job-related, for him to claim I was not coping well would mean putting me on sick leave but continuing to pay me. When the sick leave ran out we'd have to face another possibility, like using my vacation time. This option didn't appeal to either one of us, since there's very little fat in either the OPD budget or my personal one.

In a flash of brilliance — and even I have never claimed that Hen isn't smart — Hen decided to redeem part of my recovery time by sending me up to the Georgia Public Safety Training Center at Forsythe to homicide school. We have few homicides in Ogeechee, very few that call for particularly heads-up detective work, but I share Hen's belief that education is never wasted. He likes doing what he can to create the best police force possible. And he knows and appreciates the fact that I like to learn. The way he put it to me, if I recall, was along the lines of, "You can go up to Forsythe and get on their nerves for a while, raise their level of consciousness or whatever it is that makes your life worth livin' and leave me in peace till you get back to some degree of usefulness around here."

So I arranged for Teri, Hen's wife, to come feed my cats and I went off to Forsythe, never imagining how soon I'd be able to flaunt some of my new knowledge.

Hen probably enjoyed my absence as much as I enjoyed the course. When I got back he pretended to ignore my injury but continued to assign me to low energy, safe, and minimally active jobs at the station house, along with what we officially call welfare checks. These welfare checks have nothing to do with income from the county. They are to make sure that there's nothing amiss when neighbors notice newspapers spilling out of somebody's delivery box. After I kicked up enough and promised to be quick to call in for backup if it looked like anything interesting was happening, I was also allowed to go on patrol. On that particular Thursday afternoon, I was patrolling. I had put some of the requisite miles on my cruiser by driving to the south end of town where a couple of my friends, Eric and Stacy Riggs, were clearing ground to begin building their new home.

It was late June, the middle of a beautiful day, beginning to get hot and muggy. Stacy had pulled their pickup into the shade and we were sitting on the tailgate drinking some of the iced tea she'd brought out for Eric and the men he had helping him. Across the road and back toward town we could see clouds of dust rising and listlessly drifting along behind where Pootie Winkle was plowing under the last of his onion crop. The smell was enough to make my mouth water for an onion sandwich to go with my iced tea.

Corn was coming along nicely in the field between us and the old Riggs farmhouse, where

Eric's mother still lived, and the same slight breeze that was bringing the onion scent from Pootie agitated the leaves and the developing tassels on the cornstalks and created a soft rustle that seemed cooling because it sounded like running water.

As far as I could tell, except for my growing impatience to be rid of the constant chafing and nuisance of my cast, God was in Her heaven and all was right with the world. Sitting in the shade and watching Eric, who was out in the sun supervising a couple of men with a front loader, added to my sense of well-being.

"You're sure you want to live this close to your mother-in-law?" I asked, carefully positioning my elbow on the side of the truck, with my hand sticking straight up. One of the unpleasant surprises connected with my injury was discovering how hard it is to find a comfortable position for a cast.

"I don't think it'll be too bad," Stacy said. I could see her measuring the quarter mile between where we sat and the house where Eric grew up. "With the woods between us, and the back road into town, she won't necessarily be able to keep us under surveillance." She grinned. "That's why we decided to build on the dump. It's the most private place on the farm."

I could see her point. Farmers need a place to put their trash, but hardly anybody, except the really trashy ones or the ones who want to make some kind of a point about zoning and government infringement on individual liberties, puts the dump where it'll be an eyesore. The Riggs trash pile was well hidden from casual view, down a narrow lane overhung with trees. The lane turned off the dirt road that went by the farmhouse.

We watched as the front loader dumped another scoopful of years of accumulated debris into the back of a truck that would take it to the county landfill.

"What sign you reckon Miz Riggs is?" I asked.

Stacy giggled. Lately, we'd been amusing ourselves by creating a specifically Ogeechee "horrorscope" that had nothing to do with the relative positions of the sun, moon, and stars, and everything to do with our high opinion of our own wit. Under our sporadically-evolving system, sharing a birthday with somebody was no guarantee you'd share the same sign. So far we had Hen down as Catfish. ("If you are a Catfish, your milieu is the lowest levels of society. You feed off of the muck and murk of life. Your unsophisticated image serves you well. People who can get past your fearsome exterior may find you surprisingly agreeable.") I thought that was fair, since Hen does enjoy acting like a hick and giving people a chance to misjudge him. He's especially gratified when a member of the criminal element underestimates him.

Stacy and I had also been working on the wording for Vidalia Onions, my category. ("Vidalia Onions are recognized and appreciated everywhere they go for their sweetness and adaptability." Stacy insisted the definition needed more development, but I felt we were on the right track.)

"I'm thinking maybe Miz Riggs is Sugar Cane," Stacy said.

"Why's that?"

She cut her eyes toward the Riggs house and lowered her voice. Humor is humor and wit is wit, but prudence is prudence, and I guessed her horrorscope of her mother-in-law wasn't going to be completely flattering. "If you are Sugar Cane," Stacy said, "your natural sweetness is sometimes hard to extract from the tough fiber of your morality."

"Needs work," I said, when it became obvious she had no more to say.

"Yes." She sighed.

"Something about grinding, or grinding down?" I suggested, vividly picturing an old-time cane mill I had once seen. They use tractors these days, but the old ones had mules walking around and around stone grinders, a farmer feeding cane between the grinding stones, and juice running out into a barrel. "How about, 'If you aren't careful, people will decide it isn't worth the effort'?"

"Uh huh. You're gettin' there, Trudy. Grinding. That's good. I know she's a good woman, who wouldn't deliberately do anybody any harm, but she does grind me down."

"Something in particular?"

16

"Right now the big thing is she wants us to live with her instead of building our own house. She keeps grinding away at it, acting like she doesn't even know we've got a contractor and everything."

"Her house is certainly big enough," I said.

"Trudy!"

"I'm not saying I think it's a good idea, but there would certainly be room."

"Not only do I not want to live with my mother-in-law, I do not want to live in an old farmhouse. It probably won't cost as much to build a new one as it would to fix that one up. You know that."

I had to agree. The house I live in, my house, is more than a hundred years old. It was my grandmother's house, where Hen's mother and my daddy grew up. When Grandma died, she left it to me. Having lived in more modern places, I'm well aware of some of the shortcomings of the place, and every now and then I focus on something I'd really like to have re-painted, re-placed, re-built, re-furbished, or renovated, but I've had a hard time mustering the energy and the money to tackle it. A recent brainstorm, I think, was to enlist Teri to help me make a plan of attack and line up the people to do some of the work. Teri's a great organizer, but we haven't been the best of friends, so it's too soon to tell if that's going to work out.

"Why are we whispering?" I asked. "Even if

Miz Riggs is home, I don't think she could hear us from here."

"When kept cool, Vidalia Onions are long-lasting, but they sometimes lose their crispness and develop an unpleasant sliminess that people find distasteful," Stacy said.

That wasn't fair to me or the onions. "Well, pardon me!" I think Stacy is Grits. ("Grits are everywhere in the south, so ubiquitous that they are often undervalued. They almost always blend in comfortably, but are not to everyone's taste. People who don't grow up with grits may find them hard to stomach.")

"Anyway, she's not home," Stacy said. "I think she went to see Miss Sarah. How's she doin'?"

Miss Sarah Kennedy, who taught history to me and Stacy and Eric and everybody else at Ogeechee High School for at least a hundred and fifty years, had recently had a hip replacement. Naturally, with my new status as Shut-In Patrol (which the ER attendant would probably have wanted to call SIP), Stacy knew I'd be up-to-date.

"They've got her walking, if you can call it that, shuffling along with a walker. She knows she has to do it and she's trying to keep a good attitude, but it's hard. Aunt Lulu and I are going over to see her this evening. You ought to go by when you get a chance. I know she'd appreciate it."

"That place is so depressing," Stacy said.

"Every time I go, I see somebody I know — or used to know before they lost their minds."

"Well, Miss Sarah's mind is fine," I assured her. "She's spending her time reading and whipping through books of puzzles. Remember how she used to make us study history backwards?"

"I remember how hard it was."

"Maybe, but interesting, too. It taught me that whatever happens — attitudes, events, laws — everything has roots in the past. Things don't just happen out of the blue. I never thought about it before, but studying history her way is a lot like working those logic puzzles."

"No wonder I wasn't good at it," Stacy said.

"She won't hold that against you. Go see her."

"Maybe I'll wait till she goes home."

"She won't need the company so much then," I argued.

Having no reasonable rebuttal to my flawless logic, Stacy-Grits ignored me. We quit arguing and focused on watching as Eric tried to steady an old refrigerator and guide it into the scoop of the frontloader. It must have been exactly the wrong size or shape. Finally he gave up trying to get it into the scoop mechanically, and he and one of his helpers tried to wrestle it into place. At first they seemed to succeed with that effort, but as the scoop moved, the refrigerator fell away, too soon. It missed the dump truck and dropped to the ground. I heard a curse, stifled because of the presence of ladies, I presumed, as the men dodged out of the way.

On impact, a strap that had been encircling the refrigerator, holding the door closed, broke, and the door swung open. When the dust had settled, the men moved toward the refrigerator, then recoiled. I heard a completely un-stifled curse and then one of the men asked the universe in general, "What in blazes IS it?"

Stacy and I perked up.

Then, "Somebody better call the po-lice."

"Hey, Trudy!" Eric yelled. "Come here!"

Something in his tone kept me from kicking into the mulish mode I instinctively adopt when somebody tells me to do something and forgets to say "please." I slid carefully off the tailgate, holding my cast high and trying not to jolt it, and joined the men around the refrigerator. Stacy was right behind me.

I stared with them into the cavity, and the sight was so bizarre that it took my brain a second or two to make any kind of sense out of what I saw. Even then, my first thought, immediately chasing the perception of the musty but not entirely repulsive smell you might find in any old refrigerator that hadn't been opened in a while, was to wonder what a department store mannequin was doing in an old refrigerator. A lot of blondish hair, a body that seemed to be sculpted out of soap. Even as we stared, the smell grew sharper and more repulsive, suggesting swampy depths, forest mold, and something less pleasant. I realized we were looking at an oddly transfigured, curiously preserved, human body there in the old refrigerator in the Riggs trash heap.

We all backed away and gulped for clean air.

I drew myself up as tall as I could and summoned my maximum hardened, blasé, official manner, in what I realized later was an imitation of Henry Huckabee, hardened, blasé Chief of Police.

"Well, folks," I said. "It looks like my coffee break's over and y'all are through playing in this particular dirt pile for a while. Keep back from that refrigerator."

I turned toward my car and my cell phone. They all stayed respectfully back from that refrigerator, but they couldn't keep their eyes off it.

Chapter 2

Eric, Stacy, and the heavy machine operators sat on the tailgate in the shade, drinking iced tea, and watched me move into what is certainly the first, and usually the most crucial, phase of an investigation — securing the scene for painstaking examination by the experts. We know we have only one good chance at a crime scene before it becomes contaminated, so we take our time with it. I used up a bunch of yellow police tape going from tree to tree to encircle a generous area around the refrigerator, including the road and the rest of the dump.

A basic tenet of crime-scene investigation is what is formally known as Locard's Exchange Principle or "cross-transfer of evidence" — the principle that the criminal always leaves something behind at a crime scene (footprints, hair, a shell casing) and always takes something away (blood, dirt, fibers). In this case, considering that it looked like the crime had taken place quite a while in the past, there wasn't much chance that whatever the criminal left or took away would ever be discovered. A special problem of this crime scene was that there was no way to tell what of the accumulated trash of years might have something to do with the crime. The idea that we could examine an un-contaminated scene after all that time was laughable — practically punny in the context of a garbage dump. Nevertheless, I kept everybody outside my charmed yellow-tape circle while we waited for Hen and whatever other officers he could round up, including a team of technicians from Statesboro.

I wouldn't let Eric pay off the helpers and send them away — not that they'd have gone — so conversation was a little strained while we waited. It wasn't long before the others got there and we followed the book with respect to investigating the scene, even though the value was doubtful — photographs of the refrigerator and its contents, from every conceivable angle, before and after the body was removed; photographs of the earlier position of the refrigerator in relation to the other garbage; measurements from here to there and there to here; and, of course, the examination of the body itself.

She was wearing — still wearing because the airless environment in the closed refrigerator had kept them from rotting — blue-and-white-striped bell-bottom slacks and a heavily embroidered blouse. The blouse was still tucked into the waistband. I was sorry to see no jewelry — which can sometimes be traced — no shoes, nothing else. No cause of death was apparent to my eye. Maybe she'd smothered. I shuddered at the thought of her being shut up in there alive, unable to get out of a refrigerator built in the days when the door had to be opened from the outside.

By now, the smell had become offensive even at a distance, as though the decomposition that had been put on hold was making up for lost time as soon as the warm air of the June morning got to it. The body was deteriorating rapidly now. I stepped well back and let the technicians remove the body, which they lifted by the clothing, surprisingly intact. Then, holding a rubber glove in my clumsy left hand, I managed to maneuver it onto my good right hand; stretching a glove over the cast on my left hand was another challenge, not made easier by the sticky heat. Finally gloved, I bent over the body and touched a forearm. It had a slippery-slidey texture that felt something like poking a finger into shortening. I was grateful for my recent homicide training and called on that discipline to keep me focused on investigating instead of gagging.

"Let me take her prints," I said. "We won't have 'em for long."

"Have at it, lady," the youngish, greenish technician said. "I'll watch your technique from over here."

"She ain't no lady, son," Hen told him with a grin, proving he pays more attention to me than he likes to let on.

"Automatically calling all women 'ladies' may seem to be polite, but it's as dumb as automatically calling all men 'gentlemen,' " I've explained more than once. "What really gets my goat is calling men 'men' and women 'ladies,' like we're some subspecies that needs to be talked down to. If you call somebody a lady or a gentleman, it ought to mean more than just biology." Even if what I'm saying doesn't make sense to him, even if he quotes me just to get my goat, at least now I know he sometimes listens.

The entire crew watched — admiringly, I felt sure — as, one at a time, I slipped the skin off the corpse's fingertips — it came off easily, like the skin of a peach you've dipped in boiling water — and fit it over one of my own fingers. Normally — if "normal" can ever apply in situations where this technique is called for — I'd have used my left index finger. With my right hand, I couldn't do it with the grace and style I'd have liked, considering my audience, but I did manage to roll each of the corpse's fragile fingertips in the ink and onto the fingerprint card.

I don't mind telling you I was glad when I was finished and could back away.

"Glad to see you weren't wasting my money up at Forsythe," Hen said, by way of applause, as I stripped off the nasty hot gloves and turned aside for a good deep breath of the fresh, onion-scented air.

"My pleasure," I said. I figured I'd done enough showing off for one day, so I was content with watching the others work until the last

25

step — putting everything they'd found inside the refrigerator into a body bag to go, very special delivery, to a forensic pathologist in Atlanta. Much of what could be learned from the body would be learned in a laboratory, not with the naked eye of even the most well-educated, most highly-trained observer in a garbage dump. They took the refrigerator along, too.

As the last of the technicians drove away, leaving the small audience on the tailgate and the circle of yellow tape, Hen turned to Eric.

"Just in case I need to point it out to you, you're through pushing things back and forth on this site until further notice."

"But, I've rented this —"

Hen interrupted. "Further notice will be when one of my deppities comes out and officially removes that there yellow tape. You understand that?"

"How long will that be?"

"Well, now, son." Hen's a good five years older than Eric. "It's hard to say. It will be when we are reasonably confident there is nothing more we can learn from looking through your garbage dump. What we in po-lice work call examining the site. Until that tape comes down, now, I don't want to hear of anybody — anybody," he emphasized, "messin' around over here. Any questions?" He took the time to look at Eric, Stacy, and the two other men as though memorizing their faces for a potential police line-up and waited for a nod or a "yes" from each one.

"All right, then." Then he turned to me. "I reckon we might as well go have a talk with Miz Riggs now, as long as we're this close."

"My mother?" Eric was dumbfounded.

"This is part of her farm, ain't it?" Hen asked. When he says "ain't," even more than when he calls a near-contemporary "son," I know he's slipping into that folksy, neighborly mode he uses to mask his mustard-sharp intelligence and make himself appear harmless. He seems to do it by instinct, and sometimes it works even on people who know him well and should know better, like me. And Eric. And Eric's mother.

Eric nodded, acknowledging family ownership of the farm, the dump, and the body.

"Seems only polite to let her know what we found over here, don't you think?" Hen asked. "Y'all can come if you think you can behave yourselves."

Chapter 3

Eric and Stacy went with us to his mother's house and he led the way into the front hall.

"Mama?" He called. "We brought you some company."

Ethel Riggs, who could not possibly have been unaware of all the commotion at the dump site, appeared from the back of the house looking mildly curious.

"Y'all come sit in here," she said. "Eric, you be sure to wipe your feet, now, coming from that nasty old dump." I'm sure she thought she was being tactful to single out Eric, assuming the rest of us would take the hint and wipe our feet, too.

She watched while we all dusted ourselves off, then showed us into her parlor. Of course, Mrs. Riggs was too modern to call it that — she might have come as far as "sitting room" — but "parlor" fits. It was a room just off the front hall. It smelled musty from lack of use, but it most certainly was not dusty. Small, stiff, uncomfortable, it would always be presentable even when the more heavily used rooms toward the back of the house might not be. It would be saved for formal occasions like a visit from the preacher or the Avon lady or the Chief of Police on official business.

"Well, Miz Riggs," Hen began, seating himself in the place of honor she had indicated, a thoroughly overstuffed sofa with a back so low that it could not possibly have been comfortable, even for someone less bulky than Hen, even if it hadn't been covered in plastic, which it was. Hen's muscular two hundred pounds (give or take) didn't stand a chance. Stacy took one of a pair of pretty chairs with plain cane bottoms. Assuming she'd know which of the chairs were fit to sit in, I took the other one. Mrs. Riggs and Eric took the two chairs that matched the sofa. These chairs were plastic-covered, too. I wondered what she was protecting them against or saving them for.

"We're here on official business, Miz Riggs," Hen said.

"I thought you might be," she said. She cast a glance around the room, possibly to make sure we all had our feet on the floor and were sitting up straight, before adding, "What can I do for you?"

I realized she seemed nervous, and attributed it to the fact that Emily Post's book of etiquette did not address how to behave when entertaining the police after they've become interested in your garbage dump. No matter how socially rigid she was in normal circumstances, and I knew from Stacy that she could be a real stickler, this would not have come up before.

29

"Well, Miz Riggs," Hen began again. He'd given up trying to lean back and relax and was now leaning forward, sitting spraddle-legged with his hands planted on his thighs. "You've noticed all the ruckus down the road."

"Yes, I have."

"I don't want to upset you, now, but the fact is we found a body over there where Eric and Stacy are fixin' to build."

"Oh, my goodness," she said. "A human body, you mean?"

"Yes, ma'am."

She looked at Eric, not at Stacy. "I told them there was no call for them to build over there," she said, as though that was the point. "And this proves it."

"Well, now," Hen said mildly, "if they hadn't started gettin' ready to build and torn into that dump like that, we still wouldn't know some poor soul was waiting out there for a Christian burial."

"If people are killing people over there they don't have any business living there. I'm an old woman. I can't take care of myself. Eric, we'll all be safer if you live right here with me."

"Mama . . ." Eric began helplessly.

Hen interrupted. "I can see how you'd be upset with something like that turning up right down the road, but whatever happened to this woman happened a long time ago. I'm sure you're perfectly safe here."

30

"But they will have to stop building, won't they?" she asked.

"They'll have to stop working there till we're satisfied we've got whatever evidence there is to be got. This will be our top priority till we settle what looks like some pretty old business."

"You take whatever time you need," she said generously.

"We want to see if you can help us out, tell us anything that will help," Hen said.

"All I know about it," she said, "is that I told them not to build over there."

I had a vision of a mule patiently pacing around in a circle, grinding sugar cane, and decided to intervene. To keep myself from looking at Stacy and to remind Hen, gently, of my presence and the fact that I should be the officer in charge of investigation since I was first on the scene, I spoke up.

"The body has been there for quite a while, Miz Riggs. Right now we don't know how long, or who it might have been. Do you have any ideas?"

"Me? Why would I? Why would you think I'd know anything about somebody dead?" She looked genuinely puzzled.

Hen persisted. "Can you remember any strange goings-on down there?"

"All kinds of strange goin's-on, if you ask me. Havin' that road back there was an out-and-out invitation to trouble."

"Tell us about it," Hen invited. A good inter-

31

rogator relies on ambiguity to conceal from the interogatee exactly how much he knows. Taking this approach with Ethel Riggs was instinctive for Hen, I was sure. Not for a second did I imagine he thought she knew anything about the body.

"What do you want me to tell you?" she asked.

"Whatever you can," Hen said. Along with ambiguity, patience is a virtue in an interrogator. I keep meaning to work on patience, but it would probably be a waste of time. Everybody knows Vidalia Onions have a short season.

To my surprise, Hen's ambiguity and persistence paid off. Mrs. Riggs had found a topic besides Eric and Stacy's new house that appealed to her. "I don't ever go back there. If somebody dumped a body back there, I don't know anything about it. We used to use it — Woody did. Goodness knows I tried to get him to clear it out, but he wouldn't. I wouldn't have minded so much if it had been just our trash, but it was a dump before I ever married Woody; his daddy started it, so there wasn't much hope I could talk him out of it, and Woody let his friends use it, too. They all liked having a place for their trash no matter how much I didn't like people hauling stuff in there. I can't say it smelled — at least not to where I could smell it — but that wasn't the idea as far as I was concerned. Like I said, I never went back there, with all the snakes and animals and tramps and what-all. If it wasn't for gettin' to the pond, the road could grow clean up as far as I'm concerned. That's all I know about the dump. The one good thing I can see about Eric building back there is that they're finally clearing that out. About time! But I didn't kill anybody and I don't know anything about any bodies, if that's what you want to know."

She came to an abrupt stop, catching Hen off guard. His eyes had begun to glaze over under her torrent.

"Now, Miz Riggs, we aren't accusing you of killin' anybody or knowin' anything about the body," he said.

"Well, then!" she huffed. She seemed more at ease now, as though she'd gotten something off her chest with that tirade. Maybe it made her feel better to be on record as knowing nothing about the body.

Hen continued. "But you can see how it would be kind of obvious for us to talk to you, it being your property. To put it another way, it would be a bad lapse in good policin' for us not to talk to you about it at all. You can see that, can't you?"

"Of course I can," she said.

Hen leaned back, apparently still hoping to find a comfortable position, then quickly came forward again. "Let's just talk about the place where they found the body."

"I've told you everything I know about that place."

"When you say you don't go back there, does

that mean never or hardly ever?" I tapped my notepad and hoped she'd think I'd been taking down her every word.

She frowned at me. "I wouldn't say that, not 'never,' but I can't think of any particular time I ever went any further than the pond. Whoever I have doing clean-up work out in the yard or around the place might take stuff back there, but not me."

"There's an old refrigerator back there," Hen said. "You know anything about that?"

"A refrigerator? A Frigidaire?"

"Yes, ma'am. Now, how would you know that?"

"Woody put it out there when we got our new one. We got that old icebox from his mother and I never did like it. Some of the shelves were broken — Woody fixed them with electrical tape and felt real smart about it but it looked just as trashy as all get-out and I hated it. It was still running when I finally got him to get me one I liked. Served me right, I guess. The new one didn't last near as long. Of course, we got fancy when we got a new one — with an ice maker and all — and I think the more parts they have the more likely it is for something to go wrong. If it wasn't some sort of problem with the ice maker, it was something else. I've already had to re-place the new one, but I didn't do it till after Woody was gone and I didn't put it out in the dump; I made the store that sold me the new one haul the old one off."

Grind, grind. Maybe water torture was a better image than a cane mill. I began to wonder if Stacy wasn't making a mistake letting Eric build only a quarter of a mile from Ethel Riggs. If she was Sugar Cane, she'd already been turned into syrup and it was running off over the place and sticking things together, definitely gumming up the works. I tried to act alert.

"When did you get the new refrigerator, Mrs. Riggs?" I asked.

"Oh, just a couple of years ago."

That didn't make sense. Oh. Of course.

"I mean the other new one. When did the old Frigidaire go to the dump?"

"Oh. Well, let me see. I ought to be able to figure it out. We got married in fifty-eight and I think the new one was an anniversary present but I'm not sure which anniversary. It was after Eric so maybe I can think how old he was. Let me see, now, I'm pretty sure he wasn't just a baby, because I remember putting baby bottles in the door of the old icebox."

She turned to Eric, whose baby bottle days were more than thirty years in the past. "Were you old enough to remember that? Not that there'd be any reason a little boy would re-member something like a new icebox, no matter how important it was to me."

"People call them refrigerators these days, Mama," Eric said, reminding me of a conversa-tion I'd once had with Hen and Dwight over the difference between a hubcap and a wheelcover.

"But, no, ma'am," he added respectfully. "I can't say for sure I do remember the old one, but I know you had the new one by the time I started school because you'd put my papers up on the front of it with magnets, and the front of it was squared off, not rounded on the corners and the front like the one we just found."

"Yes, I remember buying those little magnets so I could put your artwork up." She smiled at her son and turned to Hen. "I never liked clutter, so I never did put recipes and cartoons and newspaper clippings of Erma Bombeck on the front of the refrigerator like so many people do, but of course Eric's school papers were different. Eric's right. We had the new one by then."

"When would that be?" Hen asked.

"He started kindergarten in 1965," Mrs. Riggs said. She seemed enormously pleased with herself, as though she'd solved the whole mystery for us.

"So the Frigidaire had been out there since . . . when would you say?" Hen prompted.

"Not much before then," Mrs. Riggs said.

When it became clear she wasn't going to be able to do any better than that, I wrote "1965?" on my pad. It was reasonable to think the refrigerator was the body's only resting place, which meant the body could have been put there any time in the last third of a century.

Hen turned to Eric. "Your mother says she never goes back to the dump. What about you?"

"Not for years." He darted a glance and a grin in his mother's direction. "I played back there a lot when I was a kid."

"Eric!"

"Yes, Mama, I know I wasn't supposed to. Truth is, it was a heckuva lot more interesting than most places on the farm to me. Probably would have been even if you hadn't tried to make it off limits."

Mrs. Riggs frowned at Eric and lapsed back into her earlier nervousness. Eric, drawing on childhood memories, grew chatty. His chattiness held together a lot better than his mother's as he explained to her. "Looking back, I can see why you didn't want us messin' around there, but it didn't make any sense at the time, not to boys. We just thought you didn't want us to have any fun."

"We?" Hen asked.

"You and that Eddie Beasley," Mrs. Riggs said, lips pursed.

Eric smiled at her. "That's right, Mama, me and that Eddie Beasley. Nobody bothered us, never even came lookin' for us. I guess it didn't occur to anybody that we'd be there, since we weren't supposed to. Eddie and I liked to mess around there, especially if we'd seen somebody go to the dump, and we'd go through whatever it was. We'd built us a fort back in the trees, used odds and ends, junk that people had dumped. We were everything from soldiers to cowboys in that fort." He laughed. "Found the wreck of it when we started clearing up for the house. Brought back memories, let me tell you!"

"Did your daddy know?" Mrs. Riggs asked, still miffed at him for disobeying her thirty years ago. Lucky for Woody Riggs he'd already gone on to his heavenly reward. Otherwise, he'd have been in for a tongue-lashing, I had no doubt.

"About our fort? Oh, no, ma'am. Don't blame Daddy. Eddie and I swore a blood oath to keep it a secret. We had piled stuff up around it so it would look like just another pile of trash, and when we were out there, if anybody came, we'd hide. As far as I know, nobody ever knew about it."

"I guess it's too late to give you a whipping over it," Mrs. Riggs said, regretfully, I thought.

"Yes, ma'am, but you'll probably get some satisfaction out of knowing I've learned my lesson. Haven't played back there in years."

His mother made a noise somewhere between a snort and a harrumph. "In fact," Eric went on, "now that I think back, I remember we did get a bad scare one day and after that we didn't go back much."

"You're lucky you got a bad scare that didn't hurt you," his mother said.

"Nothing like hindsight, is there? Looking back, I can see that what scared us wasn't nearly as likely to hurt us as some of the stuff we didn't have sense enough to be scared of — like the snakes and tramps and escaped convicts you were so worried about. We'd been down there all afternoon, setting up a battle of some kind, I imagine, and we heard somebody coming. We recognized Mr. Burkhalter's truck — Alvin Burkhalter — so we hid. We'd have hidden no matter who it was, 'cause we liked feeling like we were getting away with something and putting something over on the rest of the world, but since it was Mr. Burkhalter we really laid low. He was a friend of Daddy's and we were afraid he'd tell on us if he saw us. Besides that, we were scared of him."

"Scared of Alvin Burkhalter?" Mrs. Riggs asked, barely beating me to it. Alvin Burkhalter's one of the mainstays of the First Baptist Church of Ogeechee. A more upright, uptight man you'd never see. Then Mrs. Riggs answered her own question.

"Oh, yes. You're talking a long way back, before Alvin got saved."

"I don't know when that happened," Eric said, "but we thought he was pretty much a roughneck, and we did have enough sense to know that if he'd been drinking or something and caught us where we weren't supposed to be we might be in real trouble. He really spooked us that day — young and guilty as we were. He didn't just unload his stuff and take off like we expected him to, like people usually did. We took turns peeking out to see if he was still there — we were probably pretending he was some kind of Vietnamese Russian Red Army sniper or something — but he hung around and hung around, just like he was on to us and was waiting us out. You know how thrilling it is — or was when you were a kid — to scare yourself about things."

"No, I don't," Mrs. Riggs said, and that was that. But Hen nodded encouragingly and smiled at me. I knew Eric's reminiscing had reminded both of us of the little hideaways he'd shown me how to build in the woods next to Grandma's house, leaning branches against a tree trunk and covering them with pine needles.

Eric continued with a faraway look in his eye. "I wonder if Eddie remembers that? We were thrilled and scared for a while — peeking out to see if the enemy was still there. We thought maybe he was having a beer or something — beer cans showed up out there a lot, but he was prowling around too, like he was looking for us. By the time he finally left, we had gone from being thrilled and pretend-scared to being tired of it and really scared. On top of that, when he finally did leave and we scooted home, we were so late we both got in trouble. Daddy gave me holy hell!"

"Eric, you watch your language!"

He grinned at her. "Anyway, we didn't go down there very much after that, Mama. I guess you have Mr. Burkhalter to thank."

"I think I'll just do that, next time I see him," she said.

Hen, no doubt inspired by his overstuffed resting place, brought us back to the matter at hand.

"Eric, any chance you'd remember if that old refrigerator was there back then?"

"Oh, Lord! That poor soul got shut up in it and died!" Mrs. Riggs's exclamation hung in the air. She had finally made the connection between Hen's questions and the significance of the refrigerator.

Eric answered softly. "I don't remember it, but that doesn't prove anything. We wouldn't have been able to move it and use it for our hideout, so we wouldn't have been particularly interested in it. We had plumbing fixtures. No plumbing, but fixtures — a sink, a toilet — stuff people would take out there when they upgraded — like Daddy did with the refrigerator." He cut his eyes at his mother and added, "We loved to pee into that toilet."

She gave him a scorching look and pretended she hadn't heard. "This body you found," she asked Hen, "is it a tramp? A tramp killed by a wild animal?"

"No, ma'am," Hen told her. "Well, at this point, we can't swear it wasn't a tramp, and whoever it was might even have been killed by an animal, but it wasn't a wild animal that stuffed the body inside the refrigerator and tied a strap around it. We're looking at a murder. A very old murder."

"And it was in my icebox! I always told you

that was a bad place, Eric! You're lucky you weren't killed."

"Yes, ma'am," he said. "Maybe I am."

Hen lurched to his feet. "Well, Miz Riggs, you know where to find us if you think of anything that might be useful. I have a feelin' we're gone need all the help we can get if we're gone find out who that dead body used to be and how it got there."

"They do have to quit building, now, don't they?" she responded. Grind. Grind.

Eric and Stacy stayed behind as Mrs. Riggs ushered Hen and me out the front door.

"I think she did it," Hen confided as we walked to our cars. "A woman who'd keep chairs like that in her house, she'd be capable of anything." He was limping slightly, and flexing his shoulder muscles as he walked. "And did you notice how determined she is to have 'em quit diggin' around over there?"

I was pretty sure he was kidding. "Whoever it was probably got between Miz Riggs and her vacuum cleaner once too often. May turn out to be a cleaning lady who broke something," I suggested. "Or maybe she does know something and that's why she doesn't want them digging there."

He stopped flexing and gave me a thoughtful look.

"Just to be safe, when we do let 'em get back to work over here, I think I'll send you over to watch, in case any more bodies turn up."

"How can I ever thank you?" I asked.

"Oh, my aching back!" Hen complained.

"Can we sue Miz Riggs?" I asked.

"No. Not that. I was planning to take some vacation, starting tomorrow. Teri's gone kill me."

Or me, I thought. The Disney World vacation Hen, Teri, and their daughter Delcie had been looking forward to would be ruined because I had found a body. All of a sudden, the prospect of hanging out at the dump and watching for more bodies to turn up wasn't the worst thing I could think of. A friendship between Teri and me is doomed.

With that cheery prospect before me, I called it a day.

Chapter 4

The next afternoon we had a call about our body from the forensic pathologist in Atlanta. Hen took the call and, after what seemed like long enough to grow a crop of tobacco, harvest, and cure it, he ambled out to share with me and Dwight Wilkes, the other full-time deputy.

"Pay attention, lady and gentleman," he said as he sauntered out of his office holding a fat reference book that he kept on one of the jam-packed shelves in the overloaded bookcase in his office. He does love an audience and the opportunity to make a speech. And he was proving he knew he could safely refer to me as a lady if he referred to Dwight as a gentleman. "See what you can learn. The actual word for the peculiar waxy-soapy appearance of our Madame Tussaud is 'adipocere.' It is the result of bacteria operating on the fatty tissue in the damp closed box."

"A madam? You sayin' she was a prostitute?" Dwight asked. He's probably not really that dumb, but Hen explained the connection between wax and Madame Tussaud anyway, just in case.

"I'll call her M.T.," Dwight said, making it

sound like "empty." If brains were chitlins, Dwight wouldn't even be able to make you gag, but he is smart enough not to amuse us with his efforts at a French accent.

"Marie," I said. "That was Madame Tussaud's first name."

This is the kind of thing that passes for humor in police circles. Anybody will admit that calling the corpse Madame Tussaud, M.T., or Marie, is more humane than continuing to call the body "it," more imaginative than calling her Jane Doe, and more succinct than continuing to refer to her as "the body we found in the refrigerator out at the Riggs place." Furthermore, it neatly illustrates how close Hen, Dwight, and I come to speaking the same language. That is: not very.

With the important matter of the nickname settled, Hen went on to the pathologist's report. "According to the people whose business it is to be able to figure out these things, our body from the garbage dump was a white female — which even we small town cops had deduced from all that blonde hair. Probably late teens or early twenties. Makin' an educated guess after factoring in the state of decay, the age of the refrigerator, and the pricking of his or her thumbs, the pathologist estimates she's been dead for at least twenty years. The apparent cause of death was blunt trauma to the head, although it is possible some other cause of death might have been obscured by the passage of time. Not strangulation, though, because those dainty little bones in her throat were intact."

"That ain't much to go on," Dwight observed. "Was there anything with the body? A coin or something with the date on it?"

"We don't get that kind of luck," Hen said.

"Fingerprints?" Dwight asked.

Hen didn't exactly guffaw. "Too bad you were off overseeing a fist fight, Dwight. I know you'd have enjoyed the sight of Trudy taking the corpse's fingerprints as much as the rest of us did. Unfortunately, in spite of her initiative, investigative technique, and heroics, all we got out of it is negative information. The prints didn't match any on record, but if she was a law-abiding young lady — and don't pick a fight with me over this, Trudy, she might have been a lady for all we know — she would not have been fingerprinted back then."

"Jewelry?" Dwight asked. It's no secret I'm no big fan of Dwight, but he has learned a thing or two in a long career in law enforcement. When he retired from working at the nearby maximum security state prison he signed on with Hen, correctly guessing that it would be a comparatively low-stress way for him to continue to work in the one area where he had experience.

"No jewelry," Hen said. "No distinctive hardware. The only thing the pathologist turned up that we missed was a shard of some kind of pottery, a dish or a statuette, or something — probably whatever caused that fatal blunt trauma —

46

embedded in the skull and tangled up in all that hair. It has been carefully tagged and preserved in the unlikely event that we ever find something to compare it with."

"Anything from the clothes?" Dwight asked.

"Nothing specific," Hen said. "But the pathologist suggested that the bell-bottoms and embroidered blouse the woman was wearing placed her in the sixties."

"A sex crime," Dwight said. "An old sex crime."

"No," I said. "Not unless the killer took the time to put her back in order. Her clothing was all in place. Blouse buttoned and tucked in. Maybe a sex crime, but it doesn't look like it."

While Dwight was trying to think of another question, Hen gazed on me with satisfaction. "Looks like providence has handed us just the job for a gimped-up — excuse me, an orthopedically challenged — police officer," he said. "I know how much you've been worryin' about not being able to pull your weight around here, Trudy, so this is a godsend. You can just leave the more physical side of the job to the rest of us, now, without feelin' bad about it, and you see what you can do about finding some old case we could clear with this."

"You mean see if I can find a report of some missing woman that this could be? It would hardly solve anything."

"It would solve the mystery of why she was missing, now wouldn't it? Don't be contrary,

Trudy. It's not attractive." As though being attractive is my main motivation in life.

"Maybe the missing person wasn't missing from Ogeechee but only came to rest here. Maybe it was just somebody passing through."

"Then we'll be up a tree like a 'possum," Hen agreed. "But just to make sure we don't miss anything, you can start checking our old police files."

Hen smiled at me, very pleased. He had thought up an assignment, entirely paperwork, that would keep me off the streets, out of trouble, and reasonably tamped down. I'm sure he figured I'd hate it and be bored pure serendipity, sort of the way I feel about having me on the force irritating him.

Actually, I thought it would be interesting to look into those old files, but I didn't want to disappoint Hen, so I complained. It's a standard approach for me, behaving like Brer Rabbit trying to psych Brer Fox into throwing him into his beloved Briar Patch, but judging my protests carefully enough so that he won't actually outpsych me and think of something I really don't want to do.

"Why don't you let Dwight do it," I whined.

"Because Dwight's mean and ugly enough that he'll be more use out on the streets." I caught Hen winking at Dwight when he said this.

And that was that as far as job assignments were concerned, and we were all happy.

We don't have all that many missing persons cases in Ogeechee, just like we don't have all that many murders. Like every other place where there is any form of social interaction, we do have anti-social behavior, some of it illegal. Since I've been on the force, we've had a murder-arson and an intentional vehicular homicide that called for some pretty heads-up investigative acumen, if I do say so myself, but mostly what we do in the way of protecting the public is more along the lines of hauling in public drunks, public brawlers, drug dealers (yes, even in Ogeechee), and amateurish hold-up artists. Dwight is made for this kind of work.

Detective work is a specialized kind of problem solving, not as well defined as those logic puzzles that you can eventually solve by drawing little grids and eliminating the contradictions, but not entirely different, either. In both cases, you start by defining the problem, assisted by whatever facts you have. I like the mental challenges. In the case of the body in the refrigerator, that was practically all we knew: a body had turned up in a refrigerator. Or an icebox, but the difference that distinction made didn't seem likely to be useful.

Hen's a terrific people person, so while he sent me off to filthy, sweltering research at the courthouse and dispatched Dwight to go keep an eye on the search for more bodies or whatever else might turn up after twenty years or so, he did his part by putting in a call to the

Georgia Bureau of Investigation. As I headed out the door, I could hear him saying, "Yeah, here's what I got — a white female, about five foot five, about twenty years old . . ."

I could bore you by going into detail about how I tracked down the old case files in a cramped, hot, musty room up on the second floor of the courthouse. I could tell you exactly what unladylike oaths passed my lips as I clumsily fingered my way through spider webs and dusty cardboard boxes, where incident reports were filed chronologically, without respect to what kind of crime was being reported, banging my cast from time to time against something or other in the cramped space, constantly chafing in the heat. I could try to make you sweat and sneeze along with me, as I flipped through decades worth of incident reports, hundreds of incident reports, glancing quickly, but not too quickly, at the upper left-hand corner for a notation that would indicate the kind of crime I was interested in. But I won't. I'll excuse you, along with the teenager who paid off his community service hours by sweating along with me, since I was presently handicapped in my ability to wrestle boxes.

I'll summarize: Based on Mrs. Riggs's recollections and the pathologist's sense of style, we could assume the body hadn't been there longer than the sixties, at the earliest. It was conceivable that the body had been somewhere else before being deposited in the refrigerator at the

Riggs place, so I stuck with my orthopedically challenged police work till I got back to 1960. I might have to come back and dig deeper, but I decided to quit instead of running the risk that somebody halfway through the next century would accidentally find my long-dead and adipocere body lying behind a stack of cardboard boxes, overcome by heat prostration in the line of duty.

I wasn't surprised to come up empty. If there'd been an unsolved disappearance in Ogeechee, surely some whiff of it would still exist in community lore, especially police lore.

"You ought to keep yourself in better shape," Hen told me when I returned to the station house after my morning in archives, sweaty, dirty, wrinkled, itchy, and generally out of sorts. "Sweatin' like that ain't ladylike."

I didn't rise to his bait, but seeing him there in his air-conditioned office, still reasonably clean and well-pressed, did nothing to improve my temper.

"Either that body was a mirage or policin' around here never has been very efficient," I said. "I didn't turn up anything that would pass for an unsolved disappearance."

"I'm sure it was just careless speech that made it sound like you were disparagin' the police," he said. "I didn't think you'd find anything, but it wouldn't be efficient policin' to overlook such an obvious startin' place, and naturally, being the gung-ho policeman — woman

51

— officer — that you are, I knew you wouldn't want to leave any stone unturned and leave yourself, us, open to charges of not being thorough."

"Of course, Your Majesty; I understand, Your Majesty. It was my pleasure, Your Majesty. Anything for the force, Your Majesty."

"Glad to see you're enjoyin' your work. I like your attitude, too. You can stay around here for a while and catch up on paperwork. I thought I'd ride out to see Milton Kicklighter, see if he has any ideas." I grew up thinking "Milton Kicklighter" was a synonym for "Chief of Police." I don't know which surprised me more when he retired from the job after twenty years — what felt like a lifetime to me — that he retired, or that Henry Huckabee got the job.

Of course Hen would find a line of investigation that took the form of swapping stories with whatever old (as in "former") policemen (yes, "men") were still above ground, and trying to tickle their recollections.

"I wouldn't want to try to tell you how to approach an investigation, and I'm sure y'all will have a nice chat, but wouldn't you think something like a murder or a disappearance would have made it into the police files — no matter how inefficient they were?"

"On the one hand, Trudy, I surely do agree with you. Even old Milton wouldn't have had the gall to tear up a file just because he hadn't been able to close it."

Actually, that possibility hadn't occurred to me, and the look on my face must have betrayed my naive idealism. Hen laughed. "No, I don't think Milton would have stooped that low, but it's possible he might remember something out of the ordinary that could point us in a useful direction."

"What kind of direction?"

"Well, for instance, maybe whoever it was that disappeared wasn't missed for some reason."

"For what kind of reason?" I asked. "Never mind. Maybe the GBI will have something."

But I wouldn't just wait to hear from them. Another line of inquiry occurred to me.

Chapter 5

Here in Ogeechee, *The Ogeechee Beacon* is the weekly source of all news that touches us most closely. We pretty much leave it to *The Savannah Morning News* to cover national and international politics, the stock market, and what's happening in Hollywood, whereas the *Beacon* runs pictures of elementary school classes, articles about the garden club and church socials, and a report from the county agriculture agent. There used to be a column that tells us who's visiting from out of town and who they're visiting. Given the *Beacon*'s close focus on Ogeechee life, it seemed to me that if there'd ever been a disappearance locally — even if, for some reason, it hadn't come to the attention of the police — the *Beacon* might have mentioned it. At the very least, I figured that line of inquiry was apt to be as productive as Hen's conversation with Milton Kicklighter.

Thursday's a slow day at the *Beacon*. Since the paper comes out on Wednesday, Thursday is the day the small staff relaxes a little and tends to routine matters before they draw a deep breath and plunge into the next week's issue. It was the perfect day for me to amble over there and dig into the past.

The *Beacon* has been a Pittman family business for generations. These days the reins are slowly passing from one generation to another. Floyd Pittman keeps his hand in when he feels up to it and makes a special effort when he's called on, but his health isn't good, and his children, Phil and Molly, are taking on more and more.

When I got there, Mr. Pittman was in the front office talking with Leland Grinstead about some changes to next week's ad for Grinstead's Market.

"To what do we owe this unexpected pleasure?" Mr. Pittman looked up from the ad. "Phil's not here, you know."

Mr. Pittman doesn't usually annoy me, but his assumption did, that and the fact that the two men grinned at me. Some people would call Phil Pittman my boyfriend — even though I don't consider myself a "girl," I do not consider him a "boy," and we definitely do not engage in cutesy boy-girl behavior. I had not been thinking of him and his freckles and the way he fiddles with his glasses as I made my way to the *Beacon* offices, especially since I knew he was out of town at some kind of convention of small-circulation newspaper publishers. Mr. Pittman's comment shouldn't have annoyed me because the truth is Phil and I are both very well aware that a certain element of the townspeople don't have much of anything more important to do but speculate on our, for want of a better word, "romance." We occasionally add fuel to the fire by breaking away for a weekend somewhere outside the county, unchaperoned, and we've never seen fit to set anybody straight about how many bedrooms we rent when we go away.

In spite of my unreasonable annoyance — clearly, the discomfort of my arm was wearing out my usual sunny disposition — I returned the grins and played the role the men had assigned me. "I sure hope Phil doesn't forget how to behave himself, off on his own like that with nobody to guide him but a bunch of newspapermen," I said, doing my best to simper.

"So what can we do for you?" Mr. Pittman asked. Apparently he and Leland Grinstead weren't in any hurry to tend to their business.

"You can help out with an official po-lice investigation," I said, making two strong syllables out of po-lice in my best Henry Huckabee imitation. I even tried to hitch up my britches in his style, but that didn't work out too well, with the cast and all. "Y'all probably heard about the body we found out at the Riggs farm."

They nodded.

"We'll be wanting to get a story on that," Mr. Pittman said.

"We don't know who it was or how long the body's been there, if that's a story," I said.

"We'll want a little more than that," Mr.

Pittman said. "Phil will want to talk to Hen when he gets back. Maybe he'll know more by then."

"You could make it up without talking to Hen or bothering Phil," I suggested. "An unidentified body was discovered under unusual circumstances at a local construction site last Tuesday. Ogeechee Chief of Police Henry Huckabee declined to comment but assured the *Beacon* that the investigation has turned up several promising leads."

Mr. Pittman grinned. "Not bad. You got our style to a T. You ever want to quit being a police officer we'll let you work here."

"Do you pay any better than Hen does?"

"Not likely. I've always used family as much as I could, and paid 'em slave wages."

"Everybody in town already knows more than that, anyway," Leland Grinstead said. "It was at the Riggs place and, what I heard, it was a piece of white trash who'd been foolin' around with some black boys and they raped and killed her to keep her from tellin' on 'em."

It almost took my breath away. Almost. "Whoever knows that knows a lot more than the police do. You tell whoever you heard it from to come forward with evidence, if they have any, or keep their ignorant racist trouble-making ideas to themselves. Who told you that?"

"I don't remember exactly," Mr. Grinstead said, avoiding my eye.

I turned to Mr. Pittman, "Sounds like you'll

get a better story if you interview Mr. Grinstead and his sources."

"Anonymous sources," Mr. Grinstead said, recovering.

"Sounds like she doesn't trust the press," Mr. Pittman said, nodding sorrowfully.

"Me, neither," Grinstead said. "Caint believe a thing you read." He poked his ad with a pudgy finger and turned to me. "Says right here in the *Beacon* I'll let people have chicken breasts for fifty cents a pound."

"I told you we'd print a correction, Leland," Mr. Pittman said. "You won't lose on it. You get twice the ad for your dollar."

"Already had somebody hold me to it. You gone pay for that, too?"

"You oughta pay me for building up your business," Mr. Pittman claimed. "People go in to check out the price on chicken, they'll buy something else. What you lose on chicken you make up somewhere else."

They'd probably been enjoying variations on this same conversation ever since Grinstead's Market opened, so there was no urgency about it, but there was no reason for me to hang around and keep them from their fun. "Here's a scoop for the *Beacon*. The first thing we have to do is identify the body. I can't find anything in police files about anybody being murdered or disappearing, but it occurred to me there might have been something in the paper that would help us out."

Mr. Pittman nodded. "*The Ogeechee Beacon* Assists Police in Investigation. That would be a good headline."

"Looks like if we'd had a mysterious body, somebody'd remember it," Leland Grinstead said, looking up from the ad again. "But I never thought I'd live to see the police lookin' in the paper for that kind of thing."

"We didn't actually have a body until just recently," I reminded him.

They nodded again and Mr. Pittman offered, "I don't remember anybody disappearing, either."

"I'm not too optimistic about this," I admitted. "But I thought there might be a hint, some kind of a clue, in the *Beacon*. Going through back issues is bound to beat sitting over at the station house doing paperwork."

"You know I always say if it happened in Ogeechee you'll see it in the *Beacon*," Mr. Pittman agreed. "How far back you want to go?"

"I'll work back thirty, thirty-five years, or until I find something, whichever comes first," I said. "I don't know, really."

"You check out our ads," Lyman said. "We've always advertised in the *Beacon*, in spite of them messing up our ads every third week or so. You just check and see if we haven't always been the best place to shop."

"I'll do that," I promised.

"Molly'll help you," Mr. Pittman said. "Just go on back."

I left them and went toward the back, where I knew Molly would be waiting for me.

Molly's a little older than Phil, but they look like twins, both with reddish hair and freckles. Molly's gone to contact lenses but Phil still wears glasses — less because he needs them, I've come to think, than because he fiddles with them as a stalling mechanism whenever he needs time to think. This used to get on my nerves something fierce, but lately I've begun to think of it as kind of cute. I'm not sure, but I think that may be a bad sign. Molly turned away from her workstation at a computer terminal — yes, high tech has reached some parts of Ogeechee — and showed me where she'd cleared a space at a work table (no small chore in the clutter of the workroom) where I could lay out the big bound volumes of the *Beacon* from years past.

"You said 'at least twenty years' so this stack starts with 1980," she said, indicating the heavy black books. "You want to start there and work back?"

"That's what makes sense to me. I have no idea what will help," I said.

She went back to her computer and I positioned the volume for 1980 in front of me and started turning pages. The nice thing about my quest being so ill defined was that I had to go slowly and be alert for vibes. Not wanting to miss a clue, and not expecting a headline to proclaim anybody's disappearance, I considered it my duty to read anything that caught my eye and keep my imagination in high gear.

"Jack Boatwright Practice Teaching at Vidalia High" and "Cake Bake Sale at Cobbtown Saturday" held equal interest for me. Maybe Jack Boatwright killed one of the eighth-grade students he was practice teaching. Maybe somebody dropped dead of cake poisoning and the cook was so embarrassed she hid the body.

I was hooked. Except for the fact that I had to let the books lie flat and lean over them, instead of being able to lean back and get comfortable, I could have settled in for the summer. Maybe Mr. Pittman was right and I should be working for the *Beacon* instead of the police. I idly wondered if he really only hired family, and if that comment had been a hint in disguise, but the old newspapers quickly reclaimed my attention.

I had worked back to 1969 ("Robert McCoy in Dublin Hospital" and "Garden Club Not to Have Supper") when my attention was caught by the name Burkhalter. This was an item, accompanied by photo, announcing the engagement of Donnie Burkhalter of Ogeechee and Miss Karen Willard of Bristol. The happy couple, both students at the University of Georgia at Athens, were planning a June wedding.

"Do you know a Donnie Burkhalter?" I asked Molly.

Molly stopped typing and furrowed her brow in thought.

"It says here he's the son of Alvin and Doris Burkhalter," I prompted. The born-again Alvin and his wife Doris were prominent members of the Baptist Church, civic leaders, both of them. Alvin even served a term or two as mayor. Their son, Kenneth, had taken over the auto paint and body shop that Alvin started.

"I don't see how they could have a son we never heard of," I added.

"Maybe they keep him in the attic," Molly suggested.

"Keep who in the attic?" Mr. Pittman had finished with Leland and was rolling his office chair in our direction. Some days his arthritis is so bad it's easier for him to do that than to walk.

"Your politically insensitive daughter was suggesting that Alvin and Doris Burkhalter have a son they're ashamed of," I told him. "According to the *Beacon* in February of 1969, there's a Donnie Burkhalter who belongs to them."

"Oh, yes. My goodness, that's a ways back. Donnie Burkhalter."

"In the attic?" an unrepentant Molly asked. "That place of theirs is big enough? I guess I could believe it."

"Back then, before Donnie died, they lived in a smaller place down from the high school, when it was the high school," Mr. Pittman said.

Thanks to my recent sortie into the past, I knew what he meant. What is now the county

62

school district's administration building was the Ogeechee high school, before they built the new county high school out toward Glennville. It's just across the highway (or Court Street, if you want to be locally chauvinistic about it) from the OPD. But that wasn't the point. "Donnie?" I prompted.

"Sad, sad thing."

"This was a wedding announcement. Did he go to Bristol to live with his new wife and the family disowned him?" I asked, consulting the article for my facts.

Still shaking his head, Mr. Pittman answered, "No, there wasn't a wedding after all. Donnie was killed in an automobile accident before they ever got married. It happened at the beginning of the summer, I remember, not long after school was out. It's always hard when you see a young person die, somebody with his whole life ahead of him like that. The town was torn up about it. Seems extra bad when it's a young person, and sudden like that, not like when somebody's been sick a while."

He carefully shifted his position in his chair and looked back toward the front of the building, but I could tell that what he saw had nothing to do with the *Beacon*. His voice took on that deliberate quality that comes when you have to wait for recollections to provide the words you're after. He was in another time.

"Back then, Burkhalter's shop was right there where the road forks between the police station and the old school. They dragged Donnie's car in and left it on display there for whatever beneficial shock value it might have to all the other teenagers in town, or anybody else who might have been inclined to forget what happens when you ram a car into concrete. Couldn't hardly go anywhere in town without seeing that car and being reminded how reckless young'uns can be."

As he talked, I slowly paged through the bound newspapers. Sure enough, in a brief report under the heading "Ogeechee Man Killed" there was a picture of a mangled car and the news that Donnie Burkhalter, age twenty, had perished when his car struck a bridge on the afternoon of June seventeenth.

"Did they ever figure out why he crashed?" I asked.

"You sound like a police officer," Mr. Pittman said.

I ignored the compliment. "Had he been drinking or something?"

Mr. Pittman sighed. "Somebody had the idea he mighta got the sun in his eyes, but, far as I recall, nobody was interested in looking into it too much."

"Why on earth not?" Molly asked. Good question. I'd have thought even Milton Kicklighter would have been curious, or the county sheriff. I checked the article again, but it didn't say exactly where the accident occurred.

"You girls . . ."

It isn't everybody that can call me a girl without getting a rise out of me, but Mr. Pittman is one.

"You girls, now, a ruthless investigator and a news-hen, you might not understand about tender feelings and kindliness."

"What are you talking about?" Molly asked, clearly irked, as I was, at the notion that we were lacking in tender feelings and kindliness.

Mr. Pittman regarded the wall again. "Well, that girl had broken up with him and some people thought he might have wanted to end it all. No reason I could see to put that in the paper."

"No," Molly conceded.

"Not if there wasn't any question of foul play," I admitted.

"So that's your Donnie Burkhalter," Mr. Pittman said, beginning to roll back toward the front office. Molly and I made faces at each other and each returned to her own task.

In 1962, advertisements informed me, Leland Grinstead was selling Holsum bread for twenty-five cents a loaf and six ounces of cream cheese for twenty-nine cents.

"Grinstead's Market gets more for their bread these days," I said aloud.

Molly's used to me. She merely glanced up briefly before returning her attention to her terminal. In the same volume I learned that Miss Judith Griffin made the Dean's List at Brewton Parker and I dutifully read the lists of guests reported in "Stork Shower Honors Mrs. Lamar Harris on Tuesday Afternoon."

Much of the interest for me was in the record of changes in the town. Change happens so slowly, I'd forgotten a lot of things until the articles in the paper reminded me. I'd forgotten the big house down the block from the old post office. I couldn't remember anybody ever living there, and it had grown so dilapidated that at one point my friends and I decided it must be haunted and we'd cross the street rather than walk past it. It had been torn down years ago, maybe while I was still in college. The Pizza Place had been on that lot for years. I'd forgotten that the now empty space across from the Methodist Church had held a collection of mobile homes for sale. The trailer lot had expanded and moved east of town, near Dawson Motors.

I was finishing up what had turned into a frankly pleasant and self-indulgent foray into my hometown's past, and feeling a little guilty that it had been so unproductive job-wise, when the phone rang in the front. I couldn't make out the words, but could tell from Mr. Pittman's tone that something bad had happened to somebody, so I was already prepared for bad news when he rolled back to where Molly and I were.

He was shaking his head in wonder. "That was Miz Purvis over at the Baptist Church," he said, "to say Alvin Burkhalter's had a stroke. Lordy."

I felt a shiver. I knew better, of course, but couldn't resist the thought that all our talk about the Burkhalter sorrows had somehow brought it on.

In that melancholy frame of mind, as I was drifting off to sleep in my solitary bed that evening, I wondered what became of Karen Willard, Donnie Burkhalter's intended bride, and if she ever knew she'd been blamed for his suicide, if it was a suicide.

Chapter 6

As convalescent hospitals go, the Dogwood
Nursing Center, where Miss Sarah Kennedy
was gradually getting her new hip in gear,
wasn't the worst I've seen. A deep porch lined
with rockers ran all the way across the back of
the building, the side away from the highway.
Patients mobile enough to get out there could
gaze off into fields and woods while they got a
little fresh air. The dogwoods had finished
blooming months earlier, but the shifting dap-
pled shade under the trees was attractive and
restful.

Miss Sarah never was the kind to sit and rock,
though, and Aunt Lulu and I didn't find her on
the porch sunning herself with the others. In the
company of an aide, and with the support of a
walker, she was slowly making her way around
the building on the narrow sidewalk. She looked
up and smiled at us, but I noticed she didn't
loosen her grip on the walker.

She looked tired, but her hair, as always, was
pulled neatly into a soft bun high on the back of
her head, with loose waves framing her face.
Not many women her age scorn the softening
effect of bangs. That Miss Sarah did says a lot

about her uncompromising spirit. As far as I could tell, the only change the years had made in her coiffure was to turn the brown to white.

"Well, Miss Sarah, looks like you're doin' just fine," Aunt Lulu said. Aunt Lulu's enough younger than Miss Sarah that she uses the respectful form of address she learned as a child and has never changed, even though they've become friends and in many ways, generation-wise, they're what passes for contemporaries.

"They tell me I probably won't make the soccer team," Miss Sarah said. Then she added, with the steady good humor that had helped her survive generations of highschoolers, "But they aren't going to have to start pulling me around in a little red wagon for a little while yet, if I have anything to say about it." And of course she'd have plenty to say about it.

"You could take a rest now, Miss Sarah, while you visit with your friends. They might not want to walk around out here in the heat." The aide suggested this with tact that told me she understood Miss Sarah and her sense of discipline very well. She looked like she could use a rest in the shade, whether Miss Sarah needed it or not. No telling how long Miss Sarah had kept the poor girl out there, creeping around the building in the heat. I imagined the nursing staff was having a hard time keeping up with Miss Sarah.

"I'll call you when I'm ready to walk some more," Miss Sarah told the aide in dismissal. I almost laughed at the look of relief on the girl's face. "I'll see you back to your room, then," the aide said. I wouldn't have bet a nickel on Miss Sarah's chances of finding that particular aide again, but the girl obviously valued her job enough to be taking Miss Sarah seriously.

"Let's go inside," Miss Sarah said to Aunt Lulu and me. "I don't want to sit out here with the old people and flaunt how much better off I am than they are. Besides, we'll have more privacy in my room."

As we passed among the rockers, one or two of the people eyed us with what might have been envy. I don't normally think of myself as a novelty or a refreshing break in routine, but I'm sure Aunt Lulu and I represented exactly that to some of the people, and while I agreed with Miss Sarah's suggestion that we'd have more privacy in her room, it did occur to me that it would have been an act of charity to visit out there where we offered fresh conversation and new scenery in that fairly bleak landscape. The dogwoods and nandinas, the mockingbirds and cardinals, even the squirrels and the colorful feeders hung around the yard, would have limited entertainment value.

"I can't offer you iced tea and cookies the way I'd like to," Miss Sarah said as she settled herself into a chair in her room and waved the aide away. "I hope that won't keep you from comin' to see me again."

I've never been able to overcome my awe of

70

the woman to the extent that I can banter with her the way I do most people, but Aunt Lulu was up to it. "Law, Miss Sarah, if I want tea I can make it myself. We just came by to see if you've taken over the place yet and straightened 'em out."

"They're comin' along," Miss Sarah said with a gleam in her eye, "but let's not talk about this place. Trudy, how's your arm?"

"On track," I said. "The cast comes off next week and we'll see. I'll probably have to do some physical therapy, but that's not a big deal, not like what you're having to put up with."

She waved that away as she had waved away the aide. "It happened in the line of duty?"

"Yes, ma'am, so Hen's trying to find safe work for me to do while I'm crippled up."

"Speaking of your line of duty, I hear you've found another body."

"Yes, ma'am," I admitted.

"I don't think bodies turned up around here so often before you started working for the police. How do you explain that?"

This was a Miss Sarah I was used to, the teacher who was a genius at the "do you still beat your wife" kind of question that demanded a well-thought-out answer. Even if this question-and-answer was surely and purely frivolous, from long practice, I responded seriously.

"One idea is that I myself am producing bodies in order to keep my job," I said. "But

71

since we've been able to pin them on somebody else, I ask you to reject that theory."

"Unless you're framing them," Miss Sarah said.

"I think you must be watching too much television, Miss Sarah. Besides, we got confessions," I countered.

"And don't you dare mention police brutality, now, Miss Sarah, even in a joke," Aunt Lulu weighed in.

"Of course not, Lulu. You have other theories about the increasing number of murders?" Miss Sarah asked me.

"Of course I do. I believe that without my invaluable insights and point of view, murders were going unrecognized before I came on the force," I said. "When Reed Ritter's house burned down with him in it, people might have thought it was just an accidental fire, and not murder. And when that Atlanta art dealer got run down on the highway, it could have been an accident."

"So you're saying Hen wouldn't have recognized murder when he saw it? He's incompetent?" Miss Sarah asked, casting a mischievous glance at Aunt Lulu.

"Oh, no!" I said, doing my best to act like I thought she'd really misunderstood. "You'll never hear me say anything like that." That was the truth. I believe Hen's a very good police officer. Any comments I may make suggesting otherwise are usually for his benefit alone.

"Hen says Trudy's been good for the force," Aunt Lulu said. I stared at her. He'd never said it to me.

"What about this new body?" Miss Sarah asked. "There's no doubt about it being murder, is there?"

"None at all."

"What have they found out?" Aunt Lulu asked.

"We know it was a woman and not much more than that," I said. "Regardless of what you might hear around town."

"You can't identify her by fingerprints?" Aunt Lulu asked.

"None on file," I responded.

"Dental records?" Miss Sarah asked.

"We'd need to have an idea whose records to check. We do know she'd been dead, and in that refrigerator, for a long time."

"Whoever said dead men tell no tales wasn't up on his forensic science," Aunt Lulu said to Miss Sarah. "You'd be amazed at the tales a corpse can tell scientists these days. They can even estimate height. They take five times the length of the humerus. Which bone's the humerus, Trudy?"

"Uh. It's the long bone in the arm that goes from the shoulder to the elbow. It's the funny bone. The humerus. Get it?"

They might have gotten it, but Aunt Lulu was on a roll. "They can tell if somebody was left-handed or right-handed, too," she said.

73

"Aunt Lulu, how in the world did you know that?"

"It isn't classified information, you know," she said. "It was in a library book I was reading. The bones in the arm of the dominant hand will be slightly longer than the other arm. This woman, now, was she left-handed or right-handed?"

"I don't know that the report mentioned it. It probably doesn't matter," I said.

"Well, what have you learned about her?" Miss Sarah asked.

A little worried by these insights into Aunt Lulu's choice of reading material, I let only half my brain be offended by the implication that the police weren't as smart as these two women. With the other half I tried to think of a way to re-direct the conversation. "She'd been there a while, so I spent a couple of hours over at the *Beacon* going through old issues to see if I could get any ideas about who she might have been."

"Did you?" Aunt Lulu asked.

"No, ma'am, but it sure was interesting looking back at the changes in Ogeechee just in my lifetime."

"I'd have said nothing's changed here in my lifetime," Aunt Lulu said.

"Maybe no big changes, but there've been changes," I said. "For instance, there's a little building on Main Street by where the post office used to be — there's one change right there, a new post office — I can't remember that little

74

building ever being used for anything. What did it used to be?"

"You must be talking about the old hospital," Aunt Lulu said.

"Doctor Cummings called it a hospital when he built it," Miss Sarah said, "but then when people started going to newer hospitals he turned it into a clinic, just for routine things like office visits."

"When was it closed?"

The two older women locked eyes as though each was trying to extract the answer from the other's brain.

"I remember going there when I sprained my ankle," Miss Sarah said. "Now when was that?"

"You sprained your ankle that Halloween you dressed up like a witch and tripped over your cauldron," Aunt Lulu said. "Was that the last year you used that cauldron and the dry ice?"

"Yes. I'd been using Nona Etheridge's old wash kettle, and she got a good offer from an antique dealer over in Pembroke and sold it. I think that was the same year the movie house closed, because after that we had to find another place for the Halloween party, anyway."

"That would have been 1950," Aunt Lulu said. "That was the year the community center opened." They both looked at me. "1950," Aunt Lulu repeated. Miss Sarah nodded.

"1950 was the year of the ankle and the cauldron and the movie theatre, but the hospital clinic was still open then. My question was when the clinic closed," I reminded them.

"It probably shut down about the time Cowart Memorial opened up with newer equipment and more space and everything," Miss Sarah said.

"You could go look at the date on the cornerstone at the hospital," Aunt Lulu said.

I didn't really care, of course. My impulse had been to entertain and distract the two women, but as I listened to them sifting and cross-referencing memories to come up with a date that didn't matter in the least, I realized that they represented a vast resource that promised to outdo the newspaper when it came to opening a window into Ogeechee's past. Gossip, come to think of it, would probably be much more fruitful than the news that was fit to print. I introduced another topic, interrupting their digression into whether Cowart Memorial was going to have to close, leaving Ogeechee without emergency services, and whether it was because of bad management, Medicare fraud, or simply because so many people go to Savannah these days anyway.

"Tell me about Donnie Burkhalter," I suggested. I don't think of myself as the romantic type, certainly not sentimental, but the story of Donnie Burkhalter and Karen Willard had gotten under my skin. I was widowed after a brief marriage, and maybe having that in my history has made me especially susceptible to love stories without happy endings — and painfully suspicious of happily ever after.

"Donnie Burkhalter," Miss Sarah said thoughtfully. "Donnie Burkhalter. Tore the town up when he died. He was everybody's fair-haired boy, Trudy, a good student, good athlete, good at everything he turned to. I remember thinking Alvin was goin' to have a hard time keeping Donnie interested in that body shop, and then when he went off to school I just knew that was the end of Burkhalter and Sons. Never imagined he'd die like that."

"Kenneth settled down and took it over," Aunt Lulu said. "Nobody ever thought Kenneth would settle down like he did. Or Alvin, either, come to think of it. You'd never know it to look at him now, Trudy, but Alvin Burkhalter used to be a rounder. In those days, people weren't so alert to what you police call domestic violence, but I know more than once Doris turned up with a bruise here or a scrape there that was hard to account for."

"Alvin Burkhalter?" I asked. Eric Riggs had hinted at an earlier, rougher Alvin Burkhalter, but this still came as a surprise to me.

"Oh, yes. When he got religion he did a real turnaround."

"That was after Donnie died," Miss Sarah said. "That whole family did a turnaround after Donnie died. Doris had always been cheerful and friendly up till then, and afterwards it was

77

like she'd given up on living. She doted on Donnie and never did get over it."

"Kenneth was such a handful he wasn't much comfort to her," Aunt Lulu said. "He managed to grow up, but I'm not sure he ever straightened out."

"At least, Kenneth didn't get any worse after Donnie died," Miss Sarah said. "That's one thing. And Alvin's change for the better was so dramatic, 'born-again' was a good description for it. I remember thinking the community had traded in a promising young man for a reformed older man, and Doris wound up with a better husband, so maybe, on the whole, the community's better off."

"The community all but lost Doris along with Donnie, though," Aunt Lulu said. "I swear she hasn't smiled since nineteen sixty-nine, even if her husband did reform," Aunt Lulu said. She turned to Miss Sarah. "Speaking of Alvin, did you hear about him?"

"Hear what?" Miss Sarah asked.

"He had a stroke yesterday. They took him to Savannah, St. Joseph's. It's too early for them to tell how bad off he is, but Doris is beside herself."

"Of course she is. Nothing to do but wait and see, with a stroke. Maybe it won't be too bad."

"We can hope for the best," Aunt Lulu said. "That's all we can do."

There was no arguing with that. After a respectful moment I asked, "What about the girl who was going to marry Donnie Burkhalter, Karen Willard? Do you know what became of her?"

"Was that her name?" Aunt Lulu asked. "I'd forgotten all about her."

"None of us got to know her very well," Miss Sarah explained. "She just came that one time that I recall, for a shower."

"Louise Mathis gave a shower, and had little meringue swans filled with strawberries. Just beautiful. Louise is gone now, but she was a real good cook," Aunt Lulu said. "I wanted to model myself on her, the way she knew how to fix things up and entertain."

"So Karen didn't get hysterical and fling herself into his open grave?" I asked. Under the spell of their reminiscences, I tried, but completely failed, to imagine the young Karen Willard I had seen in the *Beacon* photograph as a now fifty-something grandmother who remembered Donnie Burkhalter, if she remembered him at all, as a brief, sad, but closed, chapter in her life.

"Oh, no. Not at all," Miss Sarah said. "I'd forgotten about it, but now that you bring it up, I recall she didn't even come to the funeral. And I'm here to tell you that fed all kinds of fuel to the fire being tended by those who thought Donnie had made a big mistake getting engaged to her in the first place."

"Doris Burkhalter first and foremost," Aunt Lulu added.

"If nobody knew her very well, why did they think it was such a big mistake?"

"He was supposed to marry Julie Todd," Aunt Lulu said. "Everybody just took that for granted — the Burkhalters, the Todds, certainly Julie — and then he went off and came back with a fiancée nobody knew anything about. Julie's the one who had a fit at the funeral, not that Karen. Remember, Miss Sarah? Julie always had been high strung and she took Donnie's dying hard."

"The Julie Todd I know?" I asked. Could she have ever been twenty years old with hopes of marriage and family? Eccentric, unpredictable, prickly Julie Todd?

"Yes, Trudy, that very same Julie Todd," Aunt Lulu answered. "She was a pretty girl back then. Spoiled rotten, but a lot of girls are, especially when they're only children, and she came late to Mabel and Walter. Oh, she always was one to throw tantrums when she didn't get her way. Remember the ruckus she caused at the funeral, Miss Sarah?"

Miss Sarah nodded.

"What kind of ruckus?" I asked.

"Screaming and fainting and all. You know how hysterical girls can be. I remember thinking she wanted to make sure everybody knew she had a prior claim to Donnie. And then when the fiancée didn't even show up, well! All our sympathy was for the Burkhalters and Julie. There wasn't much thought left over for a missing fiancée."

"Except for criticizing," Miss Sarah added.

"Well, of course," Aunt Lulu agreed. "That goes without saying." She smiled when she realized that "without saying" was exactly wrong. "She had jilted a local boy, after all, and now he was dead. Who'd have had anything good to say about her? Julie got so upset she had to go away for awhile. They called it a nervous breakdown. I don't know about nerves, but something broke down, all right, something they never could fix. She never was the same. She hadn't ever been easy to get along with, but after that she got downright impossible. Lucky for her Mabel and Walter left her something to live on. I don't know how she'd make out if she had to get along with people like she'd have to with a job."

"Lulu's exaggerating, Trudy," Miss Sarah said. "Not everybody can be a social butterfly like Lulu. Julie keeps to herself, but there's nothing wrong with that."

"It's a good idea for her to keep to herself, the way she rubs people the wrong way," Aunt Lulu said. "She never did learn to get along."

"Could be the medication she takes to keep herself steady takes the edge off her social skills," Miss Sarah suggested with a glint in her eye. "The right medication can make a world of difference. I know some people I'd like to dose up with something."

"Miss Sarah!" Aunt Lulu said, pretending to be shocked, but she smiled. I did, too, thinking that I had a few people I wouldn't mind seeing medicated into a different personality.

All in all, it was far more interesting and less of a strain than most hospital visits. By the time Aunt Lulu and I left, Miss Sarah had a sparkle in her eye to replace the grim determination that had kept her walking on that new hip, and I thought there was more color in her cheeks. Yes, our visit had done her some good.

As we walked out past the front porch crew, still rocking and watching the landscape, I couldn't suppress the thought that our gossip might have perked them up too, if they'd been in on it. Who would ever know what countless, priceless recollections were going untapped in those rocking chairs?

Chapter 7

Checking records doesn't take the Georgia Bureau of Investigation nearly as long as it takes the Ogeechee Police Department, and I'm almost certain it's a cleaner job for them. I imagined a slim, sexy, young thing (Yes, I know that's a sexist stereotype. Nobody's perfect.) with inch-long acrylic fingernails mincing into an air-conditioned office and yawning languidly as she considered the job orders waiting in her in-basket. She would stifle another yawn — she'd had an exciting, physically exhausting evening, after all — and punch keys on a computer to outline the scope of the search Hen had requested: white female about five foot five, late teens or early twenties, search records between 1960 and 1980 in Bulloch, Candler, Emanuel, Evans, Tattnall, and Toombs counties. Of course the body could have been brought from anywhere, but you have to start someplace.

She would sit there, dreamily popping her chewing gum and examining her fingernails for imperfections, while the computer printed out the information Hen had requested, whereupon she would daintily pick up the printouts and sway down the hall for a coffee break. As long as I was fantasizing anyway, I went ahead and made it good coffee, freshly brewed. Heck, throw in a clean ceramic mug.

However warped that picture might have been by my own tedious recent Ogeechee-style research into Ogeechee's old police files, it is a fact that only a day later somebody at GBI was able to give us details on six missing women, any one of whom, as far as the GBI was concerned, might have been our woman.

Even without the unusually interesting aspects this particular case presented, investigating the death of a human being shoots right to the top of our To Do list. Like any good administrator, Hen was trying to strike a balance between his own interest in the case, on one side of the scales, and giving me useful work and enough leeway to do it, on the other. It was my good luck that a spate of convenience store hold-ups all around Ogeechee was giving Hen something more urgent to think about than a body at least twenty years old, so, when the GBI reports came in, I got them.

I spread the information on the table in front of me and debated how to proceed. Would I investigate these women chronologically, in order of their disappearance? Oldest to most recent? Geographically — starting with the last-known sighting nearest to Ogeechee? Psychically — which names sounded most like someone who would wind up in a refrigerator in Ogeechee?

Optimistically — which one did I think I'd be most likely to track down? Alphabetically?

I tried closing my eyes and holding my hands over the various reports to see if some restless spirit would attract them to one of the names or faces. When that didn't work, I picked them up at random. Freely translating from the GBI files, I considered:

Eloise "Lisa" Watkins, 5'5", 115 pounds, 23 years old. She'd been working as a bank clerk in Swainsboro when she disappeared, on February 13, 1975, along with her boyfriend, Stevie Ward, and some of the bank's cash. Neither she nor Ward had been heard of since. In the photo, she looked kind of wispy and washed out, like a woman who might dream of romance and adventure but felt it was hopelessly out of her reach. I wondered if Lisa had busted loose, bought a lot of makeup and bright clothes, and celebrated that Valentine's Day with Stevie, both of them under assumed names and a colorful umbrella on a beach in the Bahamas. Or had the Stevie-man used her to help with a robbery and, not needing her any more, left her behind? If so, did he leave her in a refrigerator?

Clarisse Jean "C.J." Jordan, 5'7", 130 pounds. C.J. was eighteen years old when she was last seen, on September 9, 1969, at the Magnolia Lodge in Metter, where she had been working as a maid. Another guest had complained about the sound of an argument in one of her units that morning. Had C.J. accidentally come across something she shouldn't have — like a cache of drugs? Did she leave with the drug dealers, willingly — in search of greener pastures — or unwillingly — and become a missing person because dead women tell no tales?

Loyce Lewis, 5'6", about 115 pounds, 17 years old. She was known to have abusive parents and her friends said she'd talked about leaving home, maybe for California. She showed up at Claxton High School on March 12, 1968, with a black eye and a lame story about how it happened; she didn't show up at all the next day. Her parents said she hadn't come home from school on the twelfth, but they hadn't been particularly worried about it until one of her friends came looking for her that night. They hadn't seen her since. I hoped they were telling the truth. I hoped Loyce had hitchhiked to Savannah and taken a job as a waitress at a truck stop instead of finding death at the hands of the people who should have been taking care of her.

Lynn Elaine Reese, age 21, 5'7", about 190 pounds, of Twin City. Lynn Elaine was a misfit who was the target of a lot of teasing about her appearance, her brains, her family. On July 24, 1971, her mother reported her missing. She had told her mother she was going swimming with some friends. She didn't say where or what friends. When she didn't come home, several Emanuel County swimming holes were asked to give up their secrets, which included plenty of old tires and a 1959 Chevrolet but not Lynn

Elaine. I had a hard time thinking of a happy outcome for poor Lynn Elaine.

Shirley Yvonne Smiley, age 19, 5'4", 110 pounds, a cosmetician at Classy Coifs in Vidalia. Her distraught parents said she'd been suicidal over a breakup with her boyfriend. The photo showed a pretty dark-haired girl. It made sense that she'd be pretty, working as a cosmetician. I wondered if her hair was as dark as it looked in the photo. Maybe she'd dyed it, but generally girls think blonde is the way to go, not the other way around. Why do pretty girls, any girls, think the world must come to an end without a particular man? Her parents reported her missing on August 18, 1962, when her employer called to ask why she didn't show up for work. There'd been no sign of foul play at her apartment.

Claudine Tippins, age 23, 5'5", 135 pounds, a waitress at The Chicken Nest in Statesboro, was last seen on November 3, 1979. She'd been excited about going somewhere with a customer that day. He was a new customer, nobody local. She'd left with him and not been seen again. Maybe it had been love at first sight and they eloped, living happily ever after on fried chicken. Or maybe not.

Hen says I have too much imagination for my own good. He may be right. Even though I didn't know much of anything about any of these women, I could invent scenarios that would account for any one of them being our Madame Marie Tussaud. Maybe I was getting proprietary about the case, but somehow I felt she was somebody from not too far away. After all, we aren't on a highway between two major destinations, unless you count Bellville and Uvalda as major, and I don't know of anybody who does, and I thought it unlikely that strangers to the area would have known the territory well enough to find that isolated spot and put her where she'd been found.

I reshuffled the reports and tried to find a place to start. Shirley Smiley? No matter how suicidal she was, she didn't smash her skull in and then climb into an abandoned refrigerator. Maybe that boyfriend had the last word. Lynn Elaine Reese? I didn't see how her "friends" could have stuffed one hundred ninety pounds of her into a refrigerator. Loyce Lewis might have died at the hands of one of her parents and after all this time maybe somebody who knew something would be more willing to talk. Maybe it was wishful thinking rather than logic, but I felt Lisa was alive somewhere, enjoying herself. I got no vibes at all about C.J.

Shirley and Loyce looked the most likely. I put those two at the top of my pile but made phone calls to police in Claxton, Twin City, Statesboro, Swainsboro, and Vidalia, to see if they knew, or could find out, anything that wasn't in the reports.

They'd have to get back to me. Obviously, they had no sweet young things with computer records that go back to the sixties.

Chapter 8

What you do in Ogeechee if somebody gets sick or dies is you take food to whoever is still functioning. I'm sure a lot of that food goes to waste, but the food-ness of it, the sparing the troubled the need to give any thought to food preparation, is only part of what it's about. Mostly it's about acknowledging and sharing a loss, about creating a supportive presence.

This explains why I was knocking on Doris Burkhalter's door with a pan of Aunt Lulu's warm blueberry cobbler in my hand. Aunt Lulu wanted to be among the first to bring food, but when Hen had to cancel his plans to leave town, with the hotel already reserved and everything, Aunt Lulu decided to go with Teri and Delcie in his place. Aunt Lulu arranging to cut loose from her responsibilities is only a little less troublesome than Hen doing it, except that she is slightly more willing to delegate. A murder investigation was one of the things she could delegate and Hen couldn't.

"Doris is partial to this cobbler," Aunt Lulu explained when I asked why she was sending food to a household with only one distracted woman in it at present. "She'll be spending most of her time at the hospital, but if she wants a bite of something, or needs something to offer to somebody else, this will be there. There's not anything anybody can do about Alvin's stroke, but this cobbler will let Doris know we'd do something if we could."

I couldn't argue with that. I'd agreed to drop it off, partly to show Christian charity, partly to appease Aunt Lulu, and partly because I couldn't get the Burkhalters off my mind.

I rang the bell and waited.

I'd just about decided to leave the cobbler on the porch swing when the door opened after all, and Doris Burkhalter appeared. Much is made, especially in romantic fiction, about the immediate physical manifestations of grief, but as far as I could tell, the woman facing me looked like she always did — tired, listless, without any sparkle at all, from her dull grey-brown eyes to her flat grey-brown hair to her shapeless grey-green two-piece pant set. The lively, friendly woman Aunt Lulu and Miss Sarah remembered existed only in their memories. It didn't seem possible that even Doris Burkhalter would be able to remember that woman.

"Aunt Lulu asked me to bring this over," I said, hefting the cobbler dish. "And ask if there's anything anybody can do."

She stepped back and I followed her into the house.

"Just set it on the counter," she said. "I like it better warm."

"I do, too," I said, following her instructions. Then, uninvited, I sat in one of the tubular steel-and-plastic chairs that matched the Formica-topped kitchen table. When Doris Burkhalter lost interest in life, she apparently did a thorough job of it. The yellow Formica and yellow-flowered wallpaper in the kitchen seemed obscenely cheery, but they were of the same era as the oatmeal-colored couch and the orange-and-white striped lamp in the living room. It was the bland kind of furniture I once saw ridiculed in a comedy routine — a twelve-piece living room suite (around here we usually call it a "suit"): a couch, two side chairs, two end tables, a coffee table, two lamps, two light bulbs, one ashtray and one cigarette butt. I'd have bet there'd been orange shag carpet until it wore into unacceptability and was replaced by the beige pile. Then I remembered the Burkhalters had moved since Donnie's death, no doubt leaving behind the orange shag along with stylishly modern lime, orange, yellow, and brown drapes.

"Is there any news about Mr. Burkhalter?" I asked.

"Not real news, no. The doctor said it's still too soon to know how bad it was," she answered, sitting across the table from me. "I think he's already comin' back a little, though. Kenneth's comin' to take me over there in a little while. What happened to you?"

I've thought about giving everybody who asks that question a different answer, just for

91

variety, but in this case I opted for the bare-bones truth. "Injured in the line of duty," I said. "I'm mending."

She hadn't really cared, had asked out of politeness. She went to more important matters. "Would you like some cobbler?"

"Oh, no, thank you. I wasn't hinting. Aunt Lulu'd skin me alive if she found out I ate any of that cobbler she made for you." I smiled a little when I said it. Making little jokes — not anything really silly or slapstick, mind you — is my way of trying not to wallow in bad news but lighten it a little, if possible.

Doris Burkhalter didn't acknowledge my attempt at lightness but I knew she heard me because she took only one spoon from a drawer and dipped it into the cobbler, nodding slightly with approval when the sweet fruit met her tongue.

"Did they say how long they expect him to be in the hospital?" Aunt Lulu would skin me for sure if I came back with no fresh news at all in exchange for her precious blueberries.

"They don't know." She took another spoonful of cobbler.

"Did they give you any idea of what to expect?"

"They said it might not be a really bad one, like there could be such a thing as a good one," she said. In anyone else — Miss Sarah, for instance — I might have thought she was making a little joke like mine, making an attempt to lighten things up.

"Is there a of history of strokes in his family?"
This was hard going, but it seemed like a little
conversation was in order and empty clichés
and platitudes don't roll off my tongue as easily
as they do for some people. I'm much better at
smarting off.

She paused with the spoon halfway to her
mouth while she gave my question some thought.
"I can't tell you. His daddy got killed in a sawmill
accident and his mama died trying to give him a
little brother. There's no telling what mighta got
'em if they'd lived longer." She stared at the
spoon for a second, then let it finish its journey
to her mouth. "Maybe strokes," she said just before her mouth closed around the spoon.

"Are you doin' okay?" I asked.

"Oh, yes. The doctor gave me something."

I was glad to hear that. This zombie-like state
was a little unnerving even by her usual low
standard of vivacity.

"It's hard," I said.

"Yes," she said. She got up, covered the cobbler with foil, and slipped it onto a refrigerator
shelf.

"Is there anything anybody can do for you?" I
asked.

She shook her head. "Nothin' to do but wait
and see what the doctors can do, and I think
mostly what they do is wait and see."

I tried a platitude. "You'll just have to hope
for the best."

"Yes."

I'd been trying to think of some gentle way to approach another subject. I wanted to find out about Karen Willard and I thought the Burkhalters were the most likely people to be able to satisfy my curiosity about her. My brief marriage ended when Zach died in a hunting accident. Would it have been worse if we'd never been married? If I'd somehow been blamed for his death? I wanted to know how Karen Willard dealt with her loss. I looked around the room for some help, and I found it in the shape of a family portrait, one of those bland photographs where everybody got a haircut and put on clean clothes and froze in photographer-dictated formality and smiled for the camera. I could get to Karen Willard by way of Donnie Burkhalter.

The photograph was in a brass frame on a little bookshelf beside the table and although the color print had yellowed somewhat, and details like eyebrows had all but disappeared, it was possible to see how the two adults could have evolved into the people I knew as Alvin and Doris Burkhalter. The two adolescent boys could have been anybody.

"What a nice picture," I said. "Since I'm a detective, I'm guessing it was taken for a church directory."

Once again, my brand of humor missed its target. Doris Burkhalter didn't even turn her head.

"That was the first time the church did that, and just about the only time we had a family picture made." She studied it. "You know Kenneth, but I bet Donnie was gone before you'd remember him."

"No, I don't remember him. I think he must have died about the time I was born. I was looking through some old *Beacon*s and read about it," I added.

"He was just the sweetest boy," she told me, picking up the frame and staring into the faces. "If he'd lived he'd be fifty years old now, probably be a granddaddy, but in my mind's eye he's still twenty. Every year I bake him a cake. Alvin had a fit the first time I did that, with the candles and all. I still have a cake every year, and buy candles, even if I don't let Alvin see. You'd think I'd be able to picture him getting older, but I can't."

Not trusting my clichés and platitudes to respond to this revelation, I shook my head in sympathy. It was just as well. She needed a listener, not a talker.

"By now, if Donnie had lived, I'd have grandchildren, great-grandchildren, but I don't. It's hard, when all your friends have their children and grandchildren around them and you don't have any. You know you're missing something you should have had, something that would make it seem like there was some point to your life. Kenneth and Marie didn't have any children, and Lord knows what they'd have turned out like if they had, with the divorce and all, so I just have Alvin."

Alvin's name brought her out of her reverie, and she said in a different, harsher tone, "And there's no tellin' what I still have of Alvin."

I didn't have anything useful to say to that, either, so I tried nudging her in the direction I wanted to go.

"Donnie had been planning to get married?" I asked, to get her back on a track that could lead to Karen Willard.

"Yes. But he died."

"Tell me about the girl he was going to marry," I invited.

Her face closed down. "I won't even try to say anything nice about her. She wasn't good enough for him any of the time, one of these modern college girls. Didn't have any use for manners or morals, either one."

"It must have been hard for you." This noncommittal reflective listening was hard on me. I don't know how the psychologists do it.

"I tried to do what was right, what I knew a mother-in-law should do, to make friends with her, and help her make friends in town, but I never did really get to like her."

No doting mother I've ever known thinks her son's wife is good enough for him, but I didn't think it was the time to be philosophical or to suggest to Doris that she might have had unduly rigid expectations.

"You must not have minded when she broke up with him then," I suggested in my best bedside psychoanalyst manner.

"By the time I found out about that, he was dead. She's the one that killed him."

"What do you mean? I thought it was an accident."

"She took the heart out of him. Left town without a word and he was in such a panic when he went after her that he had that accident. She might as well have cut his heart out in the first place."

"I'm so sorry."

"She was a slut," Doris Burkhalter said, and that's when she broke into tears for the first time.

"Who was a slut? Mama, I didn't think you even knew words like that." Kenneth Burkhalter's voice in the doorway startled both his mother and me.

She turned away, wiping her tears on her napkin, so I answered. "Karen Willard."

He frowned and I thought he wasn't placing the name. After all, it had been thirty years.

"I came to bring some cobbler and we got to talking about your brother and his tragedy," I said.

His frown deepened. "My mother hasn't got enough on her mind right now without you bringing that up?" He was a big, rough-looking man getting close to fifty, handsome in a fleshy, sensual way that I found a little repulsive, and with an overbearing manner that I didn't like at all, but after all . . .

"I'm sorry about your father," I said, trying to

sound specifically sorry about that and not apologetic for my behavior. My hackles had risen at his tone, in spite of my role as charitable visitor, and I felt myself becoming defensive — a sure sign that I knew I'd been out of line.

"Yes, well," Kenneth Burkhalter said. "Well, you leave her alone about that. It was a long time ago and she's never gotten over it." He dismissed me, having expressed his displeasure, and turned to his mother. "I came to take you to the hospital. You ready?"

"Just about. You thank Lulu for the cobbler, Trudy," Mrs. Burkhalter told me. "I appreciate the thought."

"Yes, ma'am," I said.

She left the room to finish getting ready, I assumed, and I headed for the door, but Kenneth wasn't through with me. "Don't you bother her about that again, you hear?"

The words might have sounded like a loving son looking out for his vulnerable mother, but somehow, coming from Kenneth Burkhalter, that wasn't the impression I got. I sensed a bully pushing to have his own way, I sensed anger all out of proportion to my supposed offense.

"Lighten up," I said.

"You hear?" he insisted.

"I hear," I smiled at him. Sometimes my smile unnerves people, but it didn't seem to bother him. What was he so cranked up about, anyway?

Chapter 9

Having gotten the ruined romance of Donnie
Burkhalter and Karen Willard in my mind,
nothing would do but that I find out more about
her. I wouldn't want to call it an obsession, but I
convinced myself that my interest in her was at
least partly professional. As far as I could tell,
nobody I'd talked to had been in touch with her
since the day Donnie Burkhalter died. Besides
that, she'd have been about the right age. It
could have been mere synchronicity, but I managed to convince Hen that Karen Willard was a
possible on our missing persons list.

As a matter of courtesy as well as a search for
information, my first call was to the police in
Bristol, a small town about sixty miles south of
Ogeechee. According to the *Beacon*, Bristol was
where Karen Willard came from. Technically,
the Ogeechee Police Department — any city police department — has jurisdiction only inside
the town limits. Those limits are stretched if
some arm of an investigation that begins inside
the town reaches into the wider world. This was
one of those times. The Bristol police had no
missing persons report on Karen Willard. The
chatty clerk I was lucky enough to be talking to

told me she'd been working there since before God invented dirt and she knew the Willards. Or, actually, the Willard. Dinah Willard was the only one left. Oh, yes, it was the same family. Karen had gone off a long time ago and the parents had died.

My next call was to Dinah Willard. I identified myself and told her I was interested in her sister.

"My sister? You mean to tell me I've got a sister after all this time?" She had an interesting voice, low and husky, that sounded somehow intimate, confidential.

"Maybe I've made a mistake," I said. "I understood Karen Willard is your sister."

"Is? Well, yes. But I haven't seen her in years."

"Can you tell me how to get in touch with her?"

"I don't know what kind of oddball sales pitch this could be, but if you're selling something, you're wasting your time. I don't need sidin', I'm happy with my Internet provider, I don't travel, and I don't have money lyin' around to invest in a time share. Have I left anything out?"

"I told you, I'm a police officer in Ogeechee."

"Show me your badge."

I had to laugh. "How about I come to see you? I'd like to talk to you about Karen."

"After all this time? Why? What's she got to do with the police?"

"Maybe nothing." I waited.

"I'm always ready for a break in routine," she

said. "Come on and let's talk. But if you show up with a sample case and four-color brochures, I'll call the Bristol police. I have friends down there."

"No sample case. No brochures," I promised. "When would be a good time for you?"

"I'm always home. Anytime."

She gave me directions and a couple of hours later I drove up to a compact, square, red brick bungalow that looked like it might have been built in the early forties.

I pulled onto the driveway behind a miniature pickup truck. Beyond the truck was a garage with the roll-up door pulled down. Through the crusty windows I could see boxes piled high, every which way. The person who opened that door for any reason would be risking limb, if not life.

I made my way around the truck to a series of stones laid flat in the grass that led to the front door. I knocked, not trusting a doorbell that might have been around for as long as that driveway and garage, and was startled when that husky voice came from the side of the house, through the mesh of a screened-in porch.

"You're Trudy Roundtree, I expect. The car's a nice touch. I'm convinced you're not a sidin' salesman. I'm Dinah. Come on around here." She made a beckoning gesture with a hand holding a glass full of ice and a brownish liquid that might have been tea.

Obediently, I went in the direction she'd indicated, following the flat stones on around toward the porch where she met me. Then I followed her past a glider whose sagging springs and battered cushions suggested it also might have been around since the early forties, and on into the house. Like a lot of old houses in our humid part of the country, this one had a musty smell, damp and faintly chemical, like old paper, as though the fumes emitted by a paper mill in the process of creating paper were being released as the paper reverted to a more elementary state.

My hostess was wearing flipflops, shapeless plaid shorts and a knit shirt trimmed in a blue and green plaid that didn't match the shorts, and she was tethered to a long, flexible plastic tube that plugged into her nostrils and snaked its way back into the room behind her. She was about my height, but heavier than I am — say five feet plus five or six inches and maybe a hundred and eighty or ninety pounds — and if she really hoped to pass for a blonde it was time for her to do something about the grey-brown roots in her short, straight hair. The effect was of someone who once in a while could give a hoot — she'd bought the perky plaids, after all, and dyed her hair — but mostly didn't bother. I had a spooky premonition of what I might look like in another twenty years or so if I didn't watch out. I've gotten so used to wearing a uniform that my civilian wardrobe is pretty pathetic. I've never yearned to be a blonde, though, so if my natural curl doesn't desert me, when my brown hair picks up grey at least it won't be straight and have roots a different color.

Dinah Willard led me into a living-dining room dominated by a computer workstation on a dining table.

"My command post," she explained, flipping the plastic breathing tube to safety as she sat in the small swivel chair in front of the computer and pointed me to an easy chair. I sat.

"What do you command?"

She laughed a rumbly laugh, the kind that makes you want to laugh with her even if you don't know what's funny. "Not much of anything useful, unless you count keeping me in what passes for my right mind. It's not worth the effort to get out much." She waggled the plastic tube and inhaled deeply. "Emphysema. I get a disability check that helps keep me in food and drink." She hefted her glass in my direction. "My computer is my virtual social life. I don't even have to leave the house to be part of a poetry critique group and a role-playing game. Lately I've been playing canasta on-line."

"How can you do that?"

"Easy enough. Want me to show you?"

"I'd probably better tend to business and get out of your way."

That laugh again. Now I guessed the marvelous timbre could be attributed, like the emphysema, to too much smoking, and that the measured pace, which gave her conversation a

103

relaxed, intriguing feel, may have been dictated by a desire not to use up her air faster than the tank could supply it.

"Maybe another time, then. I bet you'd be surprised how interesting it can be. Interesting people, I mean. Of course, on-line you don't know the people at all, unless you want to . . . Then you only know what they want to tell you, whether it's the truth or not. The other day I was playing with somebody and after we'd been playing for a while, the question came 'How old are you?' I typed back, 'I'm fifty-four. How old are you?' . . . The answer came back, 'I'm twelve.' So we played canasta some more and then this twelve-year-old that is my social life wants to know if I'm part something. Part something? Like part tractor? 'I'm half Po-lack and half hillbilly,' the kid writes, so then I know what he means, at least. While I'm trying to figure out what my parts are, he comes back with, 'and part Catholic.' Well, I thought that was pretty funny, and said so. He comes back with 'What's so funny about being Catholic?' He won that game, honey. I couldn't concentrate for laughing."

By now, I was laughing with her.

Dinah took a slow, deep breath to restore herself after the laughter.

"He's — or she's — probably a college professor who gets a kick out of makin' up lies. That Polack, hillbilly, Catholic gag is pretty good for a twelve-year-old, don't you think?"

Before I could answer, "Can I get you some-thing to drink while we talk?"

"Tea would be fine," I said. "Whatever you're having," I added mischievously.

She grinned. "Tea. Just a sec. She disap-peared into the kitchen and a minute later called out, "You take sugar?"

"No, thanks."

She came back with a glass of tea for me and her glass also replenished — maybe it was lemon that made hers a slightly different color — and noticed me noticing the boxes stacked across the front wall of the house, effectively concealing the fact that there was a door behind them. That explained why she'd brought me in through the side porch.

"Can't seem to get ahead of the stuff," Dinah said, indicating the boxes as she set my glass down on a table near my elbow, using a *Reader's Digest* for a coaster.

"I can sympathize," I said. "My house hasn't been cleaned from top to bottom all at once in my lifetime as far as I know. Maybe I ought to just start putting everything in boxes and see where that takes me."

She laughed and did her sit-down dance with the plastic tube and the swivel chair. "Even if you're saying that to make me feel better, I like you for it. Picked up the habit of keeping things in boxes from Daddy. He never liked this house, so he never unpacked. Lived out of cardboard boxes instead of a chest of drawers till the day he died, like he was ready to take off any minute. Karen and I grew up feeling temporary about being here. I always thought that was why it was easy for her to leave."

She gestured with her drink. "What happened to your arm?"

"Fell off a beer bottle," I answered, sure by now that she had a sense of humor.

She didn't let me down. "I've done that a time or two myself. Never got hurt that bad, though." She swiveled back to the computer and then back to me before she asked, "So. What's the deal about Karen?"

"I'm not sure, exactly. It depends on your answer to my first question."

"Which is?"

"Do you know where she is?"

"Nope."

"When was the last time you saw her?"

"It's been a while." She sipped her drink.

"A long while?" I was trying not to lead the witness.

"Yes. A long while."

I gave her time to think. She sipped.

"Summer of sixty-nine," she said, finally.

I kept on waiting, determined not to show my excitement.

"She went to Ogeechee for a wedding shower or something. She was going to marry a boy from there."

"She went to Ogeechee for a shower and that's the last time you saw her?"

"That's right. The last time I saw her she was in the car with that boy, heading for Ogeechee."

"You say that's the last time you saw her. Did you hear from her after that?"

She thought about it, then shook her head and took another sip. "No. I don't guess we ever did."

"Did you report her missing?"

She didn't have to think about that one. She shook her head again.

"Why not?"

"Well, missing. That sounds so definite. Karen always was independent. Maybe you'd say stubborn. Wild. Our home life wasn't like something you'd see on television in those days, with the mother cleaning and cooking in her high heels and pearls and greeting the father with a kiss when he'd come home from his white collar job as an advertising executive or a surgeon or some crap like that." She took a breathing-thinking break after that mouthful. "Karen wanted to get away from here, from us. Independent . . . Used to give Mama fits. She just up and told us she was going to marry that boy and she was going over there for a wedding shower. It hurt Mama and they got into a fight about it. 'Who's paying for a big wedding?' Mama wanted to know. Mama had in her mind how the bride magazines said it was supposed to be done, the bride's family paying for this and that and she was afraid Karen was getting us into trouble with people we didn't even know. Karen told her she didn't have to worry about that, she'd saved up, but Mama couldn't get out of her mind that we might not be able to do the right thing, might not know how to act and what to do, or afford it even if we knew. I tried to tell her not to worry, but she said, 'I wonder if she'll invite us to the wedding.' I told her not to take it so big. We hadn't even met this boy. Why would she take for granted that Karen would marry somebody we wouldn't know how to act around?" Another pause here before she continued. "Anyway, that's all to say we weren't a close family and Karen was so independent, marching to her own drum like they used to say. We didn't know for sure when she was planning to come home, especially after the fight she had with Mama. A few days later, when Mama called over there some hysterical woman told her a wild story about how Donnie — that was the boy — Donnie Somebody-or-other — how Karen had broken up with Donnie and left, and Donnie was dead and Karen had killed him. Might as well have put a knife in his heart, or something like that.

"The only thing Mama got for sure out of all that was that Karen wasn't there and Donnie's mother blamed Karen that he was dead. We waited for Karen to turn up, but she didn't. We didn't know what to think. It's not all that far home from Ogeechee, but she didn't come. So, we thought if she'd broken up with her fiancé and was upset, she might not have wanted to come right home and explain things, maybe admit she'd made a mistake, you know, after fightin' with Mama about it. Maybe she wanted to go somewhere and get over it a little. So many kids were running off in those days, and she had a friend from San Francisco, one of her room-mates, I think, so we thought maybe she'd gone out there to the Haight-Asbury to be a hippie or something and we wasted some time trying to find that girl.

"And then Daddy got sick and Mama hadn't ever been well and it was taking all my energy trying to bring in enough money to keep us going. Well, anyway, no, we didn't report her missing. She'd gone off before and she'd've had a fit if we got the police after her. So. And after a while, when she didn't come back and we did start getting worried it was hard to say when she might have become a missing person. No, we just figured she'd turn up, or call or something, when she got ready."

Dinah's speech had gotten slower and slower, as if the heavy old memories were wearing her down. I waited a bit before asking, "But you're saying she never did call?"

"That's right. She never did. Mama and Daddy both died wondering where she was and how she was doing. Daddy figured she'd gone West and got rich and changed her name, so it didn't bother him particularly, but Mama wasn't as tough as he was, and the last time she'd seen Karen they'd had a fight, so she had a worse time with it."

"Did y'all ever think that something might have happened to her?"

"Sure. Especially Mama. But we never heard about it if it did."

"Would you want to know?"

"Know what happened to my sister? Well, sure. I mean, you've got the picture by now that we weren't 'Father Knows Best,' but we'd have wanted to know. Hey, some imposter might show up any day and want a share of the family inheritance."

She laughed and waved to indicate the extent of the family fortune. There could very well have been treasures in those boxes, but I got the point. Maybe Dinah Willard was the eccentric last (known) heir to a vast fortune, but somehow I doubted it.

"You still haven't told me what you're after," Dinah asked. "Do you know where she did go?"

"No," I admitted, "But I have an idea I'd like to check out. To be blunt about it, we recently found the body of a young woman who's been dead a long time. If you haven't heard from Karen since she went to Ogeechee, it's a possibility it could be Karen we found."

For the first time the boozy good-humored look died out of Dinah Willard's face, and without that animation I saw a lonely, sad woman.

"Dead?" She shook her head. "You're saying she might have been dead all this time, in Ogeechee? You know, awful as it sounds, I think

Mama would rest easier in her grave knowing Karen was dead, instead of thinking she never forgave her for that fight and didn't want to come back home. But why didn't anybody . . . Oh. I get it. You said you recently found a body." Dinah Willard might live on a diet of rum and coke, and she might have trouble breathing, but her brain was still working. "You just found her."

"Yes. We found somebody. I need to emphasize that we don't know who it is. It may not be Karen. But whoever it is, somebody killed her and hid the body. I'd been wondering why we couldn't match her with some missing persons report, but if it's Karen, she never was reported missing. That would explain it."

"Yeah. It would, wouldn't it."

"Can you remember if she had any broken bones, anything we'd be able to tell from . . . from what's left of her, to see if the skeleton we have was Karen?"

"Not that I remember."

"What about dental records?"

"She did have bad teeth, lots of fillings. Maybe that would help."

"It would. Who was her dentist?"

"We went to Dr. Huey, down in Blackshear, but he's retired."

"He probably gave his patient records to whoever took over for him. Do you know who that was?"

"Must have been Dr. Durrence. I started going to him maybe ten years ago."

It was a place to start. If we could find X rays of Karen Willard's teeth to match against Madame Marie Tussaud, we'd know.

Dinah Willard followed me to the door, drink in hand. "You'll be sure and let me know what you find out," she said.

"Of course. I couldn't raise all these questions and then leave you hanging. You'll hear from me."

She waved in an automatic way to whoever it was who had twitched the curtains in the window across the driveway. For better or worse, the presence of my police car in her driveway had probably made Dinah interesting to her neighbors. And been a break from her Internet social life. It had never occurred to me that I could get away from the confines of Ogeechee's social circle by way of the Internet.

Except for the chafing of my cast against my forearm, I was feeling pretty good as I drove back home. Gimped up or not, I was sure I was doing some pretty good police work.

Chapter 10

It took Dinah Willard's dentist, Dr. Durrence, a while to find the dental records bequeathed to him by Dr. Huey, down in Blackshear. Somehow I pictured him searching through boxes in the back of a garage or workshop, much as I had searched through the files on the second floor of the courthouse.

With Karen Willard's dental X rays to go on, it took the forensic odontologist far less time than it had taken Dr. Durrence to give us what we wanted. He identified our long-dead, adipocere remains as once having been an independent-minded young woman named Karen Willard who'd had wedding bells in her plans. I abandoned my fantasies about the missing women the GBI had offered me and instead tried to focus on what had happened to Karen. I called Dinah Willard to give her the news.

"I'm sorry," I said.

"Thank you," she replied. "But the truth is we gave her up a long time ago. I'm sorry to know she's dead, and it's awful to think she was murdered, but it's not like she was part of our lives, living or dead. She might as well have been dead even if she was still breathing, for all the real difference it made to Mama and Daddy and me."

That was a point of view that wouldn't have occurred to me.

"Well, now you know for sure," I said. "Not that it's likely, but if you think of anything that could help us figure out what happened to her, be sure to let me know."

That was just formula, an exit line. To my surprise, Dinah said, "After you left the other day, I got to thinking about Karen. More than I had in a long time. I remembered that Donnie's mother sent some stuff she said Karen had left there."

"What kind of stuff?"

"I don't know. Might be dirty laundry for all I know. We didn't open it. Kept thinking Karen would come home, so we just left it for her."

"It must have been something Mrs. Burkhalter thought Karen would want," I suggested.

"I don't know. Not necessarily. When Mama called over there, Donnie's mother didn't make any secret of how she felt about Karen. I don't think she'd've been trying to do Karen a favor. More likely she just wanted to get rid of any reminder of Karen, or maybe she hoped to pile guilt on Karen for dumping Donnie. How would I know? Anyway, I wondered, if I can find it, if you'd want to see it."

"Sure. I would definitely like to see it. And, Dinah, if you find it, don't open it, in case there's something in there that could be evidence of some kind."

Would I want to see it? Of course. It wasn't as

though I had a lot of leads to follow in the case, but remembering the clutter in Dinah's house, I didn't nourish much hope she'd turn anything up. Even if she could remember where she'd put something thirty years ago, what were the chances she'd be able to find it? And even if she could find the stuff, it was hard to see how it could be important. But you can never tell. And it was all I had.

After Dinah, the next obvious person to share the news with was Doris Burkhalter. Once again I knocked at her door, this time without a cobbler. She didn't look particularly glad to see me, especially when she saw I wasn't bringing more blueberry cobbler. On the positive side, she didn't look like she was on tranquilizers this time.

"I'm on police business, Mrs. Burkhalter," I said. "We've identified the body we found out at the Riggses', and I want to talk to you about it."

"Me?" She frowned in puzzlement, but she stepped aside and opened the door a little wider, inviting me in.

"Yes, ma'am. I thought you'd want to know. The body was Karen Willard."

"Oh." She sank into a chair, but she didn't look like she was going to faint, so I took a chair facing hers. Did I see a gleam of triumph and satisfaction in her eyes behind the shock?

"Well," she said, finally.

"Yes, ma'am," I said. I waited to see what she'd say next.

"What are you watching me for? What are you waiting for? After how bad she treated Donnie, you don't expect me to be all torn up about it, do you?"

"No, ma'am, you don't have to be torn up, but you should understand that it wasn't some thunderbolt from the blue that punished her. Some person did it. Some person killed her and crammed her body in that refrigerator. Some person has spent more than thirty years getting away with murder."

"I don't care," she said obstinately. "You can't expect me to care. I've got plenty else to worry about right now, and I never did care about her in the first place."

"You don't have to care about Karen Willard. But you ought to care if somebody's getting away with murder." Then I had an inspiration. "It might not matter to you much, not then, not now, but it occurs to me that maybe she didn't leave Donnie. Maybe somebody killed her instead. If that's what happened, you can blame that person instead of Karen for killing Donnie."

It was a complicated, manipulative thought, confusingly expressed, but she got the drift.

"Who?" She asked it warily.

"I don't know. Maybe we'll never know. But I'm going to investigate like I expect to find out. I'll start with you. How much did you dislike her?"

She glared at me. "It's a little late for me to

start putting on that I liked her, isn't it? You wouldn't believe that for a minute."

"No, I wouldn't. I know you didn't like her. My question is how much did you dislike her?"

"I don't know how to answer a question like that. I disliked the idea Donnie was going to marry her, but maybe it would have worked out. I don't know. She left and Donnie died so I didn't have to kill her to stop the wedding, if that's what you're hinting at."

That was exactly what I'd been hinting at, but she had a point. "Revenge?" I suggested. "Because you blamed her for his death?"

"Even if I was the kind of person to hurt somebody, to kill somebody, I couldn't have done that. For one thing, I couldn't think of anything besides Donnie. For another, I never saw her after the day he died. She left and he died and that was the end."

I didn't seem to be getting anywhere, so, reserving the comment that all I had was her word that she never saw Karen again, I moved on.

"You say she left. How did she leave? Who did she leave with?"

"Oh, I don't know. Don't think I ever heard. All I know is she left."

"How do you know that?"

"Somebody must have told me."

"Who?"

"It had to be Alvin, I guess, because when I got home he was the only one there. It had to be

Alvin that told me." She had a grimly satisfied look on her face, as though to say, "Ask him!"

"You sound real sure about that," I observed.

"It was the day my son died. I've been over that day a million times."

"What else do you remember?"

"Everything."

"Tell me about it."

"Why?" Not aggressive any more, just needing to be convinced.

"We know Karen was murdered. Maybe there's more to how Donnie died than you thought. Maybe somebody killed him, too."

She gave me a hard look. "It was a car accident." But she said it uncertainly, then sat back, settling in to her recollections.

"It happened the day after some of my friends had given them a shower. In those days, though, we said the shower was for her, not them. That was before women's lib, you know. Lots of pretty things. Truth is, showers are for the women. Men don't care about table linens and cookbooks and things like that."

I didn't comment, not wanting to break her mood.

"They were just kids, even if they did think they were old enough to get married, and they had all that energy, so a bunch of them went over to the school to play football. Alvin had gone somewhere. He was farming at the time and there's always something for a farmer to do, especially if there's something else he doesn't want to do, so he was gone a lot. And with everybody else occupied, I went to see my mother. She was at a nursing home over in Glennville then, not doing very well, and nobody else ever wanted to go with me to see her, so I always tried to find a time when everybody else was busy."

She stopped here, and I could almost see her wondering if she was going to have to put Alvin in a place like the one where her mother had been. I waited.

"I came home in time to start fixin' supper and nobody was there but Alvin, cleaning catfish in the sink. I'd asked him a hundred times not to make that mess in the house, but he took advantage of me being gone to do it anyway, all that blood and mess. He'd even cut himself on one of them. They've got mean whiskers, I guess you know. Served him right. Well, he went on cleaning those catfish and told me Karen had broken up with Donnie and left, and all I could do was watch him and think what were we supposed to do with the shower gifts and wonder if we could just keep them and let 'em do if Donnie and Julie got married after all. Then we got that call from the state patrol."

She drew in a shuddering breath. "I've never been able to look at another catfish to this day."

"So the last time you remember seeing Karen was . . ." I trailed off suggestively.

"The last time I saw my son," she finished my sentence. "All of 'em walking over to the foot-

119

ball field, horsin' around so much I didn't even think they'd make it across the street without gettin' hit by a car or something. Kids never do think anything can hurt them. They don't know anything about hurt."

"No, ma'am."

"Mama lived on three more years. If I'd had any idea, I wouldn't have spent the last day of my son's life visiting her."

We let that thought sit between us for a bit and then I stood to go. "I'll probably be talking to you about this again," I said. "I know it's been a long time, but with this new slant on what might have happened that day, with the possibility that Karen was murdered, and maybe Donnie, too, maybe you'll remember something that will help an investigation."

She nodded and I started to leave. Her voice stopped me.

"Alvin's comin' back some. He might remember something. Might do him good to have us ask him, like we believe he's still in there somewhere, not just worthless, even if it is hard to understand him right now."

"Yes. We'll sure want to talk to him." Was it just a coincidence he'd had his stroke about the time the word got around that we'd found a body at the Riggs place? Did the unregenerate Alvin Burkhalter know something that the born-again one couldn't live with? And the big question: Would asking him about that day finish him off — without giving us answers?

Chapter 11

Hen doesn't want me to get a big head, so he summoned enough self-control to pretend he thought my work on the case, leading to the identification of the body, was nothing more than routine. And he seemed to think all my joints were coming unglued when I told him I thought he ought to come with me to the hospital to interview a stroke victim about something that happened more than thirty years earlier. I'm almost certain it was an act.

"It was your arm got messed up, not your thinking apparatus, wasn't it?" he asked. I think he doesn't trust himself to know where to stop if he ever starts praising me, so he heads off in a direction where he doesn't feel like he has to know where to stop.

"Mostly my arm, Your Highness," I said, staring him down. "But it's all connected. When my aura was traumatized through fractures to my ulna, radius, and carpus, my psyche developed new access portals to the vast metaphysical knowingness." I was confident that spate of nonsense would get to him, and I was right.

He reached into a drawer, pulled out a form, started scribbling on it, and said, very convincingly, "I'm putting you on sick leave pending a psychiatric evaluation. Should be able to get you in with somebody within a month or two. You just go on home now, and lie down somewhere quiet. Somehow or other, we'll manage to take care of things around here without you."

Sometimes he can bluff me.

"Oh! You wanted it in English, then?" I asked. "I don't see what it can hurt to talk to Alvin Burkhalter. The Burkhalters knew Karen Willard better than anybody else in town and as far as I can tell they were among the last to see her that day. I've already talked with Doris Burkhalter. If we have any hope of getting anywhere on this, that hope is with them."

"Maybe it isn't such a bad idea," Hen said thoughtfully. Then, "Did I tell you what Milton had to say?"

"Must have slipped your mind. Y'all probably got to swappin' good ol' Chief of Police stories. No reason I'd be interested in hearin' about that."

Hen shook his head hopelessly. "Milton said he got to know Alvin Burkhalter and his good buddy Woody Riggs real well back when he was in charge of maintaining law and order around here. He said he used to be able to count on them to keep his life interestin'."

"Well hush my mouth," I said.

"Now there's a thought!" Hen said with more enthusiasm than he shows for most of my suggestions.

"Does Kicklighter think one of them could have killed her?"

"Hard to say. Says they were more in the line of general rowdiness and hellraisin', not vicious or violent."

"But."

"Yeah. That wrist of yours is a reminder of how rowdiness can get out of hand."

I cradled my cast. "Do you think Alvin Burkhalter killed her in a fit of rowdiness and the guilt turned him to religion?"

"I've heard of stranger things," Hen said.

"So you do think we ought to go try to talk to him?"

"I reckon." He sighed.

This explains why Ogeechee Chief of Police Henry Huckabee, Officer Trudy Roundtree, Doris Burkhalter, and Kenneth Burkhalter were gathered at the side of Alvin Burkhalter in Alvin's room at the hospital later that morning.

Oh, yes, we'd gotten permission from Dr. Bush, and he was there with us, just in case. He was a quiet little man who wanted everybody to appreciate the fact that he was taking seriously his responsibility to his patient.

"We're past that crucial period that pretty much tells the tale where stroke victims are concerned," he assured us. "The maximum swelling and deficit come within in the first seventy-two hours and after that we can begin to assess the extent of the damage. Now, Alvin's comin' along real well."

He nodded agreement with his own prognosis. Doris and Kenneth nodded. From his wheelchair, even Alvin managed a nod. Then the doctor turned to Hen and me. "The Burkhalters have agreed to let you come over here and talk with 'em, but I'm sittin' in to keep an eye on my patient. If it looks like this is settin' him back, you'll have to quit."

Hen and I joined the nodding chorus, then Hen took charge. He began by explaining what I'd already told Doris Burkhalter — we had the murdered body of Karen Willard and wanted to find out who'd murdered her.

I watched the Burkhalters as he talked. Doris sat tightlipped. Kenneth blustered a bit about us bothering his daddy, but in the face of Hen's bland but implacable authority and the doctor's agreement that it shouldn't do any harm, he finally simmered down.

It was hard to tell much of anything about Alvin. He looked better than I'd expected, not the drooling horror I'd imagined, a senseless drooping body tied to a wheelchair. He looked a little stunned, I'd have said, a little vacant and confused, tired, slack, but his eyes followed the conversation. Good.

I've been told that one of the most horrifying things for stroke victims is that information can continue to come in and be processed, but they may not be able to control speech and movement. That is, although stroke victims may understand what's going on around them, they

124

may not be able to make themselves under-stood. Other people sometimes make the mis-take of thinking there's nobody home. I felt that Alvin was at home. He might be able to follow our discussion. A look into his eyes confirmed that for me. They were intelligent, expressive of misery, anger, and frustration. Oddly, there was something about him now that looked more like the man I'd seen in that old family photo on the bookshelf at the Burkhalter home than the man I'd been used to seeing around town.

"We're here," Hen concluded his prologue, "because y'all are the ones most likely to be able to give us useful information." He turned to Alvin Burkhalter. "Mr. Burkhalter, I know it'll be hard for you to tell us what you know, if you do know anything, but I believe we'll be able to communicate. The doc says you can use your left hand just fine, so if you want to tell us somethin' — or straighten us out when we go wrong — you just wave us down. Can you do that?"

Alvin Burkhalter had our rapt attention. He raised his left hand and brought it down with a weak but definite slap against the arm of the chair.

Hen smiled at him. "Good. Good for you. Now, we're just gonna take it for granted that you'll all want to help us as much as you can."

"It won't change anything," Doris Burkhalter said. "I've been thinkin' about what Trudy told me, but I say leave it be. Whoever killed her, if

125

that body is her, and I don't guess I can argue with you about that, whoever killed her must have had a good reason. I'll go to my grave knowing she killed Donnie, whatever anybody says, so it's hard for me to get worked up over whatever happened to her."

"You might feel different about it if you'd seen what happened to her," I said. The woman was under a strain, but I thought she needed a jolt out of her self-centered world view. "Karen Willard was killed and crammed into that refrigerator. Somebody cracked her skull and took her poor dead body and folded it up — *it*, not *her* anymore — and forced the arms and legs and head into that little space and left that dead girl there to rot. Left it for the bloodthirsty little bacteria and insects that got closed up in there with the body. They've been working on her ever since. At least you knew what happened to your son. Karen Willard's parents went to their graves not knowing what happened to her. Let me tell you —"

Dr. Bush cleared his throat. Alvin Burkhalter stared at me. Kenneth was looking more and more uncomfortable as I talked. I fancied I noticed a slight green tinge to his complexion, but I'll admit I may have imagined that. I took those reactions as a compliment to my narrative ability.

"Trudy's psychic aura's got out of whack," Hen explained to the group, "so you'll have to excuse her for explainin' things in such a colorful way. She's right, though. We need you to help us out."

"I think it's a waste of time, but I'll tell you what I can so you can leave us alone." Kenneth spoke up loudly, just as I was trying to think of a way to introduce the word "adipocere" into the conversation.

"Fine," I said, relieved. I hadn't been enjoying myself, in spite of the impression I was trying to make on the Burkhalters.

"Start with the last time you saw Karen Willard," Hen instructed him.

With a sidelong look at his mother, who opened her mouth as if to speak, Kenneth hurriedly began.

"Okay, the last time I saw her was the day of Donnie's accident." He stopped and glanced at his father, who seemed to be following the conversation.

"And you told me that's the last time you saw her, too, isn't that right?" I asked Mrs. Burkhalter.

"Yes."

I turned to Mr. Burkhalter and risked a question, wondering as I did how he could manage to answer, but after all, the whole idea was to see what they could all tell us. "How about you? Did you see her after that day?"

"Once for yes, like you did a while ago? Twice for no?" Hen suggested.

With his eyes on Hen, Mr. Burkhalter slapped the wheelchair twice. I smiled, not at his answer but at the indication that he was, indeed, at home. It was the answer we'd expected, and it also showed that he understood the question and Hen's suggestion.

"I think that's the last time anybody saw her," I said, encouraged. "Go on, Kenneth."

"We'd all been messin' around, playing football, touch football so the girls would play with us." He stopped again.

"Go on," Hen prompted.

Kenneth shifted in his chair. "Karen left, said she had a headache. Said she'd go home — to our house — and lie down. The rest of us were having a good time so we let her go on by herself. Where we lived then was just a couple of blocks from the school, the football field, and she said she didn't want anybody to go with her."

He'd been explaining this to the tree outside the window, but now he turned to face Hen.

"I guess that's the last time I saw her."

"You guess?" Hen asked.

He took deep breath. "That's the last time I saw her."

"She just walked away from the football field and that's the last you saw of her, ever?" I asked.

"Uh huh." He sounded more sure of himself now. "When we quit playing, we all went back to the house. The first thing we saw when we went in the living room was this big mess, all the presents from the shower piled up in the floor, and a couple of pictures of Donnie and Karen torn up on top of the pile."

"We had all the presents at our house and they were going to store them there till after they got married and found a place to live," Doris Burkhalter interjected.

"Where was Karen?" Hen asked.

"She was gone. I told you. I didn't see her again after she left the football game."

"You say she was already gone. How did you know that? Did you look for her?" Hen prompted.

"Yes, we looked for her." Kenneth frowned even more fiercely. "She wasn't there."

"Do you know for sure she even went to your house?" Hen asked.

Kenneth shrugged. "Who else would have made that mess? Anyway, she'd been there. She left a note."

"A note? What did it say?" I asked.

"That she wouldn't marry him. Something like that."

"It said, 'The wedding is off.' " I'd been so focused on Kenneth that Doris's voice made me jump.

"No explanation or anything, just 'The wedding is off,' " Doris continued. "I thought that if she was that kind of person, the kind who could do that, I was glad she wasn't marrying my sweet son. I was glad about it for all of that little bit of time between when I heard she'd left and . . ."

"Is that all it said?" Hen asked when it became clear Doris wasn't going to finish the sentence.

She nodded.

"Were those the exact words? Nothin' about why or where she was going — or how she was goin' to leave?"

Mother and son looked at each other, confirming recollections.

"That's all," Kenneth said. "That's right."

"Mrs. Burkhalter, when we talked about this before, you said she'd left, that somebody came and got her. How did you know that?" I asked.

Her frown, though not as fierce as Kenneth's, also conveyed the effort of thinking back. "I don't know. Did you tell me, Kenneth?"

"I don't remember either," he said. "Maybe Daddy. He was there when we got there." This time he didn't look at his daddy, though. Apparently he didn't have my confidence that Alvin was keeping up. Or maybe he was counting on Alvin not keeping up. Maybe he wasn't sure his daddy would back him up.

"Mr. Burkhalter, were you there? Do you know how Karen Willard left that day?"

"Don't confuse him with too many questions at one time," the doctor said.

"Right. Sorry." I tried again. "Were you there when Karen left, Mr. Burkhalter?"

He made an inconclusive movement with his hand.

"Do you know how she left?"

His hand moved again, but indicated neither yes nor no by our newly established rules of communication.

Hen and I exchanged glances. "Who would

130

she have called? Who could she have called?" he asked Kenneth.

Again Kenneth and his mother looked at each other. Neither seemed to have any thoughts on the subject. Kenneth shrugged.

"Or maybe she didn't call anybody. Maybe she left on her own," I suggested. "Bus? Train? Airplane? Taxi?"

"You got no call to be snide," Kenneth said.

Hen gave me a quick grin. "Space ship? Subway?"

Kenneth shot him an evil look. "I think she must have called somebody."

"Any idea who?" Hen asked.

"No."

I glanced back through my notes. "Who else might remember something about that day? Who else was playing football with y'all?"

"Hmm," Kenneth said. "A whole bunch of us. Marie. Wallace Hughes. Junior Holloway. Probably Peggy and Fred Bartlett."

Mrs. Burkhalter watched me scribble names and decided to be helpful. "Wallace went off to Vietnam and didn't come back. I don't know where Junior is, but his mama still lives here. She could tell you. Fred and Peggy — that's Peggy Miller now, she married B. B. Miller," Mrs. Burkhalter said. "She lives over in Vidalia."

"We'll see how many of them we can find," Hen said.

"Marie works at the library," Kenneth offered.

131

"Uh huh," Hen acknowledged.

"Was there anybody hanging around the football field that might have followed her and killed her?" I asked.

Kenneth's frown reappeared, this time along with a strange, tight smile. "There was that kid. You know, Mama, the one who didn't have all his marbles. He thought she was pretty hot stuff. The one who wandered in front of a train a few years later."

"Leon Bell? There wasn't any harm in him. He was just simple. He wouldn't have hurt her, even if he had a crush on her. Even if y'all tormented him. Y'all did torment him, don't tell me you didn't, because he was a little different. He never did try to fight any of you, did he? No, there was no meanness in him. If Leon Bell had been hanging around watching, he was probably just wishing he could play, too."

Hen nodded in my direction and I made a note to see if there was any record of police involvement with Leon Bell. You never can tell with people, like we couldn't be sure about Alvin Burkhalter and Woody Riggs and their rowdiness.

"I'm trying to get an idea of what kind of person Karen Willard was, Kenneth," Hen said. "What can you tell us? Was she a flirt? A tease? Do you think she could have gone back to an old boyfriend? Or maybe an old boyfriend came and she wouldn't go back with him?"

"I don't know about any of that," Kenneth

answered. "I can't even really tell you what she was like. She was Donnie's girl. She was smart, I guess, being a college student. I guess she was kind of pretty, in that sixties way — no makeup, kind of a hippie look. We didn't see many like her around here."

"Did you like her?"

He looked surprised. "Never thought about that. No. I guess I didn't particularly like her, but what difference does that make now? Didn't even make any difference then."

"Mrs. Burkhalter, did you like her?"

"No. I've told you what I thought of her. She was always . . . well, flirting is the most Christian way I can put it . . . with anything in pants."

"Did she flirt with you, Kenneth?" Hen asked.

"I was dating Marie."

"That doesn't answer the question."

"Well, she was friendly."

"Uh huh," Hen said. He looked thoughtfully at Kenneth for a long moment, but left it at that.

"What about you, Mr. Burkhalter," Hen asked, turning to Alvin. "Did you like her?"

This time his answer was decisive, if inconclusive. One sharp slap, a pause, two more. Obviously, he was ambivalent. Somehow from the gleam in his eye, I got the idea that he was keeping up very well indeed.

"He didn't like much of anybody in those days, not Mama, not me for sure," Kenneth answered. "He probably didn't even notice Karen."

"Is there anything you'd like to tell us?" Hen asked Alvin Burkhalter.

This time the answer was clear — two resounding slaps. He closed his eyes and leaned back. His slaps had literally, merely, said there was nothing he wanted to tell us, but I'd have sworn there was something he could have told us. But what? It could have been anything from berating us for bothering his wife, to offering a vital clue, to accusing his dead buddy, to a confession of murder committed during rowdiness.

"I think that's enough," the doctor said.

"Yes," Hen agreed. "Thank y'all for your help. We'll leave it for now, but you can count on us talkin' to you again, knowin' your interest in the case."

As we turned to leave the sad family group, I was sure I saw tears leaking from Alvin Burkhalter's closed eyes.

Chapter 12

When we left the Burkhalters, Hen went on about police business and I went to my own doctor's appointment. The cast was coming off.

There are many things I don't pretend to understand, and most of them don't affect me or worry me. The application of a saw that is purported to cut through the cast but not hurt the arm underneath does not fit completely into that category. I don't understand it, but I did let it worry me.

Ironically, cutting the cast off went without a hitch. The magical little saw blade turned out to be something like one of those gadgets that flings a nylon cord around and chops through weeds, something that had no effect on soft stuff like my arm but battered away at the unyielding material of the cast. Maybe there's a parable about flexibility in there somewhere.

No, the part I'd worried about didn't happen. It was what I wasn't prepared for that got me — the wave of nauseating dizziness that swept over me — the nurse explained that the sudden greater flow of blood through the injured area often makes that happen — and the pain. The wrist didn't come out of the cast as good as new, oh no. The muscles that had been supported by the cast those past few weeks had given up thinking they were going to be needed again and had gone north for the summer. They were definitely not up to supporting the hand. The hand dangled as useless as a fish carcass, but painfully, vulnerably. I wanted my cast back. Instead, I was given a removable brace. I'd wear it most of the time but remove it for physical therapy and baths and for frequent applications of lotion to deal with what looked like a bad case of dandruff but was merely an accumulation of trapped sloughed-off skin that normally wouldn't even be noticed. I would have to wean myself from the brace.

Feeling more traumatized than I had in weeks, I returned to the station house to try to take my mind off myself with a little boring paperwork. There, I found a message to call Dinah Willard.

"I found it," she told me. "The box of Karen's stuff Mrs. Burkhalter sent."

"I'm flabbergasted," I said, carefully positioning my poor arm on the tabletop.

Her distinctive laugh was as effective over the telephone as it was in person. "I bet you are! Truth is, stuff accumulates around here in piles and since I hardly ever mess with the piles I had an idea which layer it might be in. I couldn't leave it alone, once I'd thought of it, so I got a boy in to help me. Didn't take as long as you might think."

136

She laughed again. I knew she had read my mind. I hadn't expected her to find it at all, certainly not so quickly.

"You want me to bring it to you?"

"I could come get it," I offered.

"Let me bring it. I promised Darrell if we found it I'd be sure he was in on what happened with it. I don't expect it to amount to anything, so I'd like to give him a trip to Ogeechee and the police department at least. He's a bright boy, at that age where he's fascinated by police work."

"He been involved with the police?" I asked.

She laughed. "Not the way I take your question. All right if we come and bring the box?"

"Sure."

"What time is it now? Let me see. I'd have to get hold of Darrell and clean myself up a little, and I don't have to tell you I don't move real fast, but we could be there in a couple of hours if that's okay."

"That's good. It'll give me a chance to round up the Chief so he can be here."

I told Dawn to get hold of Hen and I returned to my paperwork but couldn't keep my mind on it. Could there possibly be anything useful in that box? It was about as likely as that a stroke victim would recover his powers of speech and a vital piece of an old memory to go along with it. Or that he'd tell us if he did. Even so, Dinah and Darrell — whoever he was — would be a welcome diversion.

Hen and Dwight had both come in by the

time they got there. Darrell turned out to be a gangly, studious-looking boy. I guessed him to be thirteen or fourteen. He held a cardboard box under one arm and with the other he held the door open for Dinah so she could negotiate her way around it with the little two-wheeled cart that held her oxygen tank.

"Darrell's my next door neighbor," Dinah said by way of introduction. "I've put him on my payroll. We're gone get my place shoveled out if it kills both of us.

"Funny thing is," Dinah added, laughing, "we'd been playing one of those Internet games for a while, lying to each other a lot, before we found out who we really were. I'm not havin' to pay him much to help me because we made a deal. I won't tell you the kinds of lies he was tellin' me about himself, and he won't tell you mine. Mutual blackmail, you could call it."

Darrell blushed.

"Officer Trudy Roundtree," I said, extending my hand to shake his. It took him a second to respond to my formality, but he managed to rise to the occasion and shake my hand. "And this is Henry Huckabee, the Chief of Police; Officer Dwight Wilkes; and Dawn Brumby, our dispatcher."

Darrell shook hands all around, but it was obvious that Hen was the only one of us who impressed him — not young, slim Dawn; not rangy, rough-looking Dwight; not inconsequential me, of course. With his good-sized physique

138

clad in a nicely pressed uniform and a shiny badge on his breast, especially if he has his hair combed and is smiling affably, Hen does look, I'll admit, very presentable. He was the only one Darrell spoke to. "Chief Huckabee," he managed, big-eyed.

"Thanks for bringing this over, Miz Willard," Hen said, smiling at Dinah and Darrell and cementing their relationship. "We're gone need all the help we can get if we're gone find out what happened to your sister."

"I hope it'll help some," Dinah said.

"We'll see," Hen said. "Now, why don't you sit here while we take a look." He edged a chair closer to the table for Dinah.

"You can put that on the table," I said to Darrell, who was so struck with Hen that he seemed to forget he was holding the box.

The box was a cardboard shoebox that had originally held a pair of white patent leather pumps, size 6-1/2, that went by the name of Pamela. Apparently, back in the sixties, Doris Burkhalter had been the white patent leather type. Karen Willard's name and address, and the Burkhalter name and return address, were written on the outside with what looked like black wax pencil. It was tied with sturdy string. Every place pieces of string crossed, the intersection was tied with smaller pieces of string to keep them from slipping. I could picture Doris Burkhalter binding up that box, angrily securing each knot, trying to seal away her pain and every reminder of Karen Willard. Except of course there was no way she'd ever forget Karen Willard.

Darrell put the box on a table and we all gathered around. You'd have thought we were birthday guests gathering around the gift table.

"Evidence photos," Hen said, so I got the camera and took pictures, including close-ups of the postmark, the address, and the knots.

"Police procedure," Dinah explained to Darrell with a wink. He nodded solemnly.

When I finished with the photos, Hen pulled on gloves and, cutting the string, opened the time capsule. Never one to downplay a starring role, he lectured as he worked. "Now, son," he said, using Darrell as his excuse to show off, "we don't know if whatever is in this box has any bearing at all on the way that poor girl died, but in case it does, we ain't gone take any chances with it. On the chance there might be something useful here, we are going to be just as careful as we can not to mess it up."

Suiting his actions to his words, he opened the flaps of the box, releasing a stale smell. Slowly — partly to impress his audience and partly because he really is a good, careful investigator — he pulled out each item, held it up for all of us to see, and, with the assistance of his sidekick, the lovely and talented Gertrude Virginia "Trudy" Roundtree, put each item into its own zippered plastic bag. Dwight made an identifying note on each bag and added the items to an inventory list. It wasn't a speedy process, considering Hen's showmanship, the need to be meticulous, and the numerous photographs, but Karen Willard had waited this long for her death to come to light and there was no reason for us to shortchange her by being in a hurry. Besides, our audience showed no signs of being bored.

The box had been packed before the advent of those foam peanuts that Hen's daughter Delcie calls ghost poo. As Hen smoothed each piece of the newspaper that had been used as packing material, I recognized the *Beacon* and realized it was the issue that had the notice of Donnie's accident. Doris Burkhalter knew how to make a point.

I didn't think I'd been expecting much, but I was still disappointed at the small, apparently insignificant contents: A dark blue cardigan sweater with flowers embroidered down the front and around the neck, wadded around a white plastic Chanel No. 5 box that had originally contained body powder. The Chanel box rattled.

Hen slid the lid off and held up each item inside so we could all see: two little Avon sample lipsticks in pale pink shades, a brown Maybelline mascara, a green folding plastic toothbrush, an identification bracelet with an expansion band that had KAREN engraved on the outside of a flap that opened to reveal a picture of Karen and Donnie, a scrap of paper.

141

Hen held up the paper, lined white paper with ragged edges that suggested it had been torn from a spiral-bound notebook, and read. It said exactly what Doris and Kenneth Burkhalter said it would: "The wedding is off." Brutal. Blunt. Effective.

"That's funny," Dinah said.

"What do you mean?" I asked. Obviously, she didn't mean the note.

"I can't see Karen leaving that behind. She wasn't the Chanel No. 5 type, so it was kind of a joke when she bought that box in a junk store. She used it for jewelry and makeup because it was handy to carry around. She must have been in one heck of a hurry when she left, to leave that behind."

Hen looked at her, then at Darrell, then cleared his throat. "Well, now, Miz Willard, it's real likely that when she left without it, she didn't mean to be leavin'."

Dinah nodded slowly and fumbled behind her for a chair. When she spoke again, I was surprised to realize her voice was choked with tears.

"This means it's true." Dinah had put on makeup for the occasion of her visit to the Ogeechee Police Department, and now her face went pale and the makeup stood out garishly. "In spite of everything, I must have believed Trudy was wrong when she told me Karen has been dead all this time. All the time we were mad with her and thinkin' hard things about her, she was dead."

"I'm afraid that's what it looks like," Hen said.

"I'm sorry," I said.

Darrell moved over and patted Dinah's shoulder awkwardly, then stepped away and blushed. He darted a glance in Hen's direction. Hen noticed and also, then, gave Dinah's shoulder a sympathetic pat.

"I don't know why I'm bawlin' now," Dinah said, "except I guess I got used to her bein' gone such a little bit at a time that it never did really hit me. Now it's hittin' me and it feels like it's been picking up steam all this time."

"Dawn, get her some water," Hen said, because that's the kind of useless thing you say and do in situations like that.

"No, honey, don't bother." Dinah fluttered a hand in Dawn's direction and shook her head. "I'll be okay. It hit me, but it's not really a surprise. Ever since Trudy came to talk to me the other day, I knew. Maybe even before that."

She straightened her shoulders and adjusted her loose-fitting Hawaiian print dress. She rummaged in her pocket and pulled out a strip of toilet paper. She disengaged the breathing apparatus and wiped her eyes and nose. Then she hooked herself up again, squared her shoulders and looked around at us.

"One thing, though," she said, in control again. "Now we know what happened to her, we could have a funeral, or a memorial service, or something, couldn't we? We never did that. And I could bury her by Mama and Daddy."

"We can certainly have the remains released to you," Hen said. "I'll see about it."

She nodded. "Come on, Darrell. We got things to do, planning a service, trying to find people who remember her who'd come. It might seem peculiar, after all this time, but I always did say funerals are for the ones left behind and it'll make me feel better to do this."

"Good for you," I said.

"Meantime," Hen said, "we'll carry the investigation into her death just as far as we can. This box will be a help. And if you run across anything else that might help us, while you're goin' through things, you be sure and let us know."

"Thank you," Dinah said. "We sure will."

Dinah and Darrell went back to Bristol, apparently cheered at the prospect of some specific actions to take — planning a memorial service, excavating the Willard premises. Hen's suggestion of other possible items to help in the investigation would give them something to do and a way to feel useful.

"Put this stuff in the evidence room, Dwight," Hen said.

"Evidence of what?" Dwight groused. "Nothin' in here evidence of anything."

"Probably not," Hen agreed, "but it won't hurt us to hold it for a while."

Dwight put everything back in the Willard/Burkhalter box, crumpled *Beacon* and all, and locked it away in the closet we call an evidence room.

About then, Dawn took a call about a possible convenience store robbery and Hen answered the call.

I hugged my tender arm to my body and signed out for the day, thinking how pleasant it would have been to be able to go over to Kathi's Koffee Kup to have a piece of pie and talk things over with Phil Pittman. About my arm, he'd have been sympathetic but not sticky; about Dinah and her sister, he'd have been sorry, too. Yeah, I missed Phil.

Chapter 13

With Phil out of town, my next thought would have been to go collect Delcie and see what she was up to — coloring in a coloring book, playing Pokemon, playing jacks. Spending time with her is a restorative for my spirit. But she was gone, too.

Knowing how little there was in the way of food at my house, I stopped at Kathi's Koffee Kup for supper even if Phil wasn't there to go with me. Kathi has built a solid business out of offering good plain home cooking to people who could probably do it themselves but like to eat out sometimes without being too adventurous. She succeeds because she doesn't try to get above what she can handle by herself. She offers a couple of dinner choices each evening (along the lines of fried chicken and catfish, or pot roast and meatloaf, not along the lines of chicken Kiev and veal cordon bleu) and she uses the leftover vegetables as the basis for hearty soups at lunch the next day. This helps her cut costs and also contributes to the authenticity of her home cooking.

That evening, I noticed that her outdoor neon sign wasn't working as it should. Only the

"Kathi's" was lit up. I asked her about it when she took my order for a vegetable plate — fried okra, butterbeans, tomatoes, and cornbread.

"You wouldn't believe how expensive it is to fix that thing. So I'm thinking I may not get it fixed. Anyway, maybe it's time to modernize some. Don't you think that cutesy spelling is a little too cutesy?"

I remembered a dark-skinned gentleman giving me a different opinion than "cutesy" on the three big red K's that dominated the sign, but I merely nodded agreement with Kathi. "Maybe it's time to, as we say, 'update' the sign. Most people just call it Kathi's anyway, and it's not like you've got a lot of stuff printed with the whole name."

That was an understatement. Besides the sign, there was nothing printed with the whole name. The menu was a chalkboard behind the counter listing the limited daily choices, including the pies of the day, and I knew the plain napkins came in industrial size packages from Sam's Club in Statesboro.

Kathi went to see about my meal. I spoke or nodded to acquaintances who came in, all in the company of family or special friends, and was busily updating my Daytimer and trying not to look forlorn and lonesome when Hen came in and without invitation, sure of his welcome, took the chair across from me. That's what happens to a man who's grown up surrounded by women. Hen has always known he's adored. To-

147

night, though, he, too, must have been feeling a little forlorn and lonesome. With his whole family of adoring females (present company excepted) out of town, there was nobody at home to cook his supper.

"Why don't you sit down and eat with me?" I suggested.

"Don't mind if I do," he said, unfazed. "What's for supper?"

"You could turn your lazy head and read it for yourself," I suggested.

"But you already know and could help me out," he said.

"I'm having vegetables."

"What's the pie?"

"I'm not having pie."

"What can I bring you, Hen?" Kathi had arrived with another glass of water and set of eating utensils wrapped in one of Sam's paper napkins.

"I'll have the ham and scalloped potatoes with slaw, sweet iced tea, and a nice warm piece of your peach pie," he said.

"Why'd you ask me if you knew?" I asked, when Kathi had gone.

"It was a test," he said.

"A reading test?"

"A mood test. When does Phil get back?"

"Another week or so," I said, not wanting to admit I knew exactly. "After the newspaper conference he's going to visit a buddy down in the Keys and photograph some wildlife. Speaking

of moods, you're not going to win any conge-
niality prizes, the way you're moonin' around
with your family gone," I countered. I believe
the best defense is often a good offense and I'm
sometimes willing, if not eager, to be offensive,
even belatedly.

"It's my vacation gone, too," he said, as
though that was an excuse, "not just my family."

"Anyway, what makes you think my mood has
anything to do with Phil?"

"You get a little touchy when he's gone."

"Do not."

"Do, too."

This scintillating conversation was interrupted when Kathi came with our supper, and I
had completely lost the slender thread when
Kathi bustled away and Hen asked, "You hear
from him while he's gone?"

"Who?"

"Phil. You hear from him?"

"Some. You hear from Teri?"

"Some. Y'all talkin' about getting married?"

"Why? You think maybe if I got married I'd
quit my job?"

"Not you. I'd try to talk you out of that.
Wouldn't want to lose our token female on the
force."

"I'll bet you think I'd be sweeter tempered,
too?"

"Not you." He grinned at me again.

"So?"

"So, what?"

"Are you thinking about it?"

"I have no idea . . ." I'd started to say I had no idea why he thought it was his business, but my irritated gestures upset my glass of tea and jolted my arm so that unwelcome tears came to my eyes. Anyway, leaving it at "I have no idea" wasn't so bad.

Okay, so I might have been a little out of sorts. That didn't mean it was because Phil was gone.

We quit talking so we could attack the food and Kathi's cooking began to put us both in a mellower mood. By the time we tucked into our pie — I had some after all, pecan — Hen was entertaining me with the story of what he called "another one of our local geniuses," a young man who had messed up in various ways as a youth but managed to have his juvenile record sealed when he turned eighteen. Filled with the righteousness of legal rehabilitation, according to Hen, young Reggie had decided to go into a different career and applied for a job in security at the prison. Through some miraculous defi-ciency in correctional communications, Reggie was hired. I almost choked on a pecan when Hen delivered the punch line. "And then he showed up for work in a stolen car! He's gone have a job at the prison, all right, but it'll have more to do with license plates than security."

You have to hand it to Hen. He knows how to cheer me up. For the sake of the peace of mind of his nearest and dearest, this was the version of police work in Ogeechee he's always projected and encouraged me to project — all the criminals are funny and harmless. Since he's a better storyteller than I am, my adaptation is to exaggerate in the other direction, letting on that they're all master criminals and the forces of good (Hen and me, and maybe Dwight) are able to triumph only by great effort and by dint of superior intellect and zeal. Everybody knows the truth is somewhere between Hen's version and mine; we leave it to them to find a version of the truth that they can live with.

Both of us finished the evening in better humor than we'd started it. Finally, I went home.

Chapter 14

My house, as I've said before, is an old house. Aunt Lulu and my daddy grew up in it. Grandma lived there as she was growing up. I mostly grew up in it, too, because my parents were killed in a car crash when I was still young and Grandma took me in. It has all the beauties and drawbacks of a house of its time and place — high pressed-tin ceilings, tall windows, a fireplace with a distinctively different mantel in every room, a porch that reaches three-quarters of the way around, no closets, retro-fit electricity, and running water. I love every inch of it, splinters, rust, cracked sidewalk, and all. No matter where I am, when I think of home, this is it.

One of the most irritating things about having an arm in a cast is how hard it makes it to take a bath. People think they're being helpful to suggest that you pull plastic produce bags over it when you get in the shower. I decided it was easier — not easy, but easier — to use the tub, even with the extra hazard of climbing in and out of the slippery thing. My tub is easier than a more modern one would be. It's free-standing, with down-curved edges, so it's possible to get a grip on whichever side I need. A luxurious soak is out of the question, too, but I had been doing the best I could, resting the injured arm on a towel on the side of the tub and adding shampoo to give myself a bubble bath, but being careful not to splash. I had been dreaming about the luxury of a good soaking shower, running both hands through my hair, turning whichever way I like, once the dad-blamed cast came off.

Well, the dad-blamed cast was off, but any unsupported movement of my mending arm was insupportably painful. The shower was delicious, and it felt wonderful to have the hot water run over my arm, but running both hands through my hair would have to wait. I stood there and showered as though I was trying to make up for the showerless weeks. Finally, tired but clean, I made some microwave popcorn and poured myself a Coca-Cola. Then I settled onto the couch in the glassed-in room that used to be an open, screened porch, using my right hand to position my left arm carefully across my body.

Part of my inheritance when Grandma left me the house was a varying population of cats. Most of them are semi-wild, bunking down under the house or in the nearby woods as suits them. The character of cats being what it is, they don't come a-runnin' when the back door opens and I pour out cat food to supplement whatever else they live on, but my offerings do disappear. I like cats, like looking at them, like their independence, like the fact that they own themselves, so I like the wary relationship we have. There's something to be said for closer relationships, too, though, so I usually manage to promote (at least I think of it as promotion; no telling what they think) one or two cats to the status of house cats, which I can do if I get to a litter while they're fairly young. My current house cats were Biscuit and Dumplin', named, with Delcie's help, for two of her favorite foods.

I was barely settled when Dumplin' landed on my chest with a plop and repeatedly brushed the day's cares off my face with her beautiful grey-and-gold tail. Biscuit scrambled onto my feet and, true to her name, began kneading the lumps, for all the world like a cook making biscuits, before she settled down on my ankles.

There's nothing so secure as being anchored by cats. I still had my right arm free, to reach the popcorn and Coke, to hold up a book. Luckily, I could also reach the telephone, which rang as soon as I was settled.

"Trudy Roundtree," I said into it.

"Stacy, Trudy. You busy?"

"Nothin' I can't put off," I answered.

"I need to talk to you."

"All right. Talk." Dumplin' had settled down again.

"I don't want you to get this wrong."

"Get what wrong, Stacy? You haven't said anything." There's a limit to the good mood even a luxurious shower and a pile of cats can sustain.

Still Stacy stalled. I decided to help. "How's the house comin'?" I asked.

"You want to buy a lot, cheap?" There was no hesitation now.

"You're not worried about living there, are you? Grits are adaptable, remember?"

She laughed. "Actually, I hadn't even thought of that. I will now, though. Thanks a lot, Trudy. I mean it. Thanks. I may be able to use the fact that a body turned up there as a lever to pry Eric away from that spot. He might not be able to understand why I don't want to live so close to his mother, but anybody would understand why I might not want to have my house built right where . . . where . . ."

I came to her rescue. "But you said that's not it, not why you called. If that's not it, then why's the lot so cheap?"

"Because the whole thing is driving Eric crazy, that's why."

"Maybe he's just having second thoughts about living so close to his mother."

"Don't I wish! Are you eating? You sound funny."

"I've got a cat's tail in my mouth. What's Eric doing that's crazy?"

"You knew he's been keepin' an eye on the search for more bodies or whatever they're lookin' for?"

"Dwight mentioned it. That's not crazy, Stacy. It's just normal interest, I think, considering that it's his property. Actually, it's very smart. If he's cagey, he can get them to do some of the cleaning up he was going to have to do, leave piles of dirt where he wants them."

"Uh huh. I think that's what he had in mind, besides being sure if they turn up something valuable it doesn't just disappear."

"Smart boy. But they've quit looking for more bodies," I told her. "We don't have a multiple-murder site there, although if you want to pretend to think it is, I won't blow it for you."

"Thanks. But, see, well, I thought that was all there was to it, with Eric. You know, here's a body on our property and police are looking for more bodies, but that's not all there is to it. It's all out of proportion. Trudy, do y'all know who killed her?"

"Not yet," I said, trying to sound confident and glad Stacy couldn't see me. Dumplin' had decided to nap on my cradled arm, her tail tucked under my chin.

"Do you think it might be Eric's daddy?"

"Why are you asking that?"

"Do you?"

"As far as I know, it could be anybody who was living within the nearest five counties in 1969, Stacy. Do you — or Eric — know something you ought to tell me?"

"No. Anyway, I know I don't, but Eric seems worried that you'll think it was his daddy."

"Because it was their refrigerator — excuse me, Miz Riggs's icebox — and it was on their property? Or does he have some reason to think his daddy would do a thing like that?" I didn't see fit to mention the hellraising and rowdiness we'd learned about.

"I don't know. But you know how his mother's been acting about us building there. I think he thinks she might know something. I've decided Eric's a box turtle, shutting up inside himself, with that hinged shell that can snap shut with him inside so he can close out the rest of the world, or maybe a snapping turtle, with those vicious, mean old jaws."

"Stacy, you aren't telling me Eric's gotten mean? If he's . . ."

"Oh, no. I know how that sounded, but no. I think he's worried, that's all. I think his daddy was rough with him when he was a kid, and maybe that's what makes him wonder, but I don't know. But it seems to be worrying Eric. Can I tell him he's wrong, that you don't suspect him?"

"Sure. Tell him that. It can't hurt. But, honestly, Stacy, we don't know. Believe it or not, even as old as this case is we do have a couple of things to investigate, and we're doing it. We don't know much yet, though."

A sigh reached through the telephone wire. "Okay, I guess. Thanks."

Luckily the touch-tone buttons on my phone are on the handset, so I could disconnect without having to move much. I put the phone down next to the cat and grabbed a handful of popcorn. Woody Riggs? It was worth a thought. His refrigerator. Icebox. His property.

Another thought. Woody Riggs and the unconverted Alvin Burkhalter had been buddies with a rough reputation. And now we knew there was a connection between the dead woman and the Burkhalters.

I readjusted my cats and fell asleep pondering that connection.

Chapter 15

Marie Burkhalter is the head librarian in town, and since the new library, an airy, inviting brick building, is practically next door to the station house, I ambled over to talk with her.

I knew Marie by osmosis, not from personal experience. It's a subtle distinction, maybe, like the difference evangelicals will make between knowing about Jesus Christ and knowing Jesus Christ, but it's a real distinction nevertheless. It's often the case in small towns that you may know someone's name and family connections and no telling what all else about them, without necessarily ever having had a one-on-one encounter. I knew, for instance, that Marie and Kenneth Burkhalter were divorced. One of the customs of earlier generations that never has made sense to me is that a woman who gave up her natural-born name when she got married, to take her husband's name, kept his name even when she gave up the man. Here was Marie Burkhalter, who hadn't been married to Kenneth Burkhalter for as long as I knew anything about it, still going by his name. I just don't get it. Matter of fact, I don't see the sense in giving up your own name in the first place, and disappearing, when you get married. It's one of the many attitudes that keeps me from being absolutely mainstream in my own little hometown. As far as I can remember, I'd never had a conversation with Marie before, but I knew all that about her and I took for granted that she knew me in the same general way.

Inside the nearly-empty library, a bored-looking girl, whom I judged to be about nineteen, was shelving books. Marie, the supervisor, wasn't actually doing anything but presiding over the checkout desk with a book open on the counter in front of her.

"Somethin' I can do for you?" she asked, looking up from her book without closing it.

"I probably ought to get a library card," I told her.

"Well I should think so! A great big girl like you, you ought to be ashamed you don't already have one," she said, sliding her reading glasses down on her nose so she could look over them at me in the universal parody of the tight-lipped schoolteacher. The sparkle in her grey eyes and the tousled hairdo that reminded me of my own made me warm to her. "How in the name of goodness have you been gettin' along, and you a role model and all?"

"It's the uniform," I told her. "People just naturally trust me and let me take books out on their cards. My relatives, anyway."

"You mean to tell me Lulu Huckabee's abusing her powers?" Aunt Lulu's on the library board, but I'd never known that meant she had powers.

"I'm here to make things right," I said. "Unless that's an unpardonable offense."

Marie reached under the counter and came up with a blank form. "I'll need to see a picture ID."

I flipped out my police badge and identification card.

She frowned at it and turned it upside down, over, and around before handing it back. "Looks like you, all right."

"It's me, all right. Can I still get a library card?"

"Yes, indeed. You fill this out. Be sure to put your mailing address and your street address."

"Yes, ma'am."

"The mailing address is for overdue notices. The street address is so we'll know where to send the enforcers."

"Makes sense to me. Do I get my card today, or is there a background check and waiting period of some kind?"

"I'll fix you right up. You can browse for books while I do it, if you like."

"How many books can I take at once?"

She did the thing with her glasses and her nose again. "New patrons are limited to two books at a time. When we get to know you and know you'll return our books on time, you can have as many as you want."

"No kidding?"

"No kidding."

"Good policy," I said. I filled out the form and slid it back toward her. "Could I talk to you a minute, not about library business?" I asked.

"I thought your sudden need for a library card was a little suspicious," she said. "Do you really want one?"

"Yes, but there's no hurry. I can keep on using Aunt Lulu's."

She took the glasses completely off and called in the direction of the book-shelver. "Tish, I'm going in the back. You keep an eye on things out here. Call me if you need me."

Tish nodded and Marie gestured toward the door that led to the community room. I went through that door and she joined me, coming into the community room through another door, one that connected to a work area and small kitchen behind the circulation desk.

"Would you like some coffee?" she asked.

"How long's it been cooking?" I asked.

"Oh, well, if you're a coffee snob, I withdraw the offer."

"That bad, huh?"

"Definitely. I could throw it out and make some more."

"Not on my account, please."

The party room held a couple of card tables and several folding chairs. Marie unfolded two chairs and placed them on opposite sides of the table. She sat in one and gestured toward the other.

"So, besides bad-mouthin' our coffee, what

did you want to talk about? I don't want to leave Tish in charge long enough for her to get ideas above her station."

"You've probably heard about the body we found out at the Riggs place."

"Oh, yes. Beats me how the Pittmans make any money puttin' out a newspaper. Must be the legal notices that keep 'em in business."

"Phil says people don't read the *Beacon* to find out who did what. They already know that. They read the paper to find out who got caught and if they spelled the names right."

She smiled and nodded agreement. "The boy has a way with words. From what I heard it was pretty gruesome."

"Finding the body? Yes. It was an experience I won't forget for a while."

"Of course! I didn't connect, but you're the one!"

"Isn't it just like the local grapevine to leave me out! Yes, I happened to be out there when the body turned up. Eric and Stacy Riggs are friends of mine and I was watching them clear out the farm dump so they can build there."

"The Riggs farm dump. Out past the farmhouse and down a little dirt side road. I remember that place."

"You do? I always thought if you've seen one dump you've seen them all. What's so special about this one?"

Marie laughed. "In the golden days of my youth that road out to the Riggs dump was pretty much a lover's lane. It met all the requirements — not too far to go, well hidden, a little hard to find. Not the kind of place somebody would just stumble on to, especially after dark, which is just about the only time I was ever there. I wouldn't say I was fond of the dump specifically, but I do have some nice memories of the general area — me and everybody else in my generation." A dreamy smile played around her lips and her eyes took on a faraway look.

"Do those nice memories of the dump include Kenneth Burkhalter?" I asked.

The dreamy look vanished and she focused on me again, instead of the past. "Matter of fact, yes. I even have some nice memories of Kenneth Burkhalter that I associate with that place. You came over here to talk about Kenneth?"

"Only very indirectly," I said. "We've identified the body."

"Couldn't have been Kenneth. I saw him just the other day. Anyway, from what I heard, it had been there so long it had turned to soap or something and there was no way to tell who it was."

"The grapevine was reckoning without the marvels of modern forensic anthropology, pathology, criminology, and several other -ologies," I told her. "So your news is a little bit out of date. Once we had an idea who it might be, experts were able to compare some dental X rays with the corpse and make a positive identification."

"Anybody I know. Knew?"

"Matter of fact, yes. Think back. As you said, the body had been there a long time. You remember Karen Willard?"

"This is quite a guessing game. A Karen Willard somehow connected with Kenneth. You don't think he . . . Oh, wait a minute! Yes. Karen Willard. She was the girl that was supposed to marry Donnie. Right?" She beamed at me in the surprised, self-satisfied way people do when they've come up with the right answer in a trivia quiz.

"Right." I didn't rush things then, but gave her time to think about what she knew — or thought she knew — about Karen Willard. Her success at the guessing game, for the moment, was her main emotion. Any reaction to the actual death of Karen Willard would come later.

Finally she said, "But I thought she dumped Donnie and left town. You mean she . . ."

"That's what everybody thought," I interrupted. "But it looks like if she left town, she came back. That's why I wanted to talk to you."

She watched my face and waited for me to put it into plain English. "If she left town, she came back," I repeated. "My guess is she never left. Instead, somebody killed her and stuffed her into an abandoned refrigerator."

Marie kept watching me, frowning as she took it in.

I waited. When she nodded, reminding me of the blinking cursor that comes on the computer after the little hourglass has quit blinking, to in-

165

dicate that the machine is ready for the next process, I said, "I'm trying to find out what really happened to Karen Willard. The only place I can think to start is with people who knew her, trying to see what they can remember about the last time they saw her alive."

Marie nodded, cursor blinking.

"What can you tell me about the last time you saw her? Anything at all might help."

She shook her head. "I don't see how I can be much help. The last time I saw her — the only time I knew her at all — was in the summer of 1969. You're asking me to remember something that happened more than half my lifetime ago? Trudy honey, I'm doin' real well to remember to pick up the dry cleaning I dropped off last week."

"Do you remember what kind of person she was? Did you like her?"

"I didn't like her much. For one thing, she was an outsider, different, and even if she had already settled on Donnie, she seemed like competition, if you know what I mean."

"I'm not sure I do know what you mean."

"Well, I wouldn't exactly say she was a flirt, not in the old Southern-charm kind of way, but she did seem a little too sexy to me. Maybe it was just that she was a little older. I don't know. It's hard enough to try to remember what happened thirty years ago, much less how I felt about things."

"I can imagine," I said.

She laughed. "That would put you in pre-school, right? Do you remember how you felt about things back then?"

"Some things. It's funny. Looking back, sometimes I do remember how I felt about something or other — like being upset when Eric got his fingerpaint on my new white shirt, or having my feelings hurt when Hen wouldn't take me fishing with him."

"Well, for what it's worth — not much, I'm sure — I remember being jealous of Karen, whether there was any reason to or not."

"Maybe I can prod your memory a little," I said, "see if you can remember anything else."

"Okay," she said. "I'll play your little game. I don't have any pressing appointments." But she did stroll to the door and take a look at how Tish was doing. Then she sat down again, clasped her hands together on the table in front of her, and waited to be prompted.

"You could start by remembering the day Donnie Burkhalter died."

A sad smile now. "Oh, I remember that day all right. I never will forget when I heard about Donnie. I'd been mad with Kenneth about something; he'd been late for a date or something absolutely major and I was all absorbed in the kind of self-centered pouting girls get into in that adolescent romantic tug-of-war. Well, that got knocked out of me when I heard about Donnie; not that it excused Kenneth, mind you, but it blew some of my pouting clean out of my mind. I really liked Donnie. He wasn't as exciting — as dangerous-feeling — as Kenneth was, but he was nice. That dangerous side of Kenneth was what appealed to me, I think. What do girls know?"

She paused as though for an answer, but I was too smart to try to answer that one.

"So you do remember that day. Can you remember if you saw Karen again?"

"I don't think I did. I'm pretty sure I didn't. See, she didn't even come to the funeral, and people noticed that, so I think I'd have remembered if I saw her again after that. But there's no reason she'd have been around, anyway, except for Donnie."

"Okay. You didn't see her after the day Donnie died. Had you seen her on that day?"

"Let me think. Oh, yes. Yes. I do remember. You're good at this, Trudy. A bunch of us had been messin' around over at the school, playing touch football or something. Yes. Football. Not so much for the game, you understand, as for an excuse to run into each other in daylight. The emphasis was more on touch than football."

"Can you remember who else was there — anybody else I could talk to who might remember something?"

"Let me see. Who all was there? Karen and Donnie, me and Kenneth, maybe Wallace Hughes. I had a halfway crush on him, but I was going with Kenneth. Yes, Wallace was there, but that won't do you any good. He didn't come back from Vietnam. Probably the Bartletts. Peggy had a crush on Wallace, too, so she'd have tagged along with Fred. Just a bunch of kids."

"So you were all playing football."

"Yes, I do remember some things about that day. I remember Karen quit playing, left before any of the rest of us did. Said she had a headache or something. The Burkhalters lived just a couple of blocks away and she said she'd walk. She didn't want Donnie or anybody to go with her, said she'd want it quiet when she got there, so we all just kept playing. But after a while I noticed Kenneth wasn't there, and I decided he'd followed Karen."

"Did you think he liked her — I mean boy-girl stuff, like he had a crush on her?"

"No, not really. For me, it was just generalized jealousy. When it turned out he hadn't followed her — he'd twisted his knee and crawled under the bleachers and fallen asleep — I was already half-mad at him and didn't get over it in a hurry. Wouldn't have wanted him to think I was too easy. And then he turned up late for our date and I got more upset. You know how teenage queens are. Sometimes you'd pick a fight so you could make up. You ever do that?"

"Not for a while." But I had to smile.

"You're right, Trudy. That wasn't just any old day. It was a very significant day. Looking back, I wonder why on earth it didn't dawn on me that if I was so jealous of Kenneth even then, and didn't feel like I could trust him even then, I didn't have any business marrying him. Anybody should have been able to see how it would turn out."

"Maybe it was hard for you to see any alternatives," I suggested, thinking of the appallingly small pool of eligible men in Ogeechee. It can't have changed much. I thought of how Aunt Lulu and Miss Sarah had said everybody in town expected Donnie Burkhalter to marry Julie Todd. "And sometimes it's hard to go against what everybody seems to expect you to do."

"Too hard for me, anyway, so I married Kenneth and then had to divorce him. I might have been wrong about him going after Karen, but if I was, she's the only skirt he didn't chase."

"Did you see Karen again after she left the football game?"

"No, I'm sure I didn't. When we quit fooling around at the football field, we all walked over to the Burkhalter house, to see if she was feeling any better, but she wasn't there. Instead, what we found was a big mess. Somebody had thrown a shower for the happy couple a day or two before, and all those shower gifts were piled up in the floor in the living room — the pillowcases my mother had embroidered for them, and everything — and a note from Karen saying she was leaving."

"What did you do?"

"None of us knew what to do, or even what to think. Donnie took off in his car looking for her, and after a while the rest of us kind of went our way. Kenneth and I had a date later, like I said, and I wanted to get on home and primp a little after all that unladylike football playing. And that's it." She looked at me sadly.

"Did y'all talk about what could have happened to make Karen take off like that?"

"Sure did. We couldn't figure it out. Mainly, nobody could see how, or rather when, they could have had a fight. They seemed to be gettin' along okay at the football field. But from all the mess, it looked like she'd had a real fit. I'd have guessed she was too cool a customer for that, but there it was. Something serious. It must have looked like that to Donnie, too, for him to take off after her like that. But then it didn't matter, because it was just a few hours later that Donnie had his accident, and Karen just didn't seem important any more. People liked Donnie and we didn't really know her."

"Was there anybody she'd made friends with? Anybody she might have confided in or talked to?"

"Not that I can think of. I'd have been as likely as anybody, I think, since I was dating Kenneth, but I can't say we were really friends. She didn't confide in me, if that's what you're after."

"Did anybody know how she left?"

"I never thought about that. I have no earthly idea."

At this point our *tête à tête* was interrupted. Tish tapped on the door, opened it, and stuck her head in. "Julie's here now, so I'm goin'. I told her she was in charge."

"How'd she take it?" Marie asked Tish.

Tish shrugged. "She likes bein' in charge; she don't like me tellin' her anything."

"Okay. You go on. I'll see you next week. Tell Julie I'll be out in a minute."

Marie looked quizzically at me and I nodded. Tish made a sour face and went away.

"Julie's never been known for her patience and sweet temper," Marie explained. "And she doesn't like Tish at all."

Something clicked. "Julie Todd?" I asked.

"Small world, isn't it? Yes, Julie Todd, the very Julie Todd who had planned to marry Donnie Burkhalter. She's one of our volunteers."

Marie leaned back in her chair, apparently not in a hurry to go relieve Julie of her responsibilities. "Young people think they know how life is going to work out for them, but nobody really does, do they? Julie thought she was going to marry Donnie and live happily ever after; then it was supposed to be Donnie and Karen who got married and lived happily ever after. If life had worked out differently, either Karen or Julie and I would have been sisters-in-law. At least until I divorced Kenneth. It's hard to imagine. I guess it's a good thing we can't see what's coming. I should have been able to see what was coming with Kenneth, though. Honestly, kids are so stupid."

"Do you think if Donnie hadn't died — if Donnie and Karen — or Donnie and Julie, for that matter — had married — do you think it would have made any difference to you and Kenneth?"

"That's an interesting question. Hmm. No, I don't think so. Kenneth always was a macho, selfish jerk. Took after his daddy too much, I think. Funny thing is, after Donnie died, Mr. Burkhalter changed. Kenneth just got worse, but I couldn't see it, not in time to make any difference."

"In that happily-ever-after life, would you and Karen have been friends?"

"No, I don't think we'd ever have been close, even if we had been sisters-in-law. We might have found a common interest in books, but I think she was also a selfish, detached person. Probably she and Donnie wouldn't have lasted, either. Then we'd have had that in common, too, being divorced from a Burkhalter."

"What about Julie?"

"What about Julie? Do you mean would we have been friends? Probably about like we are now, if that's friends. One thing about old friends — I guess I mean people you've known a long time — is that you've learned how to get along with them, what you can expect and what you can't. You can avoid the sharp edges, and you can get along. Maybe you aren't old enough to appreciate that yet. With Julie, now, when we were growing up she always had a 'my way or no way' attitude toward life, that I found hard to take. She seemed to think she was so special the universe was supposed to kowtow. That hasn't changed. I suppose if she'd gotten married she'd have been a different person by now, had some of those sharp edges worn off, like me, but I don't think we'd ever have been what we'd have called in those days 'best friends.' "

"Her way or no way? Is that a good trait in a volunteer?"

Marie laughed. "It's not the worst trait I've seen, believe me, not half as bad as not knowing the alphabet well enough to shelve books by author, or showing up hung over, and we've had some volunteers like that. Oh, Julie and I get along fine. If she doesn't do something the way I want it done, I just get Tish or somebody to do it over."

"Why put up with her if she won't do things right?"

"Firing a volunteer can be tricky, especially one who's famous for her temper fits. And one who's a big financial supporter of the library. You'd never know it by the way she lives, but Julie's well off. And she's on the library board. Wants to make sure we don't get too backward, I guess, and make sure we keep her in the kind of books she wants to read. She's done a lot of good. One of the things she thought up was taking books to patients at hospitals and nursing homes. Sort of a specialized bookmobile. Anyway, I didn't say she won't do things right."

Marie made a face. "She does when it suits her. She's not a big fan of doing anything just because it suits somebody else. Never was. That isn't a particularly bad approach to life, when you think about it."

"No, it isn't," I agreed.

With a flash of humor, Marie added, "Julie doesn't always do things the way I want her to — but I'm not the kind to think my way's the only way."

One of the lesser known benefits of small town life, if you happen to be in one of the snoopy professions, is that people assume you already know everything about everybody, so they don't bother being discreet. Of course, it was possible that Marie's indiscreet comments about her volunteer and library supporter had to do with my ingratiating manner and her nostalgia about her high school days and Donnie Burkhalter.

"Actually, Donnie might have gotten off easy," Marie continued thoughtfully. "Being married to either one of those women wouldn't have been a bed of roses. Maybe he got off easier than I did, marrying Kenneth." She smiled. "Don't pay attention to my cynicism, Trudy. I never grew out of it, I guess. I get along pretty well here, after all. Working at the library may not be a glamorous job, but it's a job, and it keeps me in touch with people who like to read, so it isn't all bad."

"I'll keep that in mind," I said. "Thanks for your help."

"Such as it was," she said.

She opened the door for me, but went back the way she had come, through the other door. As I left, I saw her bent over Julie Todd, who was seated at a computer console at the main desk.

I was back at the station house before I realized I'd forgotten to pick up my library card after all.

Chapter 16

On patrol again — basic, routine chores have to be handled even in times of more momentous investigations — and thinking to kill a whole flock of birds with one casual-seeming little pebble, I drove out to the Riggs place. Stacy's concern about Eric's worry had caught my interest and I was hoping to find out if Eric had any real reason to think his father could have been involved in Karen Willard's death.

Nothing was happening on the building site. The forensic teams had satisfied themselves that this wasn't a mass grave site, and Dwight had taken down the yellow tape that marked it off as a crime scene. The area was noticeably cleaner than the last time I'd seen it. The spot no longer looked like a farm dump. It looked like nothing more than a building site awaiting a contractor. Even so, I couldn't help but notice a couple of cars dawdling along past the site, occupants rubbernecking like out-of-towners in the Big Apple.

Doubting that the investigators had scraped the whole thing off and carted it away for analysis, I concluded that either Eric had managed to have some influence on the way they left the place or he'd been hard at work since they left. My next obvious conclusion was that Eric was proceeding with plans to build there, regardless of the now-known history of the spot as well as his mother's and Stacy's objections. On the other hand, there was nobody at work at the moment. Maybe Stacy had managed to slow, if not completely halt, the project.

Eric's truck was parked at his mother's and before I knew what I was doing, I'd pulled in behind it. Thinking of how unpleasant Mrs. Riggs had been at our last interview, I was taking my time getting to the door, waiting for my spine to stiffen, when the front door opened.

At first, Eric's back was toward me; he was apparently bidding his mother goodbye. Then he turned and saw me. I was caught.

"Hey," he said.

"Hey," I said. "Looks like I've got you blocked."

"That's okay. I'm not in a big hurry. You need Mama?" he asked, turning back to the house without waiting for an answer.

I shrugged. As far as I had thought it through, my approach was going to be that I was just being friendly, seeing that everything was okay with them and the police hadn't done any damage. I hadn't worked on actual dialogue though, so I followed him without answering.

"Mama?" he called, "I'm not gone yet. Trudy Roundtree's here again. I don't think it's a social call."

"Is that why I don't rate the parlor?" I muttered, following Eric past that door, now closed. "Or was it Hen that rated?"

Mrs. Riggs, holding a coffee mug, stood in the kitchen doorway. I didn't think she looked particularly friendly.

"Mornin', Miz Riggs," I said, trying to sound like Hen. "Thought I'd see how you're doing. Things settlin' down okay?"

"Well," she said.

"You want some coffee, Trudy?" Eric asked. "I guess I'll have some more."

"Thanks."

Sitting round the kitchen table with mugs of coffee, we were far more relaxed than we'd been in the parlor, and I don't think it was the absence of Hen's intimidating presence that did it.

It wasn't a social call, so I got down to business. "Just in case you've been hearing things on the grapevine, I wanted to let you know, officially, that we've identified the body we found on your property."

"I'd heard that," Mrs. Riggs said.

Eric nodded and sipped coffee, looking at me over the mug.

"It was a woman named Karen Willard. She was engaged to marry a son of Alvin and Doris Burkhalter."

"I remember her," Mrs. Riggs said. "Is that all you came about?" She glanced at Eric.

"Yes, ma'am. I don't have much more to tell

you. We haven't found anybody who saw her after the day Donnie Burkhalter died."

"That was an awful day," she said shakily. Using both hands to steady her coffee mug, Mrs. Riggs managed to set it down without upsetting it, but not without several black drops splashing onto the quilted floral placemat in front of her.

"Yes, ma'am. I'm sorry to upset you." I was sorry, but since she was already upset, I decided not to waste it. "I need to ask you something."

She took her hands off the coffee mug and put them in her lap.

"When Hen and I were here the other day talking to you, you said you didn't want Eric and Stacy building over there. Now that we know more about it, I want to ask if you had some reason to worry about what they'd find if they started digging."

"Trudy!" Eric slammed his mug down, messing up his own placemat in the process.

I held up a hand to forestall his protests. "Eric, we're investigating a murder here and I'll be asking a lot of people questions that might not be acceptable in polite society, but that need to be answered. Miz Riggs?"

Her chin came up and she gripped the mug. "I didn't and I don't want them building. Period."

"Mama!" Eric protested. "We don't need to go into that for Trudy." Eric wanted to build on that lot; Stacy wanted to build, but anywhere else; his mother didn't want them to build anywhere at all. There was no way this trio of different wants would ever be able to make beautiful music. My life seems so simple by comparison.

"I want them here, with me," Mrs. Riggs said, now looking at Eric and ignoring his protest. "That's all there is to it."

"Okay," I said, taking a sip of my own coffee and carefully setting the mug down. I thought it would be nice if I could manage to leave my placemat clean. Then Mrs. Riggs surprised me.

"You mean that girl, that body, she's been out there all this time?"

"As far we can tell, that's right," I said.

"Ever since that day? The day Donnie Burk-halter died?" she asked.

"Maybe."

"I remember the day Donnie died. I'd been in to the grocery store and saw Doris, and then later when we heard about Donnie all I could think of was that she might have been at the grocery store when her boy died and how would she ever get over it. Woody was upset because Eric wasn't here like he was supposed to be and I didn't have supper ready. I had a bad time then, worrying about why Eric wasn't home and if something had happened to him while I was off at the grocery store, like Donnie."

When she came to a stop, I said, with a sideways glance at Eric, "This seems like a good time for me to tell you that we know Mr. Riggs and Alvin Burkhalter used to have a reputation

181

around town, and a way of attracting the attention of the police. I'm going to ask you, Miz Riggs, just to be absolutely clear. Were you afraid they'd find something better left hidden when they started digging there?"

"No. Nothing but trash and snakes," she said. "That's not why I don't want them building there."

"So you have no reason to believe your husband was involved in Karen Willard's death?"

"No."

She was adamant, but I recognize denial when I see it. She had taken a position and was sticking to it. It was a standoff. "I think I've taken up enough of your time for now, Miz Riggs. If you do think of any little old thing that would help us find out what happened to Karen Willard, let me know. Okay?"

"Of course I will," she said, but somehow it didn't encourage me.

"Eric, come on with me and I'll move my car now," I said.

"But," Eric said, before I caught his eye and my blue iceberg gaze convinced him I wanted him to leave with me.

"Yeah, I better be goin' too, Mama. See you tomorrow." He gave her a hug, then led the way back out the front door.

We stopped at his truck.

"Now that you've cleared Mama," he said with a pitiful attempt at nonchalance, "are you gettin' anywhere on this?"

"Mainly clearing away underbrush, sort of like you and that dump," I said. "Looks like you got the crime team to help out with your cleanup."

He smiled. "Didn't seem to matter much to them where they left things when they were through, so I made some suggestions. Lucky it was a garbage dump in the first place. Hard for 'em to mess that up any."

"So everything's okay?"

"Heck, yeah."

A car drove past and we watched the dust settle. "I'm thinking of puttin' up a lemonade stand and makin' a tourist attraction out of it."

"You can't blame people for being interested, Eric. I expect the more work you do, the less it looks like it used to, the less interest it'll have for anybody."

There was no way to ease into my next subject so I decided to be blunt. "Stacy thinks you're worried that your daddy might have had something to do with killing Karen Willard."

He heaved a great sigh. "It occurred to me. He was mean enough. And she was found on our land, after all. He'd've dang sure known about that refrigerator. Trudy, this is hard to talk about, even after all this time. We never talked about it when Daddy was alive. He knew how to behave himself when other people were around, but he was a mean ba—. He was mean. Sometimes he'd hit me — more than just a run-of-the-mill whipping like I probably deserved, I mean. Sometimes for no reason besides he'd been out drinking with some of his friends — like Alvin Burkhalter — or Mama didn't have supper ready when he wanted it."

"Did he hit your mother, too, or just you?"

"He'd hit her once in a while. Not a lot. Sometimes. I was afraid of him and I think she was, too. He's been gone a long time, and I know I shouldn't say this, but I wasn't real sorry to see him go."

"We were in junior high, weren't we?"

"Yeah, old enough that I felt guilty for not feeling worse about him dying, and young enough that I felt guilty for wishing him dead."

"We've got to keep on investigating this," I said, "wherever it takes us."

"I know." He absentmindedly rubbed at a spot on a fender. "But you know what?"

"What?"

"I do have trouble thinking of him as a killer. Maybe I just don't want to believe it, don't want to think it was in him to do that kind of thing. Because . . ."

"Because then it might be in you," I finished for him.

"Yeah."

"Yeah."

As I drove away, I kicked up a cloud of dust for Eric to drive in. I couldn't help wondering where we'd all be in this when the dust settled.

Chapter 17

"You ask me, it's a big waste of time trying to find out who killed this girl," Dwight said.

"Woman," I said.

"Huh?" Dwight said.

"Never mind, Dwight," Hen cautioned him.

We were in the file room at the station house, going over assignments.

"Why?" I challenged. "You think she was just a girl, not important, not even from Ogeechee, so we should just give up?"

Dwight leaned away from me, on the two back legs of his chair, exactly the way Grandma used to tell me would ruin the chair and bring about my early death from bashing in the back of my head. He raised his hands and rolled his eyes in a parody of astonishment and retreat.

Hen decided to protect him from me.

"He didn't say that, Trudy. He said, and I'll paraphrase here, Dwight, if it's all the same to you; he said he thought it would be hard to learn enough about what happened all that time back to make a case."

I took a threatening step toward Dwight and was gratified to see the chair wobble. "That what you meant, Dwight?"

The chair legs came down with a thump and Dwight snorted. "Yeah," he said. "That's what I meant. But whoever did it's probably dead by now, anyway. Like I said, we're wasting time."

Before I could turn on Dwight again, Hen stepped in and took his side.

"Trudy, I don't think you're bein' fair to Dwight," Hen said, like a schoolyard monitor stepping into a squabble. "We all know that most of what we do is routine and boring, and another big hunk is keeping the peace, but Dwight knows as well as anybody that when we get down to where the gristle meets the bone there's nothing more important about our job than protecting human life and, when we can't do that, bringing to justice those who harm others."

"So, why aren't y'all more interested in investigating this case?"

"Interest ain't the point," Hen said. "I didn't know you better, I'd think you were complaining that I'm letting you lead an investigation for a change." The hypocrite didn't even give me a chance to sputter. "Even with your imagination, Trudy, you caint call this a fast-breaking case after all this time. In spite of what they show on TV, most good police work is a matter of grinding routine, and I caint remember the last case we wrapped up in under an hour."

"Minus commercials," Dwight contributed.

They make a great team.

"Even if I forgot to tell you that, you should have figured it out for yourself by now," Hen continued. "And we do have to keep on taking care of other things."

"Like the Chief says, I'm just saying we don't have much," Dwight said.

"Matter of fact, seein' as how this case is so stale, I think we're comin' along pretty well. Come on now, Dwight. Admit Trudy did some good work, finding out so quick whose body it was."

"Uh huh," Dwight said. "But what else we got?"

"We're piecing together her last day," I said. "We know she walked away from the football game and we haven't talked to anybody who says they saw her alive after that."

"Okay, let's work with that," Hen said. I seemed to sense his relief that we'd reached the point where we could move into his usual method of evaluating an investigation. I call it his Hencratic Method. He questions every blessed thing we think we know, which forces us not to take anything for granted.

"How do we know she got to the Burkhalter house?" he asked.

"We have that mess and the note she left," I answered.

Dwight grunted acceptance of that evidence.

"How do we know she's the one who did that?" Hen asked next.

"We don't, do we?" I asked, amazed that we

187

hadn't questioned it before. "Everybody says she did, and we've been taking their word."

"Might be worth looking at," Hen said.

"You saying maybe she didn't make it back to the house?" Dwight asked. "Maybe somebody else did that to make it look like she got mad and left town?"

"It's a possibility we gotta keep in mind," Hen answered.

"That could be where Woody Riggs came in," Dwight said. "Maybe he offered her a ride."

"It wasn't that far," I argued. "Just a few blocks. And we don't know if she even knew him, so why would she take a ride from him? And even if he did pick her up, why would he kill her?"

"We know he was her future father-in-law's good buddy," Hen suggested. "Not much of a stretch to think she knew him."

"Made a pass, she didn't like it, he roughed her up. More than he meant to, maybe." That's one of the advantages to being the kind of man Dwight is. He has no trouble at all looking at things from a low-life perspective.

"Okay, say that's what happened," Hen said, holding up a hand to forestall my objections. "That doesn't account for the mess at the Burkhalter house. Dwight, you sayin' he'd take her there to make a pass?"

"And she was so taken with him she decided not to marry Donnie?" I asked. I'll admit I used sarcasm, but it's lost on Dwight.

"There'd have been no reason for Riggs to go to the Burkhalters'," Hen said. "He mighta been a hellraiser, but nobody's said he was stupid. Anybody saw him there, they'd remember it."

"I don't know about that, about goin' to Burkhalters'. But you gotta admit she turned up in the Riggses' garbage dump," Dwight persisted.

"That argues against it being him, in my mind," I said. "He couldn't have known it would be thirty years before she'd be found, so if he killed her, I think that's the last place he'd have put her."

"Maybe. But maybe he put her there just till he could get a chance to move her, and he never got that chance," Hen said.

"But somehow we have to account for that mess at the Burkhalters'," I said.

"Maybe that didn't have anything to do with Karen's death," Hen suggested.

"Riggs and Burkhalter coulda been in it together," Dwight said. "That woulda made it easier to get her in the car. Then, Burkhalter's job was to cover their tracks. Didn't you say his wife came home and found him with blood on his hands?"

"Catfish blood, she said," I confirmed.

"They're bloody, mean suckers all right," Dwight said.

"But why?" I asked. "Why would he do it?"

"Same as for Riggs," Hen said, "but if her future father-in-law was in it, then we get more of

189

an incentive to keep her quiet. Maybe she threatened to tell and they did it to keep her quiet."

"Well . . ." I said, but Dwight snorted again.

"Nah. Hellraisers? They ain't got no reputation to look out for. They wouldn'ta cared what she said. A bank president, now, a preacher, that woulda been something else."

"I think we've milked that cow dry," Hen said. "Let's move on, long as we're talking about suspects and motive. Who else we got?"

"Miz Riggs?" I hazarded.

"Caint see it, myself," Hen said. "Caint see any hint of a reason for her to do it."

"More likely she'd kill Woody. Miz Burkhalter?" I suggested.

"Doesn't sound like she liked her prospective daughter-in-law very much," Hen said, "But that don't usually amount to murder. At least not before the weddin'."

"But if she was angry, it could account for the mess at the house," I said.

"But how'd she get the body in the refrigerator?" Dwight asked. "Maybe it was her and Alvin. He drove the body out there, she made the mess, to throw everybody off. A woman by herself would leave the body where it was and try to lie her way out of it."

I didn't admit it out loud, but I thought he was probably right again.

"Kenneth Burkhalter?" I suggested.

"Big strong boy," Dwight said. "Yeah."

"Maybe he came on to her," Hen said. "Then it plays out the same way it might have for Woody Riggs or Alvin Burkhalter. Everybody says Kenneth took after his daddy."

"That's a pretty weak 'why' and I don't see 'how' at all," I objected. "Kenneth was playing football with the others."

"But he disappeared for a while," Hen reminded me. "And it wasn't very far to the house."

"We're about out of likely suspects. The only other name to come up is Julie Todd," I said.

"Spooky Julie?" Hen thought about it. "Don't see how that scrawny little thing coulda killed Karen and hauled her body off and put it away like that, no matter how mad she was about losing Donnie."

"Maybe she wasn't always a scrawny little thing," I said.

"Maybe it was a conspiracy," Dwight said. "The whole buncha those kids ganged up on 'er."

"Miz Odum over by the armory says there's a pack of dogs running loose in her yard and don't we have a law against that." Dawn's voice came as a shock but was a welcome interruption.

"Dwight, go see about it," Hen instructed. "We're not getting anywhere on this."

Dwight unwound himself from his chair and headed for the door. "Bet you money, whoever did it's dead and gone," he said over his shoulder.

"Probably Donnie Burkhalter. Decided he didn't want to marry her after all, killed her and then ran himself off a bridge."

"Neat, clean, and nothing for us to do. Right?" I asked Dwight's back. "But we do need to find out, not just take for granted that who-ever killed her is beyond our reach."

He turned slowly and spoke just as though he hadn't heard me. "Maybe that retard, what was his name? The one who hung around, the one they wouldn't let play with them? Maybe he did it."

"Just as long as it's somebody dead?" I asked as Dwight turned away.

"He may be right about not being able to make a case against anybody," Hen said once Dwight was on his way to the dogs.

"I know," I admitted. "But even if we can't make a case, I don't see how we can rest if we don't do everything we can to find out what happened."

"I caint argue with that, but you better be pre-pared to face up to not being able to find out. Whoa, now! I didn't mean we won't try! We'll keep on it, however we can figure to investigate it. But you got to remember, we need some kind of evidence if we're gonna bring a case, not just some kind of mumbo-jumbo feeling, not just some wild-eyed science fiction conspiracy theory that stretches around what we think we know."

"Right now I'd settle for woman's intuition," I said. "I want some theory that explains everything. If we had that, then we'd know what kind of evidence to look for and where to look."

Here was Dawn again. "Pauline Ford from over at the Cut-n-Curl called and said Miss Kate Waters missed her hair appointment, and doesn't answer her phone."

That qualified as one of my welfare checks, so I lit out.

Miss Kate's house sits on a big lot, quite a way back from the dirt road that passes in front. She's well along in years but not well, health-wise, and Aunt Lulu told me her daughter, who lives over in Warner Robins, has been after her to sell the place and come live with her. I could understand Miss Kate's reluctance to give up her home and go live, as she put it, at somebody else's mercy, but I could also appreciate the daughter's dilemma, trying to come see her mother every week or two and take care of her own family and business at the same time.

Miss Kate's car was in the carport. I rang the doorbell and could hear it echoing through the house but I didn't hear that it stirred up any movement. I banged on the door and called out. "Miss Kate? Miss Kate? It's Trudy Roundtree." Nothing.

I tried the door. Locked. The curtains were pulled over the windows near the front steps, and the side windows were too high off the ground to offer me any glimpse inside. I went around back.

The door into the kitchen from the back

porch was unlocked. I opened it and called out again. No response. Trying not to think of the car in the carport and what that might mean, I looked through the small house. Nothing.

I had just about decided to get Dawn to call Miss Kate's daughter, to see if she knew of any travel plans, when I noticed a quart jar of tea sitting on the kitchen counter top, with the tea bags still in it. Nobody would go off on a trip and leave the tea bags soaking.

Okay. What next? The front door had been locked, but not the back. No sign of a break-in. The place looked to be in order. Nothing to suggest vandalism or a hasty search for valuables. No signs of foul play.

I went to the back door and surveyed Kate Waters's domain, trying to think. At the back of her lot she had a little garden, with some eggplant, squash, and a couple of tomato plants. A hose trailed from a faucet bib in the middle of the yard to the garden. I realized I could hear the faint sound of running water. Good grief!

There she was, lying in a pool of water behind the tomato plants. She was conscious, but barely. "Don't tell Donna," she whispered. "Don't tell Donna."

Much as I hated to go against her, I didn't see any way to keep her daughter in the dark about it.

I rode in the ambulance with her to the hospital, learned that Miss Kate had forgotten and left the water running on the garden the day before, and slipped in the mud when she went out to see about it. She'd broken a hip. After I made arrangements to let Donna know about her mother, I went back to the station house.

It was the quiet time of the afternoon, the time of day I go into low gear unless there's something very stimulating in the air. Typing up my report on Miss Kate didn't qualify as stimulating. I kept wanting to clear my mind and let the facts we'd uncovered in the Karen Willard case rearrange themselves into something that made sense.

I closed my eyes, sure there was something . . .

"You nappin' on city time?" Dwight asked.

I must have dozed off. I certainly hadn't heard him come in. "In a righteous trance, Dwight."

He snorted.

"I'm trying to dream up something that would resolve all the discrepancies, or I should say inconsistencies, in the story we've pieced together."

"Can't be done. No way, long as it's been. You can't get witnesses to a shooting last Saturday to agree on what happened."

"I hate to say it, Dwight, but you may be right for the third or fourth time today. I sure hate to give up, though."

"Yeah." One thing, maybe the only thing, I really like about Dwight, considering that I rarely agree with him about anything, is that he isn't especially chatty.

"Surely we can solve this!"

"Don't call me Shirley." That's Dwight's sense of humor.

"Thanks for your help."

"Ungh." He ambled off. I finished my typing and was about to call it a day when I had a bright idea and intruded on whatever Hen was up to in his office.

"I've thought of a way to tell if Karen Willard went back to the Burkhalter house," I told him.

He looked skeptical.

"We'll ask Dinah to see if she can find a handwriting sample to compare to that note."

"Not bad, Trudy. Not bad. But strictly speaking, that would only prove she wrote the note. She could have written it somewhere else."

"I'm thinking there wasn't a lot of time between when she left the game and the others came to the house. Not time for too much planning and sleight of hand," I argued.

"See what you and Dinah can come up with," Hen said. "Whatever it is, it'll be more than we know now."

I gave Dinah Willard a call.

"It'll make Darrell's day to get back into police work," she told me. "It kind of left a hole in his life when he found out I was his on-line Spice Girl. He's tryin' to be brave about it, but he's beginning to mope. This is just the ticket!"

That night, as I drifted off to sleep under my security blanket of cats, instead of counting sheep I decided to put myself to sleep by concocting horrorscopes for some of the people in the case. Stacy and I weren't being very systematic about this, and I wasn't sure what-all we'd used. Some plants, some foods, some animals. Had we used kudzu? Dinah Willard could be Kudzu. "Kudzu isn't bound by convention or concerns about the opinion of others. What appears to be a lack of discipline and self-control masks a deep-rooted instinct for staking out territory and fighting for survival. Kudzus dominate whatever landscape they're in." That wasn't too bad, but I could tell I was having trouble keeping her personality separate from the kudzu-like clutter in her house.

I fell asleep while working on Doris Burkhalter. Squirrel? "Squirrels are always busy about the work of gathering food and providing for the future. Their apparent playfulness masks strong territorial instincts. They can be vicious if they think they're being threatened." "Apparent playfulness" didn't apply to her, but "territorial instincts" might. Could Doris Burkhalter have been so squirrelly that she didn't want her son to marry away from Ogeechee? Maybe Mockingbird. "Mockingbirds are hypocritical, deceptive, and always pretending to be what they aren't. Generally considered to be harmless." That didn't seem to apply to anybody I knew. Was it my definition that was at fault, or . . .

Chapter 18

The next morning I was out on patrol and had just finished checking on Miss Kate Waters when Dawn gave me a call to say Dinah Willard was on her way. I made a broad sweep around some of the more notorious hangouts for ne'er-do-wells, just to make sure they don't forget that the Ogeechee Police are ever vigilant, and then returned to the station house.

I had barely started making use of my time by trying to write up useful notes on my activities of the day before, Hen helpfully reading over my shoulder, when Dinah Willard and her buddy Darrell arrived.

"Well, if it ain't the Bristol branch of the OPD," Hen greeted them.

Darrell pulled himself up and stuck out his hand manfully. "Good mornin', Chief; good mornin', Officer Roundtree," he said.

Dinah looked upon him fondly for a moment. The boy apparently spent a lot of time with computers, but not so much that he had forgotten how to act around actual people.

"Took us a little more digging," Dinah said. "And Lordy do we have a mess, but we had a mess anyway, didn't we Darrell?"

"Sure did," he said fervently.

"What we came up with is a letter Karen wrote to Mama from school," Dinah continued. "Darrell and I didn't pay much attention to the handwritin' on that note the other day, so we don't have an opinion about whether it matches or not, do we Darrell?"

"Not yet," he said.

Dinah held out an envelope. Darrell took it from her and reverently passed it on to Hen.

"Fast work," I said, ignoring the flagrant idolatry.

"Not fast, slow and hot," Darrell said. "But we didn't mind much."

"We got on it right after you called," Dinah said.

"Trudy, go get us that note, for comparison," Hen said, obviously unwilling to deprive Darrell of his presence even for the short time it would take to go to the evidence room.

When I returned with the "The wedding is off" note, sealed inside its plastic bag, Dinah was settled in a chair near the table. They had spread out a letter handwritten on a sheet of unlined paper that looked like it might have come from a notepad, about six inches by nine. I put the note on the table beside it.

We all gazed at the note and the letter. I don't know much about handwriting analysis, but the samples didn't look alike to me, even apart from the fact that one was written in pencil on lined paper and the other in pen on unlined paper.

Trying to analyze the differences in the writing itself, I noticed angular letters with narrow loops, or none at all, in the wedding note; rounded letters with tall, wide loops in the letter. I glanced at Hen, and was disgusted to see that both Dinah and Darrell were looking at him as if he were an oracle. He didn't let any of us down.

"Sure looks like two different handwritings to me," he said.

"Me, too," said Darrell.

"But we're not experts," Hen cautioned. "It might not mean a thing that they don't look alike to us. Could be Karen was in a hurry and scribbled the note instead of taking her time with her penmanship like she did when she wrote to her mama. You think about it, your handwriting doesn't always look the same way, does it?"

"No sir," Darrell agreed without a moment's thought.

"Another way of looking at it, if that note doesn't look like Karen's writing, it could mean that somebody else wrote it, couldn't it?" Dinah asked. "Somebody like Donnie Burkhalter?"

"Yes, it could," Hen admitted. "Donnie or anybody else under the sun. Anyhow, no matter what it looks like to us, we'll have to see what it looks like to an expert. What they are really good at is comparing handwriting, and we need somebody who can give us some assurances about whether this document — for police purposes, Darrell, this scrap of paper is a document — is authentic. That is, was it written by the person we think it was? Now, if an expert compares these two handwriting samples and says they could not have been written by the same person, then we'll know something."

"What? What'll we know?" Darrell asked.

Dinah and I exchanged glances. We'd both noticed Darrell picking up on the "we." Hen noticed it too. He spoke directly to Darrell, leaving it to Dinah and me to eavesdrop. "Well, son, for one thing, it'll tell us we're right smart to have figured it out ourselves. If that's what happened, another thing we'll know is that somebody besides Karen wrote that note. We don't have any reason to think she didn't write the letter."

"Then what? What'll we do then?" Darrell persisted.

"Well, son, think about it. What do you think we ought to do?" Hen asked.

Darrell took in a deep breath, blushed, and stood up so tall I thought he was going to fall over backwards. But he was up to the challenge. "I think we'd want to find out who wrote the note, and why they wrote it."

"Smart boy," Hen said. He turned to Dinah and grinned. "Smart boy. You caught yourself a good fish with that there Inter-net."

I thought Darrell was going to explode.

Hen de-electrified the situation by relapsing into lecture mode. "Experts in handwriting analysis can do two kinds of things for us. The obvious thing, what we've already talked about, is to tell us whether two samples are written by the same person. The way I understand it, even if you're trying to disguise your handwriting, you'll do some things that will give you away without you even realizing it. Some experts say, the thing that most often gives people away when they're trying to disguise their handwriting is the length of the stroke they put at the end of a word."

"Why?" I asked in spite of myself. "What does that mean?"

"That's the stroke people make when they're through thinking about it," Hen said. "So whether it's long or short, turns up or down, or whatever, people do it unconsciously."

"That's interesting, isn't it, Darrell?" Dinah asked.

She might as well have asked if he wanted to keep on breathing. "Oh, yeah!" he said. "What's the other thing? You said two things."

Hen smiled benevolently. He eats up hero worship, and with Delcie, Teri, and Aunt Lulu out of town, he may have been feeling deprived. "The other thing is less scientific, not as reliable, and I'm not sure how much I go along with it, but some people will tell you a handwriting expert can figure out character traits from handwriting."

"How can they do that?" Dinah again.

"There's something about the way you cross your 't's' and dot your 'i's' that tells them as much as goat's blood and turkey feathers tell the witch doctors," Hen said. "So, even if we caint find a match for this handwriting, we might be able to get an idea what kind of person we're looking for."

"Or what kind of person that person was thirty years ago," I said. "I've sure changed a lot in thirty years, and my handwriting has, too."

"There's a school of thought that says people can change their personalities by changing their handwriting instead of the other way around, but the goat's blood and turkey feather school would say that barring some kind of traumatic event, your basic traits don't change much." Hen grinned at me. "Reckon your grade school handwriting coulda given us a clue how you were gone turn out?"

"I don't know about all that, but I do know I'm twice the person I was then," Dinah said with a laugh, placing her hands on her wide hips.

"I wasn't any kind of person," Darrell volunteered.

Hen grinned at him. "Well, son, you remember this conversation and aim to make sure that when you look back on it thirty years from now, you're happy with the changes in yourself and your handwriting." I wanted to gag.

"Yes, sir," Darrell said.

"Well, I reckon y'all have other business to see about," Hen said, "so we'll let you get on with it, and we'll see what information we can get the experts to milk out of the things you've brought us. We want to thank y'all for being so helpful." Hen handed me Karen's letter and the note with the disputed authenticity, assuming I'd run back to the evidence room with it, so I didn't.

He shook hands with Dinah and Darrell. "We'll let you know when we need your help again." To some ears that might have sounded like dismissal, but obviously not to Darrell's.

"Just let us know," he said. "We'll get right on it."

" 'Preciate your attitude," Hen said. Then he looked at Dinah.

"Why don't I give you a sample of my handwriting?" Dinah asked. "So you don't waste any time on thinking I had anything to do with Karen's murder."

"Thirty years too late," Hen said.

"I wasn't in grade school thirty years ago," Dinah said. "My handwriting hasn't changed all that much."

Darrell looked from Hen to Dinah, worried, hoping he wasn't going to have to choose between them, but it was okay.

Hen slapped him on the back and smiled at Dinah. "Nah. That wouldn't tell us what we want to know, now would it? If we decide we need a contemporary sample, we can get that any time, can't we?" He smiled.

Dinah smiled back but rummaged in her shoulder bag. "I don't have a spiral notebook to tear a page out of, but I think I've got a pencil in here somewhere."

I ripped a page out of my notebook and handed it to her.

Dinah wrote, "The wedding is off." Smart and confident. It didn't seem like bluster. "Of course, I could be deliberately changing the way I write. Would one of your experts be able to tell that?"

"I'll ask 'em," Hen said, unperturbed. He grinned at her, and he didn't seem to be blustering, either. "You want to give us something useful, reckon you and Darrell could find us something you wrote thirty years ago?"

Dinah gave him a steady look. "I didn't go off anywhere and write home, not that I remember, but we could sure take a look. Come on, Darrell. Looks like it's just as well we didn't take time to clean up our mess before we brought this over. We'd just have to mess everything up again."

"Yessum," he said.

Darrell followed Dinah out, stopping at the door to throw a puzzled look in Hen's direction. Like Darrell, I was a little unsure about how much of a confrontation we'd just witnessed, if any at all. We watched Dinah crawl into the driver's seat. Darrell handed up her oxygen tank and tucked the breathing tube out of the way of the closing door. Then Hen turned his attention to the two pieces of paper in his hand.

"Good God Almighty," he said.

"Meaning?"

"Meaning, the good Lord himself's gonna have to tell us what to do with this stuff."

"What about that lecture you gave your adoring audience about all we'll be able to learn from expert handwriting analysis?"

"Can't hurt," he admitted, "but dogged if I see how it'll help. I don't hold with goat's blood and turkey feathers, no matter what it sounded like. I just said that to cheer them up." He heaved a sigh. "Trudy, this is all thirty years ago."

"How much of that hocus-pocus about what can be learned from handwriting was just to dazzle Darrell?"

"Did you notice it didn't scare Dinah Willard?" Just like Hen to answer a question with another question.

"You're cranky and taking it out on this case because you haven't been getting all the coddling and attention, much less all the home-cooked meals, your enormous ego has led you to believe you deserve. Buck up! The sun will shine again. All is not lost. It's always darkest before . . ."

Instead of interrupting me, as I'd hoped and expected, he let me rail on until I ran out of clichés and came to a sputtering halt. Worse, he was grinning the whole time, even when he asked, "You think we're gone solve this case based on thirty-year-old handwritin'?"

"If we solve it at all it'll be a miracle. Anyway, Dwight's probably right. The likely thing is that whoever did it is already out of our reach."

"Gone on to whatever reward was waitin' on

the other side of this vale of tears?" He loves sounding like a preacher.

"Don't you think so, Hen, long as it's been?"

"Could be. But we might as well send that handwriting up to Atlanta for comparison. And while they're at it, they can check for finger-prints. If Karen Willard didn't write that note, it might have prints from whoever did. That's one thing, anyway. What you can do in the mean-time, whenever your other work slows down and you have time on your hands, is set about col-lecting handwriting samples from anybody else we think it might have been. Thirty-year-old samples, if you can find them," he added.

"How likely is it, now she knows what you want, that Dinah will be able to find a sample to bring us?" I had to ask.

Hen shrugged. "Same as with any of 'em, if you think about it. We'd have to take their word for it they couldn't find anything they wrote that far back. Not to mention what even a half-witted lawyer would be able to do with their Fifth Amendment rights against self-incrimination."

It struck me that most people wouldn't even pretend to be trying to dig around for an an-tique handwriting sample, especially since they had no way of knowing what significance that sample might have in unraveling this murder case. To save my life, I couldn't have said what I hoped it would prove, either. I had to credit Dinah, at least, with having a clear conscience. Or faking one, knowing we'd probably never know the difference. Well, maybe I'd wait and see if she brought something in. Even then, we'd only have her word that it was her old handwriting, so what would we know for sure? For sure? Nothing. Still, unpromising as it seemed, it was about the only thing I had to work on.

My internal grumbling was interrupted when I thought of a great untapped resource.

Chapter 19

When Hen told me to start trying to collect thirty-year-old handwriting samples when my other work slowed down and I had time on my hands, I naturally interpreted that to mean I should give it top priority. The only problem with that was that I didn't know how to go about it.

As a stalling maneuver, and one that more or less fit with my actual job description, I decided to visit Miss Sarah Kennedy again. It's a stretch to try to apply our "welfare checks" to somebody like Miss Sarah, whose welfare is being attended to, but I'm nothing if not flexible. Besides, it made me feel a little less like a hypocrite, considering my lecture to Stacy about how much Miss Sarah needed company. I had the bright idea that I could combine business with pleasure and present some of the clues in my jumble of a case to Miss Sarah's logical mind. Unless I misjudged her, it was just the thing to brighten her day. I thought it might tend to my welfare, too. Welfare is such a versatile word.

I found Miss Sarah in what the folks at Dogwood Nursing Center called the solarium, a room with plenty of windows, some game tables, and a television set. She was sitting with her back to the television set, her chair positioned so that sunlight came through a window over her left shoulder to illuminate the book she held.

"Trudy!" she said, closing the book. "What a treat! You caught me taking a break from my physical rehabilitation."

"Are you wearing the staff completely out?"

"Don't get snippy with me, young lady," she said.

"No, ma'am, I won't. Especially since I've come to ask for your help."

"Help? Whatever you have in mind, I'm interested, as long as it doesn't involve running and jumping. Nothing could please me more in my present circumstances than to be made to feel useful," she said. I was glad to see the alacrity with which she set the book aside. I was amazed to see the title: *Crime Science: Methods of Forensic Detection*.

"A little light reading?" I asked.

"It takes my mind off my own troubles," she said, "and it's doing wonders for my vocabulary." She held the book up for my inspection. "Lulu brought it for me to study while she was gone. She's worried I'll lose my mind, cooped up like this, and she's making sure I keep it exercised." She gestured toward the book. "This one isn't too bad. We tried *The Encyclopedia of Forensic Pathology*, but had to give up on it."

"Were the words too big?" I asked innocently.

"No, the pictures were too graphic. But you said you came to ask for help. What kind of help can I give you?"

"Brainstorm with me," I invited.

"I'm probably capable of a good brainstorm," she said. "What's the topic?"

"Karen Willard's murder," I said. "Don't look at me like that. Dwight frankly thinks we're wasting our time, and even Hen doesn't act like he thinks there's anything urgent. Since it all happened so long ago, I'm afraid if I don't come up with something soon, the case will just fade away, and it isn't one of those times when rules and guidelines will be much help. Maybe the freelance detecting you and Aunt Lulu are dabbling in is what we need." I nodded at her book.

She shook her head. "I doubt you're going to convince Hen there's any urgency. You don't have a hot trail to follow."

I laughed. "Not exactly! And if whoever did it is still alive, he or she has managed to behave all this time. But that was before anybody knew there had been a murder. Now we're stirring things up. Who knows? What I hope you'll do is go over the little bit we have, the little bit we know for sure, and see if you can help me find something significant we've missed."

"It sounds unlikely."

"But neither one of us has anything to lose. Are you game?"

"I am game," she assured me. "What is it that you do know for sure?"

"Not much," I admitted. "We went over it all yesterday, including trying to come up with a suspect with some kind of motive — even the remotest smidgen of a motive."

"I don't see how I can be of any help there," she said.

"I wouldn't expect you to be any better at police procedure than the police," I said. "Even if you have been boning up on forensic science. No, I see you more like Jessica Fletcher or Miss Marple, somebody with an analytical mind, who knows human nature well enough to sense possibilities and make connections that science can't. With your help, maybe I can come at it from a different direction, like we did in your history class, and see what led up to the murder."

"You aren't bad at human nature, yourself, Trudy. I've always admired the way Agatha Christie drew Jane Marple. I'm flattered."

"It isn't flattery, Miss Sarah," I said. "It's an honest compliment. It's the simple truth that you, like Miss Marple, know how to observe and draw logical conclusions from what you observe."

"You have something for me to observe, then?" Her good manners had kept her from ogling the box I had under my arm, but now she gave it a ladylike glance.

"Yes, ma'am. Here's the situation. We've been

told that Karen Willard suddenly left town, leaving behind a pile of shower gifts at the Burkhalter house along with torn photos of Donnie and a note saying the wedding was off. That's what we've pieced together from old recollections. Besides the little bit the forensic pathologist could tell us from examining Karen's body, we have just this one thing — a box of odds and ends that belonged to Karen that were left at the Burkhalters'. More precisely — no. I'll leave it at that, and see what ideas come to you."

Miss Sarah smiled. "All right. I accept the challenge. As you say, what have I got to lose? What do I do?"

I gave the box a thump. "I want to see what your fresh eye and impartial intellect can make of this. If anything." I shrugged. "Even asking some questions we haven't thought of asking might be useful. Here's the box and what was in it. Don't take the things out of the plastic bags."

"I understand. The bags prevent us from contaminating the evidence."

"Yes, ma'am."

"All right. Let me see," she said. I put the box in her lap and tried to be patient as she slowly examined each item.

I looked out through the solarium windows at a nurse's aide slowly pushing a very old man in a wheelchair. His left hand waved aimlessly as they moved along. I removed my wrist brace and grasped my left hand in my right. As Miss

213

Sarah examined the box and its contents, I used my right hand to push my left hand forward and backward, stretching the lax muscles in my wrist as far as I could, holding it each time as long as I could stand it, as I'd been told to do if I want to get my strength and flexibility back.

"Who prepared the package for mailing?" Miss Sarah asked, holding up the plastic bag with the string in it.

"Doris Burkhalter." As soon as I'd said it, I realized that was an assumption, a logical assumption, but not something we knew for sure. I'd have to check.

She nodded. Next she took up the bag with the sweater in it, read the label, squinted at the embroidery, held it up to the light. She set it aside and subjected the Chanel box, lipsticks, mascara wand, ID bracelet, and toothbrush to the same scrutiny.

I smiled. She was going to give me exactly what I needed — a fresh look through intelligent eyes. The intellect that terrified generations of ill-prepared students was now working for me, the Ogeechee Police Department, and the cause of Justice!

"It's limiting not to be able to touch and smell these things," she said. "I know I could tell a lot more if I wasn't working with two of my senses tied behind my back, so to speak."

I smiled at her way of expressing herself. "Do the best you can. We don't want to add or subtract even the smallest thing from the evidence.

In case any of it turns out to be evidence. In case we ever think of any kind of evidence to look for on any of these things."

"I understand," she said. She stared out the window. "Hmm."

"Yes, ma'am."

She smiled. "All right then, working with what we have, let's ask ourselves why Karen Willard took everything else with her and left these things behind."

"I've been asking myself that. Her sister says she wouldn't have left the Chanel box."

"That could mean she didn't pack up and leave the house under her own steam," Miss Sarah said.

"That's what I think," I said.

"What other possibilities occur to you?"

"She could have left in a hurry. But it would have had to be a big hurry."

"Yes. The toothbrush suggests that."

"That's exactly what I thought. When I visit somebody or stay in a motel, I keep my cosmetics and toiletries all in one place. If I do leave something behind, it isn't likely to be my toothbrush."

"You'd be more likely to leave something like a sweater," she agreed. "Something that wouldn't necessarily have its own place."

"Yes." I agreed. I waited for her next observation, unwilling to taint her perceptions if I could help it.

"This bracelet," she said.

"Yes, ma'am?"

"I believe you said she tore up the photos of Donnie. Why would she keep this one?"

"Maybe she forgot it was there?"

"You're saying she forgot it, along with her toothbrush and the Chanel box she was supposed to be so proud of?"

"Hard to believe, isn't it?" I asked.

"Yes." She picked up the photographic copy of the note and gave me a questioning look.

"We've sent the original off to the forensics lab. No telling when we'll get a report. They're always backed up."

She studied the photograph. "This note suggests that she wasn't calm, that something had upset her enough to make her suddenly break off her engagement. Do you know if they had quarreled?"

"No, ma'am. I mean, they hadn't quarreled, not that we know of."

She glanced at the note again and then looked at me over the top of her bifocals. "It isn't signed. Are you sure she wrote it?"

"Ah!" I said.

"Ah?"

"Ah ha!" I amplified. "Well, actually, no, we aren't sure she wrote it, in spite of what everybody has assumed. That's one of the reasons we sent the original off to Atlanta. You realize this must be confidential? It wouldn't do any good for people to know what I'm after."

"Of course."

"I think we need to be sure who wrote the

216

note. All the handwriting experts will be able to do is tell us if it's likely that Karen Willard wrote it. They won't be able to tell us who did, unless we have some other writing to compare to it. How would you go about finding samples of handwriting — authentic samples," I added, thinking of Dinah Willard and how easy it would be for her to bring in any old scribbles, or none at all, "Authentic samples that people wrote thirty years ago?"

"This isn't one of your games, is it? Like the horrorscopes you and Stacy are making up?"

"How in the world do you know about that?"

"I overheard Stacy laughing about it with Linette Crowell, one of the nurses."

"If I needed anything to tell me I was right to come to you, that was exactly it! This is just something Stacy and I have been playing with, and you know all about it! My gosh!"

Miss Sarah looked modest.

"About those horrorscopes, Miss Sarah."

"Yes, Trudy?"

"Well, we were trying to be clever and amuse ourselves," I said, feeling very much like a sophomore who forgot to do her homework and couldn't claim the cat had eaten it.

"Yes. I'm sure you were."

"We didn't intend for anybody to know about them. Not everybody would be flattered to hear what we've concocted."

"I'm not surprised to hear that."

"We wouldn't want anybody to get their feelings hurt," I said.

"Of course not." She relented. "I don't know any details, Trudy. I couldn't tell anybody what you concocted, and wouldn't if I could."

"Thank you."

"You are quite welcome," she said. "Now. About the handwriting samples."

"Yes," I said, relieved that we'd gotten back to that.

She pursed her lips and tucked a stray wisp of hair neatly back into its bun. "All right, then. It would depend on whose handwriting you need. Different people write down different kinds of things."

"To be thorough, I'd need handwriting samples from everybody in town who knew Karen Willard. People like the Burkhalters."

"Alvin and Doris? Does that mean you suspect one of them?"

"Not necessarily. Just trying to be thorough."

"Oh, yes. I see. Handwriting samples from the Burkhalters. Who else?"

"I wouldn't want to leave anybody out. Anybody whose name has come up. Kenneth and Marie Burkhalter. Woody Riggs."

"Woody Riggs!"

"The body was on his property," I reminded her. "For that matter, Miz Riggs."

"Ethel Riggs? Surely not!"

"Probably not," I amended. "But it can't hurt to rule people out. Besides, the more we look for, the less obvious it'll be who we're really after," I said. "If we knew who we were after, which we don't. I've been trying to think of the kinds of things, handwritten things, that people might keep around that long. Most people don't do much writing by hand these days, with e-mail and computers. Maybe they didn't thirty years ago, either."

"All right, then. Let's see." Miss Sarah thought for a minute. "Diaries," she murmured. "Love letters. Records. Business records. Or . . . several of those people were in high school then. I'm trying to think of school records . . . school papers . . . That's a long time. Yearbooks!"

"Yearbooks?"

"They would always pass them around and get their friends to write notes to them. People do keep their high school yearbooks. If you could get your hands on two or three yearbooks from back then you might be able to find some of the handwriting samples you need."

"That's brilliant! I knew you'd think of something."

"I was trying to think where I'd look for something I wrote thirty years ago," she said. "Something that would still be around."

"That might do it for Donnie, Kenneth, and Marie. What about Doris and Alvin, or Mr. and Mrs. Riggs?"

"Here comes my tormentor," Miss Sarah said, looking past me down the hall. "You could go ahead and start with the yearbooks. I'll see what else I can think of. It'll give me a place to send my brain while she's torturing my body. You keep me informed of your progress, now, you hear?"

"Oh, yes. Miss Sarah, you've been a lot of help. You've given me several good ideas. I'll be back," I said, watching with sympathy as the nurse trundled her off for physical therapy. Physical therapy does hurt, but, as the athletes say, "No pain, no gain." The alternative, when you're talking about physical rehabilitation, is to give up and be crippled, but it's probably also true of many of life's emotional aches and pains. If you don't work through it, you don't get better. I'm sure there's a lesson in there somewhere, something about embracing the pain, working with it, about how working through pain makes you stronger.

Thoughtfully bending my left hand backward and forward with my right hand, I went back to my car.

Chapter 20

I couldn't ask Donnie Burkhalter to share his yearbook with me, but Kenneth Burkhalter was a possibility. Maybe even Doris. She might well have been the kind of mother who'd hang on to those things for both her sons, but I was reluctant to bother them again so soon. Then I remembered Marie. I called her at the library.

"You forgot your library card," she said when I identified myself. "Is that what you're callin' about? I'm holding it for you at the desk. Of course, you'll have to produce a picture ID again to claim it."

I had to laugh.

"I'm reading Aunt Lulu's copy of *The Corpse in the Choir Loft* so I'm not in a panic yet, but she went out of town and took her library card with her, and I'm just about finished, so I'll come get my very own card. Actually, that's not what I'm calling about."

"Really?" Not even mild surprise. "Something told me your interest was more in Karen Willard than in books."

"I confess."

"So, what's that got to do with the library?"

"Actually, it's you, not the library, unless the

library keeps back issues of the high school yearbooks."

"We don't, but the school probably does. Why do you need them?"

"You're right about my interest in Karen Willard. I'm on the verge of getting obsessed with her, with this case," I said, "and I'd like to see what y'all looked like back then. Maybe it'll help me get a sense of the times." This much was true, and for more than one reason. I was just plain interested — as though it would be possible to guess the mind's construction from the face and know anything about what those kids had been like. Even Will Shakespeare knew that kind of thing was impossible. Oddly, too, I specifically wondered what Marie had looked like, if I'd see any resemblance between her picture and my own. But mostly, of course, I wanted to look at any handwritten notes the books might have, and any the school had would be pristine copies, hardly any use to me at all.

"How about you? Do you have the yearbooks from when you were in school?" That's what I really wanted.

"I don't."

My heart sank.

"But I'll bet my mother does, and I'll bet she knows exactly where they are."

My heart lifted.

"It would be a kick, a blast from the past, a trip down memory lane, whatever the phrase is, to look at them again after all this time," she continued. "They seemed so important right then, when none of us really thought there was life after high school, but I doubt if I've opened them since. You want me to bring them to the police station if I find them and if I'm willing to let you see what I looked like in high school?"

"I'd appreciate it. You could call me and I'll come get them."

After that, I twiddled my bad thumb with my good one for a few minutes, then I called Eric Riggs. I thought I could be a little more straightforward with him.

"Eric, Trudy. I've been thinking about our conversation, the one about your scary day at the dump, which might have been the day Karen Willard was killed."

"Uh huh," he said, sounding like a box turtle about to snap shut.

"I couldn't help but think you'd want to know for sure, either way, if your daddy had anything to do with Karen Willard's death."

"You think you can tell me?"

"No. Not yet, but there might be a way."

"Good. Be my guest."

"I need your help. Yours or your mother's. We have a handwritten document that might bear on the case, and I need handwriting samples of all the people involved. It can help us clear out the underbrush, stop wasting time."

"Yeah, you better not waste any more time on this. What is it now, thirty years? Thirty-five?"

"Eric, I'm bringing you into my confidence

here, trying to bring you a little peace of mind if I can and you don't seem to appreciate it."

He sighed. "What do you want?"

"I need something in your daddy's handwriting."

"This what passes for modern police work?"

"Don't get snippy with me, mister. You're talking to the law. Come to think of it, we only have your word for it that somebody else put the body there."

"Trudy, I was five or six years old."

"Okay. I'll go to your mother. She can find a sample of your daddy's handwriting and yours, too. I'll bet she still has your kindergarten papers."

"Of course she does! What kind of mama you think she is?"

"She's the kind who'd kill for her young, no doubt about it. Maybe I need a sample of her handwriting, too, while we're at it."

"Is it too late for me to take back my crack about the police?"

"Not if you'll help me out."

"With handwriting samples? So you can pin this on Daddy?"

"Good grief, Eric, haven't you been listening? Not to pin it on him, unless he did it, but to clear him. And your mother. And you."

"Okay, okay, don't start off again. I'll see what I can do."

"I could ask your mother, if you'd rather do it that way."

"No point in upsetting her for nothing, is there? Let me poke around first. I'll ask her if I have to."

That left Alvin and Doris Burkhalter. I tried to think like Miss Sarah, tried to think of something each of them would have written that long ago that, for some reason or another, would have been saved.

I've found that, sometimes, when I don't seem to be getting anywhere on a puzzle the best thing I can do is back off and try to come back at it later from a different direction. I leaned back and closed my eyes and tried to think of something else besides old handwritten documents. Documents. Body. Refrigerator. Business records, Miss Sarah had said. Business. Wait. Everybody kept saying the Burkhalters used to live near the old school. That meant they'd moved since then, which meant there might be deeds or other official documents from when they bought land, hired a contractor, built a house, paid taxes.

"I'm going over to the courthouse," I told Dawn.

As always, the clerks at the courthouse were helpful, probably happy for the break in routine represented by a police query, but it wasn't a productive quest. Not knowing what kind of legal document I was looking for or when it might have been recorded made it impossible to know how to go about finding it; and even though the clerk kept on being polite, I could tell she was getting frustrated right along with me, like the clerk in a bookstore with a customer who asks for "that new book by the romance writer. I'm pretty sure it has a blue cover."

I thanked her and went back to the station house. It had been a slim hope, anyway. I'm no expert in handwriting analysis, but I do know that signatures can be very artificial. People often draw, rather than write, their signatures, to make them look right — that is, to make them look like the writer would like to present him(or her)self. Even the capital letters aren't necessarily like the capitals they make in ordinary writing.

I was out of ideas on the Burkhalters' handwriting, but I did have another idea I could try while I waited to see what Marie Burkhalter and Eric Riggs could turn up.

"The idea is that we round up all the suspects and put 'em in a room together and you whirl around pointing your finger at each one until somebody cracks? I think I read that book. Struck me as pretty phony." Hen, it is understatement to report, wasn't immediately taken with my suggestion.

"No," I said defensively. "I have no intention of whirling. The idea is that if we get everybody together they might jog each other's memory and help us fill in some of the blanks."

"Some of the many blanks."

"Some of the very many blanks. We'd get Eric and Miz Riggs, Marie Burkhalter and the rest of them, try to go over things systematically and see what happens." Hen likes to be systematic, so I thought that word might bring him around.

"I'll go along with it if you'll wear a deer-stalker and an Inverness cape," he said.

"I'll quit complaining that you aren't taking the case seriously," I counter-offered.

"You've got a deal. Set it up."

"But I'm going to wear my uniform," I said. It was a weak exit line, I admit.

Chapter 21

Nowhere is it written that police inquiry has to take place at the police station, although that is often a good idea. It is axiomatic that an interrogation is more likely to be successful if the interrogatee is not in his (or her) own element, not completely at ease. In this case, since we didn't really have a suspect we needed to keep off balance, we'd decided to go with informality, hoping that a comparatively relaxed atmosphere would produce something useful.

So there we were, over Hen's mild objections (which I had cruelly countered by reminding him he didn't have a family to go home to right then, anyway) and Dwight's derision (which, from long habit and on principle, I ignored). We'd opted for a conference room at St. Joseph's hospital in Savannah so we could include Alvin Burkhalter.

"This is Trudy's show," Hen announced to the guests. It might have sounded like he was disclaiming any responsibility for how it turned out, but since he had helped himself to a cup of coffee and taken a chair in front of the closed door, I took it for support.

"Is this legal?" Kenneth Burkhalter asked.

"Interrogating everybody without Miranda or anything?"

"You sayin' we ought to consider you a suspect?" Hen asked.

"I'm saying you don't have any business upsettin' Daddy."

"Let me put your mind at ease on the Miranda business," Hen said, as though he really believed that's all Kenneth was concerned about. "That's when we get us a suspect. We get any idea one of y'all killed that gir— woman, we'll come to a screechin' halt and do the Mirandizing," Hen assured him. "Where we are now, we're taking it for granted you'll want to help us sort things out, seein's how she was almost part of your family. Trudy got it in her head it might help if we sort of shuffle your stories together about what happened that day, so we organized this field trip. Did I say how obliged we are to y'all for being so cooperative? Maybe everybody jigglin' everybody else's recollections'll shake somethin' loose that'll turn out to help. No big deal, is it, Trudy?"

"Not to me," I said. "Not unless you think trying to find a killer is a big deal."

Hen shook his head in disgust at my stubborn attitude, or, just possibly, at my undercutting his attempt to put them at ease.

I looked around at the people we'd invited to the party. Alvin Burkhalter, still in a wheelchair, looked much healthier, if not happier, than he had the last time I'd seen him. He'd made progress in recovering from the stroke, but the doctors weren't quite ready to send him home. His left hand massaged his right wrist as he looked apprehensively from Doris, sitting next to him in one of the hospital's square, wood-framed chairs, to Kenneth, across the room in an identical chair. Was Alvin's anxiety a lingering effect of the stroke or was he worried about the outcome of this meeting?

Kenneth was leaning forward, elbows on thighs, head turned so that I couldn't read his lips, saying something under this breath to Marie, sitting next to him. Marie, noticing my noticing, smiled an indulgent smile and winked at me.

Eric, Stacy, and Ethel Riggs were crowded together on a loveseat under the windows across from Hen. Hen and I had debated inviting them, and I'd insisted that they had something useful to add.

I massaged my left wrist with my right hand in sympathy with Alvin Burkhalter, and began my spiel.

"Once I watched Grandma unravel a mess the cats had made when they got in her workbasket and tangled up three or four balls of crochet thread. She didn't rush and she took her time, just working with one thread at a time as far as she could. Then she'd put that ball down and pick up another and work with it as far as she could."

"That's interesting," Kenneth Burkhalter

said loudly in the direction of the carpet, meaning it wasn't.

"Well, sir," Hen interpreted, "What Trudy's sayin' is everybody's got a different story to tell about what happened the last time anybody saw Karen Willard and we're gone follow them one thread at a time and see how things connect up."

It was a nice, homey analogy, designed to help everybody relax and it was almost true. It would have been more like the truth to say we'd decided to pick one thread and pull on it till it broke. Or until we were hopelessly tangled up, which seemed just as likely.

"To stretch that yarn a little more," I joked feebly, "it didn't seem to matter where Grandma started with the untangling as long as she was patient and kept after it. We've got a tangle here. We've talked to all of y'all, and we still have a tangle, so we thought we'd try it this way, see if it will jog loose anything new."

"The official police attitude, unless and until somebody convinces us otherwise," Hen said surveying the room, "is that everybody here would like to get this untangled so you can put it behind you once and for all."

"Put it behind us?" Doris Burkhalter asked in a well-worn voice on a well-worn theme. "Put it behind us! You're raking up the dead and tellin' us to put it behind us?"

"Well, now, Miz Burkhalter," Hen said mildly, but giving her the iceberg glare from the family blue eyes, "we didn't set out to rake up Karen

Willard, but now she's been raked up, along with the in-con-tro-ver-ti-ble fact that somebody didn't mean for her to be raked up, we got to look into it."

Doris couldn't stand up to the glare. She darted a glance in her husband's direction.

"You didn't like Karen Willard, did you?" I asked Doris Burkhalter. For being the first to speak up, Doris Burkhalter won the right to be the first one we questioned.

"I told you that," she said.

"You're not saying Mama killed her to keep her from marryin' Donnie?" Kenneth erupted. "That's about the stupidest thing I ever heard."

Doris flashed him a glance. Gratitude? Surprise that he was taking up for her?

"Actually, I'm not saying that," I admitted. "Miz Burkhalter, you sent a box of Karen's things to her family." Feeling a little like one of those fictional detectives Hen had teased me about, I lifted the box, which had been hidden behind a chair, into full view.

Doris Burkhalter nodded. Her eyes and everybody else's were on the box.

"Why did you do that?" I asked.

"I didn't want her stuff in my house. There was a sweater like one I had. I threw mine away after that. Never could wear it again."

I pulled out the sweater for all to see. "And you sent the note she left. Why didn't you just throw it all away?"

"I wanted her to feel guilty."

232

"One thing we need to find out is if it was Karen who left those things," I said, "or maybe somebody else took her other things to try to make it look like she left in a hurry."

"I always leave something behind when I go somewhere," Marie said. "I don't think that proves anything."

I reached inside the box and took out the Chanel box.

"Karen's sister says this would have been the first thing she picked up if she was leaving."

"I wouldn't know about that," Doris Burkhalter said.

"What are you driving at?" Kenneth said.

I seemed to be getting nowhere, so I went in another direction. "We've been over and over the skimpy evidence in this case, and the strongest theory of what happened is that Donnie killed Karen. When he left the house after the football game, he took the body out to the Riggs place and then, either by accident as everybody has always thought, or out of remorse, deliberately committed suicide by wrecking his car."

There was a strangled sound from Doris, but Kenneth drowned her out.

"Are you out of your mind? He was with a whole bunch of us every minute after she left the football field until we got home and found —"

"Found what?" I asked. "Found her note? Found her gone? Karen Willard didn't know many people in Ogeechee, and most of the time strong feelings are involved when somebody

233

gets worked up enough to commit murder. What is more likely than that Donnie went after her, found her, and they quarreled? Maybe he didn't mean to kill her."

The air conditioner came on, giving us cool air and something to listen to in the long silence that followed my speech. Except for the slight movement of the curtains in the air stream, there was profound stillness as everyone considered, I assumed, not only the likelihood of the scenario I'd outlined, but their ability to live with it.

"You didn't know him," Doris Burkhalter said. "You want to blame him because he's not here to defend himself. She killed him, not the other way around."

"Okay, then," I said. "Let's test that. Let's try to fill in as much detail as we can about the day y'all played football and came back to find a pile of shower gifts, but no Karen. Since that's the day Donnie died, it's a day everybody can remember."

Various snorts and sighs assured me I was right about that much, at least.

"When Karen Willard walked away from that football game, she walked to her death, so —"

"How do you know that?" Kenneth Burkhalter interrupting, and putting me on notice, in case I hadn't already figured it out, that he wasn't in a helpful frame of mind.

"It's an assumption we will keep on testing," I said. "Right now it's based on the fact that nobody has said anything about seeing her after that."

"You just keep on askin' questions if you think Trudy's goin' too fast," Hen said genially. "We don't want to take anything for granted here." He leaned back in his chair and took a sip of hospital coffee.

"So let's see how we can do about filling in some of the details of that day." I finished my sentence as though Kenneth and Hen hadn't interrupted. "We'll just do the best we can," I added quickly, to forestall Doris Burkhalter's objections. "And it doesn't really matter where we start. Anybody got a good idea about what time anything happened that day? Anything at all?"

To my surprise, it was Ethel Riggs who spoke first. "We had just set down to supper about seven-thirty when somebody from the church called and told us about Donnie."

It wasn't much of a start, and didn't seem likely to add to our stock of useful information, but it was a start and I was grateful. "Thank you, Miz Riggs. That'll help us get a sense of when things were happening that day. But we don't want to take anything for granted." I darted a glance at Hen and Kenneth Burkhalter. "We need to know how you're so sure it was seven-thirty."

"We always had dinner at seven o'clock, and I'd fried catfish," Mrs. Riggs explained. "Remember, Alvin? You stopped by and brought us some catfish. When Woody came in, ready for dinner, the catfish was ready but Eric wasn't there and I knew there'd be trouble. Woody liked to have things his way, and he didn't like cold catfish. I had a bad time then, worrying about why Eric wasn't home and if something had happened to him."

"You're sure that was the same day?" I asked.

"I'm sure. You remember, Alvin? Well, maybe you don't. Anyway, when Eric did come in, all late and dirty, Woody had worked himself into such a temper he gave Eric a whippin' and wouldn't let him have any supper. I sneaked you up some biscuits later, Eric — remember? — because I was so glad you were still alive."

"I do remember, Mama," Eric said softly. "Give a boy an inch and he'll take a mile," he explained to the rest of us in what I took to be an approximation of his father's voice.

Ethel Riggs must have decided to come clean about the whole unhappy story that was her marriage. "And I was sittin' there chokin' over my supper — I had to sit and eat with Woody — when the phone call came and I thought here we were about to eat Alvin's catfish and his boy was dead and we had a live boy and Woody wouldn't even be good to him."

There was a small silence when Ethel Riggs's story faltered to its close, but Eric, at least, remembered why his mother was telling it — to establish the time.

"I wouldn't have been particularly interested in what happened to Donnie Burkhalter," Eric said, "so I wouldn't remember that, but what I do remember is that it was the same day."

"The same day as what?" I asked.

"The day Eddie and I got the pants scared off us at the dump. I've just put it together!" There was no disguising his excitement. "That was the same day. I was late getting home that day because we were trapped out at the dump, waiting for Alvin Burkhalter to leave."

Bedlam.

"Wait just a . . ." Kenneth Burkhalter yelled.

"No," from Alvin Burkhalter.

"Oh, no!" from Doris Burkhalter.

"Hold it!" Hen's voice dominated the furor. "Everybody hold it! Okay. Now. One at a time. Eric, you through?"

"I can't tell you times, except it was just before I got home that night, but Eddie Beasley and I were out at our hideout at the dump.

"I've talked to Eddie Beasley," he said to me. To the others he explained, "Eddie and I didn't know Donnie Burkhalter, but we knew his daddy. It wasn't that little old Volkswagen of Donnie's — the one they had on display in town after the accident — that scared the livin' pee out of me and Eddie. It was Alvin Burkhalter's truck. I'm sorry. I'm sorry, but I'm sure of that."

Alvin Burkhalter had quit rubbing his bad hand. His head was wagging from side to side, in what could have been a lingering effect of the stroke but looked to me like he was saying no.

"We were cornered," Eric said. "Scared to

leave." He shot an apologetic glance in Alvin Burkhalter's direction. "Mr. Burkhalter, in that old red truck you used to have."

"No!" The word had a strangled sound, but it was emphatic and it cleared up any lingering questions about whether Alvin Burkhalter understood what was going on.

Mrs. Riggs, sounding less shaky now that she was on less personally upsetting ground, said, "You've got to be wrong, son. Either it wasn't Alvin or it wasn't the same day. Wild as Alvin used to be — and I'm sorry to say it, Alvin, but you were, you know it's the truth, you and Woody both — wild as he used to be, Alvin wouldn't have been botherin' with hauling trash with his son just dead."

"Maybe he didn't know his son was dead," Hen said.

"No," Alvin Burkhalter repeated.

"Maybe he was on his way back from fishing?" I suggested.

"No."

"No," Mrs. Riggs agreed. "He brought those fish by a lot earlier in the day."

"Eric must be wrong about the day," Ethel Riggs said. "He was just a little boy."

"Ethel's right," Doris Burkhalter said. "Alvin was home and had already cleaned those catfish when I got home from seein' Mama. And he stayed there. He didn't go anywhere after that, not that day. He was home when the State Patrol called."

"We need to be sure if we're talking about one day or two," I said. "Can you remember what time you got home that day?" I asked Doris Burkhalter, frankly tiptoeing around the central bombshell — Alvin Burkhalter at the Riggs dump on the day Karen Willard died? Could Eric be right?

She didn't answer immediately, but I could tell from her frown that she was thinking about it. From the way her glance darted from her husband to her son and back, I guessed we might never know whether she was trying to remember the truth or trying to think of what the right answer ought to be. "Must have been four, four-thirty," she said finally. "I left Mama in time to get home and start fixin' our supper. I knew Kenneth was supposed to be going somewhere with Marie later and they'd all be hungry so I didn't want supper to be late. Then, when I got there the kitchen was a mess from Alvin cleaning those fish in the sink." She looked at her husband for confirmation. "Blood and fish innards all over the place. Never did like catfish much."

"Just boys," Alvin Burkhalter croaked.

"He means —" Doris Burkhalter began apologetically.

"He means we — he means the recollection of a couple of kids can't be trusted, but we knew that truck," Eric insisted. "Red, with a scrape across the tailgate that we thought looked like a lightning strike. I talked to Eddie about it just the other day, and we know we're right about that. And I know being so late is what got me a whippin' that night."

I was glad Dwight wasn't there. I could just hear him saying, "Whose word you gone take? The stroked out geezer or the spooked little young'uns?"

"I know you think you're right, Eric," Marie Burkhalter said, "But there is something wrong here. I don't see how Mr. Burkhalter could have been at your farm in that truck. Kenneth and I had a date to go to a movie in Vidalia that night, and we went in that truck. I was such a priss in those days I was furious at him for bringing the truck, when I'd been expecting him to have the car, and on top of that I was upset about his being late. We fought the whole night long, didn't we, Kenny? We were on our way home, between there and Lyons, when the Sheriff stopped us and told us about Donnie." Her voice softened. "At least we quit fightin' then."

"Eric?" I asked. "You still sure?"

"Unless that truck had a clone!" He wasn't defensive, just sure of himself.

"Son, I notice you keep sayin' 'that truck.' You didn't see who was drivin' it?" Hen asked.

"Maybe we didn't see. We were hiding, didn't want to be seen. Whoever it was stuck around a while."

"Eric's sure it was the truck," I said. "But not sure who was driving it. Let's see if we can pin that down. Miz Riggs, you say Eric got home about seven-thirty."

"That's right."

"Marie, you said Kenneth was late picking you up. What time are we talking about?"

"Maybe eight. We missed the first part of the movie."

"Kenneth, what time did you leave home in the truck?"

"No idea," he said. There was a challenge in his voice.

"Miz Burkhalter?" I asked.

"Even if it was Kenneth there in Alvin's truck, even if it was, that doesn't mean anything," she said.

"Do you know what time he left the house?"

"No." And wouldn't tell me if she did.

"Kenneth, you disappeared from the football game for a while. Did you have time to follow Karen to your house and kill her?" Hen likes those direct questions.

"I never left the game. What are you talking about?"

"Marie?" I prompted.

"You dropped out, Kenny. When I asked where you'd been, you said you had a twisted ankle or something."

He turned on her angrily. "I was there all the time. I never went home till we all went together and found . . ."

He stumbled over saying what they'd found. It seemed like a thread worth pulling.

"You found?" I asked.

"That pile of stuff. Shower presents. The note. You know what we found."

"Did you find Karen?"

"No," Marie said, trying to help. "She was already gone."

"And Donnie had been with y'all the whole time?"

"The whole time," Kenneth said. "And I was there the whole time, too, Marie."

Alvin Burkhalter's left hand began to beat against the armrest of his wheelchair.

"Alvin!" Doris Burkhalter cried. "Somebody get a doctor!"

"No!" At least he knew how to make that word. "W— wait!"

His wife didn't need to translate that. He wanted to say something and he didn't need a doctor.

"See what you've done!" Kenneth said angrily.

Alvin's right hand waved in his son's direction. "No." He said again. "No. Ken."

"I think he's all right," Doris said, tentatively.

"Not Ken." Alvin said. "Not Ken."

"You're saying it wasn't Kenneth in the truck at the Riggs dump?" I guessed.

Alvin looked me in the eye and nodded.

"Do you know who it was?" I asked.

With his strong left hand, Alvin Burkhalter thumped his chest. "Me. My truck."

"He's lying," Kenneth said.

"Kenneth!" His mother was aghast.

"Kenneth?" Marie was confused.

"You're calling your daddy a liar?" I asked.

"I gotta admit, Trudy," Hen said, "this is turning out to be a lot more interestin' than I thought it would."

"He's had a stroke," Kenneth said. "He doesn't know what's going on."

Maybe not.

Alvin Burkhalter thumped his chest again.

I turned to his wife. "Miz Burkhalter, you said your husband was there when you got home that afternoon. Who else was there?"

She glanced from Alvin to Kenneth again, looking for the right answer in one of their faces. Not able to guess what to say from that, she consulted her memory. "Nobody. Just Alvin."

"Was the truck there?"

"I don't know. Maybe somebody stole it?" She glanced hopefully at her son after this suggestion.

"Did Kenneth come home later?"

"Mama, you don't know. You don't remember." From Kenneth.

"Kenneth had the truck," Marie said. "I remember."

Kenneth turned angrily in Marie's direction and Hen came to his feet, assumed an imposing stance, and cleared his throat.

Kenneth raised his hands in surrender. "Okay. Okay." He gave Marie one last angry look. "Okay. Here's the deal. We came home from the football field and found that mess in the living room, the presents and stuff. Daddy showed us Karen's note. Donnie took off. Everybody else left. I don't remember why any more, but Daddy and I got in some kind of dust-up. We used to have a lot of those. And I just left, took the truck. I was tearing down some dirt roads, burning up gas and kicking up dust, when I noticed there was something in the back."

He certainly had our attention. Alvin Burkhalter was still hitting his armrest, automatically but gently. Apparently, he was mesmerized by Kenneth's story.

After a glance around the room to see how we were taking it, Kenneth resumed. "It was Karen." He drew a deep breath.

"But, uh, I didn't know that. I screeched to a stop and she fell out and got banged up. Bad. Hit her, uh, head. She was hurt bad. But she told me she'd been hiding there so I could give her a ride out of town."

Even the air conditioner was quiet.

"I tried to get her in the truck so I could get her to the hospital, but she was hurt worse than I thought. When I picked her up, she went limp. I, uh, I think maybe that's when she died."

"So it was you in the truck at the dump?" Eric asked. "Not your daddy?"

Kenneth stared at him. "Uh."

"No," Alvin said.

Kenneth re-grouped. "Uh. I knew I was in

bad trouble. I remembered that old refrigerator at the Riggs dump and so I took her there. I thought I'd figure out what to do later, but then there was Donnie. So I didn't. Tell. Till now."

"Good God, Kenny!" Marie said, putting her hand on her shoulder. "No wonder you weren't fit to be with that night!"

"Not bad for spur of the moment," I said. "But if you think about it, it doesn't hold up. What about her luggage?"

"Luggage? What luggage?"

"Where was Karen's luggage, if she was leaving? Your mother sent a few things — all that was left at your house — to Karen's family. What about the rest of her stuff?"

"She had a suitcase with her. I dumped it too, I guess."

"You guess?" I asked.

"You're asking us to believe a woman who was having a destructive fit had the patience to pack her bags, sneak around after your daddy came home, and go wait in the truck?" Hen was frankly skeptical. "The only part of your story that sounds like the truth is the part about you putting her body in the refrigerator."

"I swear."

"Swearin' don't make it true," Hen observed. "But you were right about bein' in trouble."

Kenneth tried bravado. "Yeah. Well. Long time ago. Kid. I'll get me a good lawyer."

"Good idea," Hen said. "You want to make the arrest, Trudy?"

"Not yet, if you don't mind. You know how balky I get when people try to tell me what to do."

"Lordy, I do," Hen said. Then to the rest of the group. "We might as well humor her. It'll be quicker in the long run."

"I want to go back to that timetable I was working on," I said. "Any idea what time it was when y'all quit playing football and went to the Burkhalter house?"

"Middle of the afternoon," Marie offered after thinking about it. "I know we didn't start till sometime after lunch, and we'd been there a while."

"Two?" I suggested.

"Later," she said, after glancing at Kenneth, who didn't appear to be at all interested.

"Three?"

"Maybe. Maybe later."

"And Mr. Burkhalter was there when y'all got there?"

"Wait just a minute!" Kenneth said. "You think he can't defend himself, you think —"

"You hold your horses, hoss," Hen told him.

"No," I said. "That's not where I'm going with this."

Kenneth held his horses, but with a visible effort.

"Marie says you left the game for a while, Kenneth," I reminded him.

He turned on Marie. "I told you I was under the bleachers. I never left."

"All I said was I missed you," she said. "Remember how jealous I used to be? I looked for you and couldn't find you."

"I was under the bleachers."

"Or maybe you followed Karen to your house and killed her," I suggested.

"I told you what happened."

"It's time for a little show and tell," I said, springing my one real surprise on the group. I held up the fragment of pottery the lab had taken from Karen's skull. "This was embedded in Karen's skull." I turned it this way and that, to catch the light. "Can everybody see the nice bright orange glaze? The pebbled surface? Good. I know it's hard to see. If you want to, you can see a much bigger piece of the same stuff in the Burkhalter living room."

Alvin slumped. Doris looked stricken.

Kenneth, of course, was verbal. "What? You out of your mind? What are you talking about?"

"I'm talking about the lamp in your mother's living room. I'm guessing there used to be two of them."

Doris Burkhalter was nodding. "It got broken during some of their rough-housin'. You know boys."

"I think it got broken during Karen's murder." Think? I was sure of it. "I believe she was killed right there in your living room, not by falling out of a truck."

"I might be ready to arrest Kenneth for murder, now, not just a measly old thirty-year-old negligent vehicular homicide and whatever else we might be able to connect to that," I said to Hen. "You have the right to remain silent," I said to Kenneth, "Anything —"

"No." It was Alvin Burkhalter again. He was sure good with that word.

"Me," he added. "I did it. Ma. Ma." He shook his head and pounded his wheelchair in frustration while we watched, stunned. "Mirandize me!" he finally managed.

Automatically, I recited the Miranda warning.

It took a while, but with a combination of our yes-no signals and halting words, he told his story.

Alvin Burkhalter's story was essentially that he had broken the lamp over Karen's head and, knowing the others would be coming home soon, had hidden her body in the truck to dispose of later, but then Kenneth took off with the truck and he never saw the body again. "I was a . . . heller . . . in those days," he said. He'd kept quiet all these years because he hadn't known what to think when the body disappeared.

He also kept quiet when we asked him why he'd done it. "Wait for . . . my lawyer," he said.

"He's lying," Kenneth insisted again.

There I was, robbed of an arrest because we had two confessions and no immediately apparent way of proving — or disproving — either one.

"That's all for now," I said in disgust.

"We're gone take all this back and see if Trudy's cats can unravel it for us," Hen said. "So we don't want any of y'all leavin' town until further notice."

As Hen and I left, I saw Stacy Riggs bending toward her mother-in-law with a kinder expression on her face than she usually had in that context. Maybe we'd have to revise our horrorscope for Sugar Cane, and put a more positive spin on all that fiber.

The Burkhalters, including Marie, were clustering together conspiratorially. My bright idea hadn't done our investigation much good, but I realized the families involved — for better or for worse — had all moved into new territory.

"Nice party, Trudy," Hen said. "You've got a real flair for entertainin'."

Chapter 22

When you're as pampered as Hen is, being on your own even for a little while can seem like being totally bereft. Taking pity on him, and calling on that part of our relationship that has nothing to do with police work, I asked him if he'd like to eat supper with me that night. I'm sure the invitation had nothing to do with my observation that recent events were pulling the Riggses and Burkhalters closer together and I was feeling left out.

"What time?" he asked, without even asking what I might be serving, validating my assumption that anything he didn't have to contend with all by himself would be welcome.

"Whenever you can get there," I answered.

"You don't need two or three hours in the kitchen?" he asked wistfully.

"You're kidding," I said. "The invitation is for supper, not Thanksgiving dinner."

He sighed. "Six-thirty?"

"Fine."

Hen and I both grew up thinking of my house as the center of home and family, so it's a fairly recent development that anything as formal as an invitation has figured into things. When

Grandma was living, she was almost always there, and even if she wasn't, you could still count on finding the door open and something good to eat in the pantry or the refrigerator. Since the house has been mine, and Hen has his own home anyway, that easy-come attitude has gradually changed. I don't like to think I'm selfish and cold, but I do like being able to call my home my home and not having to keep the welcome mat out all the time.

All that is to say that having him to supper, even if I tried to act casual about it, was something of an occasion, especially since the rest of the family wouldn't be there.

I told myself it was an act of charity to give Hen a good meal, but the fact is, having a decent meal wouldn't be such a bad thing for me, either. For me, it isn't making a meal that's hard, it's wanting to make a meal. When I'm on my own, my meals are likely to be cereal; tomato, banana, or grilled cheese sandwiches; or maybe some canned clam chowder. It's not that I don't know what a real meal is supposed to look like, I do: cornbread or biscuits, some kind of meat, three or four vegetables, iced tea, and at least one kind of dessert — the kind of meals Kathi puts out. As I said, it isn't hard. In the summer in Ogeechee, vegetables are especially easy. On my way home I went by Aunt Lulu's yard and helped myself to some tomatoes and squash. I'd hoped for one of those little Japanese eggplants she was trying this year, but they weren't ready.

I stopped at Grinstead's Market for some pork chops and some canned biscuits and as soon as I got home I poured a can of mushroom soup over the pork chops and put them in the oven to cook while I slapped together a banana pudding out of instant pudding, vanilla wafers, and bananas. In spite of what I'd said about Thanksgiving dinner, I realized I was fixing too much food for only two people, but I didn't seem to be able to stop myself. I had a clue to the reason when at the last minute I decided to make the Huckabee salad — something Aunt Lulu swears nobody outside our family has ever eaten. It could be that nobody outside our family has ever been that desperate, but for us, that salad is comfort food. Hen might not need it, but I did. When I tell you what's in it, you'll think you understand why nobody else has ever tried it, but you ought to try it before you gag: Pour a can of tomatoes into a bowl and crumble enough saltines into it to soak up the juice without making it too dry. Add a chopped hard boiled egg and diced sweet pickles, salt, pepper, and mayonnaise until it tastes right. Part of what's great about it is that there's no real recipe to worry about, no way to be mechanical and business-like. You just relax and mess with it till it tastes like you want it to.

I put the salad aside, then chopped the squash with some onion — using my left hand, carefully, as much as I could — and put it on to cook. I was slicing tomatoes when Hen arrived.

"Pour yourself some tea. Supper'll be ready in ten minutes," I predicted, hastily sliding the biscuits into the oven so that he wouldn't be able to tell anything from their suspiciously regular appearance. If they didn't taste like what he usually got, maybe he'd just think it was the difference in cooks. "We'll eat on the porch."

While we waited for the biscuits, I poured myself some tea and took it out to the porch with some plates. I took a sip and left it on the table, returning to the kitchen for butter and a jar of Aunt Lulu's strawberry preserves.

"We gone eat over the well?" Hen called after me.

When I was a child, it terrified me to eat out there on the porch, because I knew the part of the porch where the table sat had been built over an old well. I would try to get a seat around the edge so that when (not if) the floor gave way, I'd be able to save myself by holding on to the curtains. I fantasized that somehow I would be able to rescue the others, who hadn't had my foresight. Telling me that the well had been filled in and covered over and even if the floor should for some unknown reason break open I wouldn't fall far did nothing to calm my fears. A well meant only one thing to me — a watery death, unless I was vigilant.

Involuntarily, I shivered. "I used to wonder what was down there," I admitted. I set plates and silverware on the table.

"Rocks," he said. "Dirt."

"You never did have much imagination. There could be bodies."

"Yep."

"Do you know when they filled it in?" I asked, trying to lighten things up. "And why?"

"Mama would know. Probably when the city got on a water system."

The oven timer went off.

As a matter of policy and principle, Hen and I don't usually talk business when we're together off duty, but now, without Aunt Lulu, Teri, and Delcie around, there was no reason not to.

"There could be bodies all over town," I said as I put the pork chops and biscuits on the table. "Think of all the old barns and smokehouses and dumping grounds in the woods around here."

"You are abso-tively right. Not to mention the ones that might be stuffed down in old wells," Hen said, helping himself to everything in reach while I went back to the kitchen for the vegetables.

"Even a town this small has plenty of secrets," I said with a shiver, thinking not only of my childhood fears, but of Karen Willard's body.

"Most of 'em wouldn't be all that interestin'."

"Looks like the Riggses had interestin' secrets," I answered. "Even if it's too late to have anything to do with anything, I can't help but wonder if Woody Riggs could have been brought up for domestic violence, child abuse."

"Thirty years ago? Nah. Good old fashioned

discipline. Nobody's business but their own." In police work we see plenty of the kind of "discipline" of children, even wives, that can leave them damaged physically and emotionally, so I understood the sneer in Hen's voice.

"And Alvin Burkhalter, too," I said. "It's too late to nail Woody Riggs, but I wish I could arrest Alvin Burkhalter, even if he is a sick old man."

"Arrest him for what? For bein' Woody's friend and a rounder? He's not the man he was thirty years ago, Trudy. You'd be punishing an innocent man." Hen's look as he made this comment wasn't innocent. He was deliberately baiting me.

"Okay then, how about Kenneth? Let's arrest him. I got the feelin' he was makin' up that confession of his as he went along. You didn't believe him, did you?"

"No. So what do we arrest him for?"

"For lying to us."

"Now, Trudy, trouble is, I don't think Kenneth Burkhalter would object much to lyin' to the po-lice or anybody else, but he'd have to have a good reason to confess to a killin' he didn't do."

"Maybe he's lying to protect his sick daddy."

"You saying you believed Alvin's confession?"

"No, I'm not saying that. I didn't."

"So now you've got Alvin lyin'. Why would a good ol' church-going man like Alvin Burkhalter confess to a murder he didn't commit?"

He glared at me as he wiped some mushroom soup gravy off his chin.

"We didn't believe Kenneth, but we're trained professionals. Maybe Alvin did believe him. So he might have lied for the same reason Kenneth might have lied. To take the blame. Maybe Alvin thinks he's about to die and figures God'll forgive him for a pious lie, so he's trying to make up for being a crummy father. I don't know," I said in frustration. "Maybe Alvin did do it and isn't lying at all. He's probably not as much of a liar as Kenneth is."

Hen picked up another biscuit and studied it before he suggested, "What if they're both lying?"

"I like that! I like it a lot! No. Wait. If they're both lying — if they're both confessing to protect the other one — it would mean that neither one of 'em really did, wouldn't it?"

Hen nodded agreement.

I savored a bite of the family salad while I thought it over. "You know, I'm really having a hard time coming up with a credible reason for anybody wanting to kill her. Or managing to do it without being caught in the act. We didn't learn much from that group meeting, but we did learn that there wasn't a lot of time for the killer to have done the deed."

"What do you figure?"

"If I'm right about Karen being killed at the Burkhalter house — and that piece of pottery sure makes it look like somebody hit her with the Burkhalter lamp — and if we assume Alvin didn't kill her, in spite of his confession, then it had to have happened between the time she walked away from that football field and the time Alvin got home. An hour and a half, at most, for her to decide to break up with Donnie, make plans to leave, trash the shower gifts, write the note, and incite someone to murder her."

"If she hadn't already made up her mind to break up and leave," he said, "or written the note, if she wrote the note. How you comin' on handwriting samples?"

"Still working on it. It's pretty pathetic to be pinning any hopes on that."

He stabbed the air with his fork. "Maybe the killer was another boyfriend, somebody she'd dumped for Donnie. He was waiting there, but instead of leaving together, he killed her."

"That's not bad except that it would have been rushing things a lot. It does explain one of the more mystifying elements of this case. Everybody says Karen and Donnie seemed to be getting along fine at the ball game so they didn't understand why she'd have left. And there's still the problem of her luggage," I said.

"What do you mean?"

"What happened to her other stuff, the stuff Doris Burkhalter didn't send to Bristol?"

"Kenneth says the rest of her stuff was in the truck."

"Why would we believe him about that if we don't believe the rest of his story?"

"Beats me, you know, an outsider would have had no reason to make it look like she'd left. But her body was in the Burkhalter truck, Trudy. We do believe that much, don't we?"

"I do. I think. Even if Alvin and Kenneth are lying about something, they seem to agree on that."

We ate in silence for a bit.

"What about this," I offered. "Kenneth and Alvin were both telling part of the truth. It was Kenneth at the dump in Alvin's truck. The timing would have been tight, but it could work. Kenneth put her in the refrigerator but he didn't kill her. He might have been trying to cover up for Donnie. And maybe Alvin found her body and thought Donnie had killed her. Alvin might be trying to take the blame for Donnie." I was getting excited about this new theory.

"That doesn't work," Hen said. "Donnie was with the football players the whole time."

"But Alvin wouldn't have known that. He could have thought Donnie did it," I countered.

"Why'd he let Kenneth take the truck if he'd put the body in it?"

"Kenneth sneaked off in the truck. Said they'd had a fight, or something. I think they both agreed on that, too," I reminded him.

Hen thought it over. "Okay. And then, when Kenneth came back in the truck without the body, Alvin didn't know what to think and got so confused he got religion?"

"Works for me. And, Hen, that would explain

why each one of them thought the other one did it — has thought so all this time."

"We've been goin' in circles so long we're both dizzy."

"That's a sugar rush you're having," I told him.

"Pass the banana puddin' again, will you?"

I passed the banana pudding. "Maybe it was Leon Bell, after all, and the Burkhalters covered up for him instead of Donnie."

"You admitting Dwight's conspiracy theory wasn't completely off base?"

Before I could think of a way to keep from giving Dwight any credit at all, Hen's cell phone rang. More and more in police work we've moved to using cell phones because they're easier to carry around and harder to intercept than the radio. This wasn't business, though. It was Teri. Rather than eavesdrop on the squawk that was all I could hear of the conversation, I started clearing the table.

"No, doesn't look like it," Hen said.

I imagined the question: "Are you going to be able to get away at all?"

Squawk.

Hen: "You remember that three-legged dog we used to have that we thought had brain damage from when he managed to catch the UPS truck?"

A squawking laugh. Teri understood Hen's point — we were chasing our tails. She must have asked him how things were going in the investigation.

"Yeah, Trudy's feedin' me right this minute."

The question? Are you eating right?

I accuse Hen of being a sexist, with rigid ideas of gender roles in life, and he is that. But what chance did he have? Obviously he grew up, and was still, surrounded by women who had strong ideas about their roles. The idea that anybody needed to take care of him didn't offend him, it made him feel loved. The idea that I was one of the ones who was taking care of him made me drop a dish.

Crash. Squawk.

"That salad Mama says nobody outside our family has ever made."

That was a no-brainer. She was checking on what I'd been feeding him. "Trudy?"

That was the answer to another question.

"She's right here. Trudy!"

That was a summons. Me to the telephone. Surely Teri wasn't going to grill me about what I'd fed him. But it wasn't Teri, it was Delcie.

"Hey, Sweetie."

"Trudy, why don't you solve that murder so Daddy can have his vacation?"

"He didn't tell you to ask me that, did he?"

"No. Why?"

This was making my day. Here was a pure friend with a high estimate of my capabilities.

"I'm sure working on it. I'll do what I can."

"Okay!" She shouted, away from the telephone, "Trudy says she's working on it!" Bless her little heart.

Then Aunt Lulu came on. "Trudy? Thanks for takin' care of Hen. I know it goes against your feminist grain."

"Yes, ma'am, you're right, and you're welcome."

"I've been wondering if you've found any fingerprints on that note."

"When did you get so interested in police work?"

"When it occurred to me that modern police methods and procedures may be very well in their place, but I don't see how they can help you with something that happened that long ago."

"Yes, ma'am. You've got a real good point." I didn't tell her Dwight shared her opinion.

"And since two of the most important people in my life are dedicated to it, I thought it would make me a better conversationalist if I learned to speak their language."

"Aunt Lulu, I think you must have had one ride too many on Space Mountain. Don't they have a caution up there about how that can make people sick?"

"Never you mind about that. What have they done to get fingerprints off that note? Laser? Magnetic-sensitive powder? Chemical fuming? Or since it's paper, and old at that, ninhydrin solution?"

"Uh. We usually leave all that to the guys at the lab," I said, choking back the smart alec suggestion I'd have made to anybody else, along the

261

lines of how I'd give them her number in case they needed help. I wasn't about to get into explaining forensic analysis to her, or the technicalities of lifting prints off a piece of paper that old. "They did find prints on it, but none they could match with any on file."

No way would Hen be able to reconstruct the other end of my conversation! Heck, he wasn't even trying. He was digging into the banana pudding again. It's better if you make the vanilla pudding from scratch, but my shortcut method obviously isn't bad.

"Let me talk to Henry, then," Aunt Lulu was saying.

"Yes, ma'am." I handed the phone back to Hen and dished up the rest of the banana pudding for myself, telling myself I needed the potassium.

"Mama asked me about ninhydrin solution," he said when he disconnected.

"Me, too."

"I don't like it. It's bad enough having one woman in the family who thinks she knows more about policin' than I do."

I smiled. "You going to try to stop her?"

He snorted.

"Maybe you should make her up an approved reading list," I suggested. "You don't want her to be out of date."

"She been getting books from the library on this?"

"I could ask Marie Burkhalter."

"Better not. She'd tell Mama and, depending on what she's been reading, she might sue us for invasion of privacy, unauthorized prying into her library records, no tellin' what. Mama also says we should pull Miss Sarah in as a consultant. A little learning can be a dangerous thing, Trudy."

I decided not to take that comment personally and began to think I was enjoying myself a lot more than Hen was.

"Did you tell her we already thought of consulting Miss Sarah?"

"No. She'd be so jealous it would ruin her vacation."

"It wasn't supposed to be her vacation, remember? It was yours."

"Yeah, I remember that."

"Hen, if you wait to take a vacation till we get this Karen Willard case cleared up, you may never leave Ogeechee again."

He grunted, not happily.

"When are they coming back?"

"Couple more days. Pass the banana pudding."

When I showed him the empty bowl he grimaced and decided the party must be over. He was gone and I was just about finished in the kitchen when the phone rang — my phone this time.

"Daddy tells me you let a murder case break after I left," Phil said.

"Uh huh. We sat on it till the sensation-mongering media had left the premises. You having a good time?"

"Matter of fact, I am. It wouldn't be everybody's idea of fun, but sitting around swapping lies and war stories with people in the same business, especially when it doesn't happen every day, does happen to be my idea of a good time. Not as good as visiting Atlanta with a fellow art lover, but not bad," he added, too late.

"I don't think there's any danger of the *Beacon* missing the scoop on this, so don't let that worry you," I said, a little miffed.

He laughed, and I could imagine him adjusting his glasses, a mannerism he might use to stall for time even without anybody there to appreciate it.

"Want me to meet your plane?" I asked.

"Thanks, but Molly's got to be in Savannah anyway for something or other. She'll pick me up."

"Okay, then. See you in a couple of days."

The conversation didn't exactly go wrong. It just didn't go anywhere.

I had another helping of Huckabee Salad and entertained myself working out Phil's horoscope. Boiled Peanut? Boiled Peanuts are complex and hard to figure out, since they go by the name of nuts, and seem to be nuts, but are actually peas. Most often seen parched or roasted, the true Southern version is boiled in brine and is an acquired taste. Hmm. Is Phil more complex than I'd realized? Is he actually a friend who seems to be a sweetheart? Or vice versa?

Chapter 23

"A message from Marie Burkhalter," Dawn said in greeting when I got to the station house the next morning. "Said to call her at the library. Somethin' about a book bein' a year overdue? Here's the number."

From her portentously serious look, I could tell that Dawn was making a joke. Book. Year. No doubt about it. It is so seldom that Dawn tries to make a joke that I try to encourage her when she does. I've just about given up thinking I'll be able to teach her the fine art of insubordination, but I'm still hopeful about the sense of humor. She might be able to have a full and rewarding life even if she remains in awe of Hen, but she'll never be able to succeed at much of anything that matters if she doesn't develop a sense of humor. As this example shows, though, she still has a long way to go. I did what I could to show her I recognized the effort.

"Good grief! I can't be in trouble with the library! I haven't even picked up my library card yet. She didn't have to call the po-lice on me!"

Dawn giggled.

"I'll walk on over there and give myself up," I

said. "Might as well pick up my library card at the same time."

Sweet Dawn was still smiling when the door closed behind me.

"Good mornin'," Marie Burkhalter said when I walked into the library. "If you'd called, I could have saved you a trip over. I was going to tell you that I can't get hold of my yearbooks. Mama kept stuff like that out in the garage, but they had that fire last summer when Daddy was burning some trash a little too close to the garage and then went inside for a nap before he made sure it was really out. My whole childhood went up in smoke. Lucky it was just the garage and my childhood and not the house and my parents. Sorry."

"Me, too," I said. "But it was just an idea, probably not important at all. Let me get my library card, then, so my trip won't be a complete washout."

Marie went to look for my card.

"You talkin' about school yearbooks?" The disembodied voice startled me.

"What?"

Julie Todd rose from behind one of the low mobile bookshelves across the room. I knew she was almost exactly Marie Burkhalter's age, and I was struck by how differently the years had treated them. Marie, I thought, had aged well. Her appearance and manner showed an awareness of an individual self, and an appreciation for that self, hard-won, no doubt from some of the circumstances life and Kenneth Burkhalter had sent her way. Marie's half-amused take on life would make it fun to be around her, unless you happened to be the no-nonsense type.

Julie Todd's scrawny figure was dressed entirely in black. Not chic, high fashion black, I hasten to add. A long, loose, uneven gauzy black skirt with a shapeless black T-shirt pulled over it, black hose with reinforced toes peeping through heavy black sandals, flat black hair with a dullness that suggested shoe polish rather than Clairol in a severe chopped style that suggested Main Street Barbers rather than Pauline's Cut-n-Curl. No makeup. At Halloween, green eye-shadow and a broom would be all she'd need. She would definitely not blend right in at a church potluck. Not that she'd have tried. Maybe she'd always been so sure of herself and her family's position in the town, and so protective of both, that she'd expected the universe to kowtow, as Marie had said. For some people, the other side of that "social position" coin might have translated into *noblesse oblige* or a need for the good opinion of her neighbors, to her adopting a *grande dame* persona. That obviously wasn't how it worked with Julie Todd.

Aunt Lulu and Miss Sarah said Julie made a scene — had a fit? — at Donnie Burkhalter's funeral. So there was a passionate nature behind this apparently careless appearance and the go-to-the-devil attitude Marie had described, an at-

267

titude and appearance that would practically guarantee a buffer zone from the social life of Ogeechee. Definitely more off-center than Marie.

Her voice was pleasantly raspy. Cigarettes. I thought of Dinah Willard. I guessed Dinah would be a few years older, but even tethered to her oxygen tank she looked healthier than Julie Todd. I pictured Julie piled up in a recliner near a reading lamp, drink at hand, cigarette dangling from her lips, devouring book after book in unlimited supply, thanks to the Ogeechee Public Library. She spoke again just as I was about to indulge in creating a horror-scope for her.

"I don't know what you want school year-books for, but it seems like the school would be the place to look," she said.

Except that the ones at the school wouldn't have all those cute little handwritten notes in them, I thought.

"That was my first thought," I lied, "but bein' summer, I didn't know how easy it would be to find somebody over there who'd be able to help me."

She gazed at me, blinking slowly. Maybe that medication Aunt Lulu and Miss Sarah had mentioned kept her in a slo-mo world. She seemed to be thinking something over. "What years did you want?"

"Sixty-nine, sixty-eight, sixty-seven. In there."

"I might have those, but what do you want

them for? Research for one of those retro parties where everybody dresses up like the sixties?"

"No, but that's a good idea." When she said that, I pegged her look — sixties. Hippies. Flower children. She was frozen in that time frame. She was definitely not the Garden Club type, but I wondered if her slo-mo had anything to do with an illegal garden plant in the hemp family. I brought my thoughts back to the moment. "You've heard about the body we found out at the Riggs place?"

"In a refrigerator. Everybody in town's heard about that by now."

"We've identified the body. It was a woman named Karen Willard and she was engaged to a local boy, Donnie Burkhalter, back in the sixties."

"I hadn't heard that." She gave her head an odd, quick shake, like someone who is disoriented. The gesture made me think of a chicken, a little bantam hen. "Karen Willard. Karen Willard. I wondered what happened to her," she said. Then, "In a refrigerator?"

"That's right."

"I don't understand. Everybody thought Karen Willard left town. Ran out on Donnie. That's what everybody thought."

"Looks like everybody was wrong," I said.

She nodded and seemed to make an effort to get a grip on herself. She gave her head that odd shake again, as if to clear it, and said in a businesslike tone, "Well, she wouldn't be in our yearbooks, if that's what you were thinking. She wasn't from here."

I nodded. "I know. I thought the yearbooks might give me more than just pictures — might give me an idea what was going on in the lives of people that age back then." It sounded thin even to me, even though it was pretty much the truth. "The Civil Rights movement, hippies, all that." I shrugged and tried to sound casual and naive. "I don't know how to go about investigating a case this old, and I thought the yearbook might give me some ideas. Seeing Donnie, Kenneth, Marie . . ."

"Me."

"Yes. You'd all be there."

"You wouldn't recognize a one of us."

"Maybe not. It's been a long time." She wasn't making this easy for me, but I stuck with it. "I thought seeing y'all might give me some ideas about where to start on this case."

"This case?"

"It happened a long time ago, but it's still a murder case. There's no statute of limitations on that."

"Murder?" She seemed to think that over. Then, "How do you know that? How can you tell?"

"For one thing, if you think about it, you'll realize she didn't put herself in that refrigerator."

"I've heard of kids doing that, before they made a law about how refrigerator doors close."

"She was dead before she was put in there."

"They can tell that?"

I nodded.

She seemed to accept that and turned back to our earlier topic. "I might have the yearbooks. We've all changed. I used to be very pretty. That used to be important."

How do you respond to a statement like that? You still are? No kidding? What's important to you now? I smiled.

"Life is change," I said. "Everybody gets battered by life's ups and downs, and that makes its mark." I was thinking not only of Julie Todd, but of my widowhood and return to Ogeechee, of my husband Zach and Donnie Burkhalter, who both died young. Of Phil Pittman.

"Tell me about Donnie Burkhalter," I invited impulsively. "From what I've heard he was a great guy, popular and well-liked. Of course, the main person I've talked to is his mother, so that's not exactly an objective opinion."

"I probably thought as much of him as his mother did," Julie Todd said. "I'd planned to marry him, in case you didn't know. But I have a feeling you did know that."

"Yes, I'd heard that."

"He was really in love with me, you know."

"It must have broken your heart." It sounded so trite I was ashamed of myself.

"His engagement to Karen? No, I knew that was a mistake. He never would have actually married her, you know."

"I meant his death," I said, but her comment

271

made me wonder if Donnie's engagement to Karen had hurt Julie worse than his death. "Was Donnie much like his brother?"

Her eyes glittered and she opened her mouth. I was sure something juicy was going to come out, but she clamped her lips together and shook her head.

"Not like Kenneth, then?" I suggested.

"No. Not a roughneck. Not the ladies' man Kenneth was even then. Donnie was smarter. Not as rough. Much nicer. Much tamer." She did smile then, but it didn't reach her eyes. "Better looking."

"What a shame," I said when she stopped. "Have you ever thought about how he might have changed if he'd lived?"

She looked startled. "No."

"People who die don't get to change any more, they're fixed in memory just as they were." I smiled and tried to lighten up a little. "Except that we may tend to gloss over their failings and exaggerate their good qualities."

"Here's your card," Marie said, coming from the back.

"I'll bring the yearbooks tomorrow," Julie said, and returned to shelving books. "If I can find them. Now that I think about it, I'm not so sure I do know where they are. It's been a good long while since I've given 'em a thought."

"Well, I'll appreciate it if you can. Thanks," I said, again, including them both, and went back to the station house with my new library card.

Chapter 24

"Trudy? Sarah Kennedy here." She'd caught me at home just before I left for the station.

"Good morning, Miss Sarah. You giving the nursing staff a few minutes' peace?" I'm gradually learning to tease Miss Sarah, but I'm still careful about it.

"Not only that," she responded, "but I'm doing your job for you at the same time."

"Dare I ask?"

"You remember we talked about high school yearbooks?"

"Yes, ma'am, I do."

"Doris Burkhalter stopped in this morning. I asked her if she still had the yearbooks from when her boys were in school and she did. Matter of fact, she went right home and came back with a stack of them. We spent a good while looking through them, reminiscing about all the young people and their families and the different school activities through the years, not to mention how things have changed. Well, you'd expect that. Trudy, it seems as if this business has broken some sort of emotional logjam for Doris."

"I hope that's good," I said.

"I imagine it will be, in the long run if not the short run. She's kept a lot of things bottled up inside for all this time, and now with Alvin's situation, too, she's reached the point where she'll . . . Oh, yes, I meant to tell you, I wouldn't have asked her about the yearbooks except that I've decided she can't be the one who killed Karen Willard."

"You really are doing my police work, aren't you? I forgot to caution you that this is something that should be left to professionals, not something you should try at home."

"Fiddlesticks." I could picture her sitting straighter and frowning into the telephone. "Sitting here between therapy sessions, I have nothing to do but think. Are you interested in knowing why I've eliminated Doris from suspicion?"

"Of course I am, and stop looking at me like that."

From the other end of the phone line, she laughed. "If Doris had been the one who killed Karen, she would have known she was dead."

"Yes, I'm with you on that," I said cautiously, glad she really couldn't see the expression on my face.

"What I mean is, if Doris knew Karen was dead, she wouldn't have mailed those things to Karen," Miss Sarah explained.

"You're right. Of course. Unless —"

"Unless she was being subtle, or simply couldn't abide the sight of anything that would remind her of what she had done. But then she'd have thrown everything away. No, that isn't it. If my memory serves, there is evidence even the police will appreciate. I'd need to see the note again, but I believe the handwriting on that note exonerates Doris."

"It does?"

"There was no need to hunt all over creation for a sample of Doris's handwriting, Trudy. It was right there on the package."

"Of course it was. She addressed it. You're good!" And I'm stupid.

"But I'm afraid my other conclusion is troublesome."

"What's that?"

"That whoever did kill her was someone at the Burkhalter house."

"And you've based this on . . . ?"

"Obviously, somebody, somehow, got rid of all the rest of Karen Willard's things," she said.

"Assuming that Karen Willard did not actually leave and take her things with her," I said.

"Of course she didn't," Miss Sarah said. "It had to be somebody who thought he knew which of the things at the Burkhalter house were Karen's, because whoever it was took those things away, trying to make it look like Karen had run off. The things that were left behind — the things Doris mailed to Karen Willard's family — were things that could easily have belonged to Doris. They're the kinds of things a man wouldn't be likely to be sure about — Alvin, or Kenneth, or even Donnie."

"That makes a lot of sense, Miss Sarah." I remembered Doris Burkhalter saying the sweater of Karen's she'd boxed up and mailed was like one she had. "You and I are seeing that in the same light and, as a matter of fact, we already have two confessions from assorted Burkhalters. From a police standpoint, though, we could use some evidence. You don't happen to have any of that, do you?"

"Not yet. I haven't got it all completely sorted in my mind, but once we know where to look we should be able to find evidence. Don't you think so? Fingerprints and handwriting, for instance. Once you have fingerprints or handwriting to compare to those on the note instead of . . ."

"Miss Sarah, I hate to interrupt, but I have to point out that writing a note is one thing and killing somebody is something else. We can't afford to assume that whoever wrote it is the killer."

"But it would be progress to identify that person, wouldn't it?"

"It would be progress," I agreed.

"Good. What would you say if I told you I think I know who wrote that note?"

"I'd caution you against jumping to conclusions."

"Of course," she said. Then she sighed. "It would be so convenient if we could blame it on Donnie," Miss Sarah said.

"You mean because he's dead?"

"Yes. Instead of causing more pain."

"Even if he didn't really do it?"

"Of course not," she bristled at the thought. "But if the killer is still alive after all these years, he or she is no longer the person who killed Karen Willard. A murder conviction would be convicting somebody who no longer exists."

"I understand," I said. Hen had said almost the same thing, but I thought he was just teasing me. I thought of Alvin Burkhalter's confession and his about-face in lifestyle.

"Well. You can come get the yearbooks whenever you like. I asked the library to get me a book on handwriting analysis and Julie Todd will be bringing it by this afternoon, so if you time your visit right we can have a party."

When we disconnected, impressed with Miss Sarah's ability to look at what we had and draw reasonable conclusions from it, I was suddenly anxious to get to the station and take another look at everything myself.

I spread everything we had out on a table. What I found supported all of Miss Sarah's conclusions.

Comparing reports, I confirmed that there were no shoes with the body and none with the things Doris Burkhalter mailed to the Willards. The lack of shoes indicated that Karen had not walked away from the Burkhalter house. It also shot down Kenneth's story — not that his story had much going for it in the first place. The absence of shoes suggested that Karen had, as she had intended, gone back to the Burkhalter house and taken off her shoes so she could lie down with her headache. It did not suggest that she had gone on a tearing fit, created the mess, and written the note. Instead, then and there, somebody had killed her and tried to make it look like she'd gone away on purpose.

From what we'd learned at my party at the hospital, it seemed likely that it was Kenneth who had put the body in the refrigerator. I believed that Eric and Eddie recognized the truck, and there was no doubt that Kenneth had that truck and was later getting to Marie's house than he should have been.

But since he and Alvin both seemed to believe the other had killed her, I suspected neither of them had.

Back up. Break the loop. Think outside the box. Look at the evidence again — the reports, the box of Karen's things, the note.

Wait a minute! There was something else missing besides shoes, something that should unquestionably have been there, something important, something that called for an explanation.

Calling on my memory and the detailed information about the state of the body and what had been contained in the refrigerator, I knew who had killed Karen. Not only that, I had the answer to the question that had seemed unanswerable. I knew why. Proof? That was another thing. Good Lord! Proof! That was what Miss Sarah was up to.

I hightailed it to the hospital.

Chapter 25

The woman at the reception desk told me I'd find Miss Sarah in the solarium and that she had another guest. She was telling me how well Miss Sarah was coming along when I rudely turned away, half panicked over what scheme that dauntless old woman might have hatched.

A broad hallway leads to the double doors that open into the solarium. As I approached, I could see Miss Sarah, seated facing the door. She was talking to someone who was seated, back to the hallway. They held a book between them. Miss Sarah gave a quick jerk of her head when she saw me. I took it for a warning. I stopped outside the door where I could watch and listen.

"You were always such a pretty girl," Miss Sarah said.

A sardonic laugh and, "Was I? I don't remember," in a raspy voice I recognized as Julie Todd's.

My blood ran cold at Miss Sarah's next words. "Even in that other life, so long ago, you had a strong, clear, distinctive handwriting."

"What made you take an interest in handwriting?" Julie asked.

Miss Sarah answered obliquely. "You can tell so much about people from the way they write."

"I've read some of those books," Julie said. "If you make tight lower loops it means you had a dark relationship with your daddy. If you cram your words together it means you're impulsive. You don't believe in that garbage, do you?"

"Oh, no, not that. I do see why people want to believe it's significant, since everybody's handwriting is so individual, but I think it's more likely to be arthritis or affectation than attitudes about one's father that determine how a person's handwriting looks. You can tell whether somebody is careful or careless, neat or sloppy, even whether they want people to be able to read what they've written. I do believe everyone's handwriting is unique. So do the police, you know."

Did I imagine an edge in Julie's raspy voice when she said, "Are you working undercover for the police now? I wouldn't think Ogeechee would need or be able to afford undercover cops, but I had been wondering, with the kinds of books you and Lulu Huckabee have been asking for."

Miss Sarah darted me a glance but kept Julie's attention focused on the book by turning a page.

" 'To my favorite guy — just kidding — lucky Julie,' " Julie read aloud. " 'Your platonic friend, Peggy Bartlett.' She always had a crush on Donnie. Here's another one 'You'll go far — but

281

don't go too far, lover boy.' Wally was getting a little risqué with his sophisticated teenage humor," she added, no longer reading.

"Oh look, here's yours," Miss Sarah said. " 'Love, always. Julie Todd.' Simple and tasteful." I could detect a sad, gently teasing note in her voice, but I doubted that Julie could appreciate it. The teasing note disappeared with her next words. "I imagine you've heard the police have a note that was allegedly written by Karen Willard all those years ago, saying she was leaving town."

"Allegedly," Julie said, without emphasis. "How did the police get hold of that note after all this time?"

"Doris Burkhalter sent it to Karen's family, along with some other things of Karen's. It's ironic — but good, appropriate, providential — that it will help catch Karen's killer, when probably all Doris intended was to make the poor girl feel guilty about leaving Donnie."

"Did that note say she was leaving town?" Julie challenged.

"Now that you mention it, it doesn't. Not specifically. Everybody just assumed that's what it meant, but no, Julie, that's not what it said, not exactly."

"What did it say, exactly?" Julie asked.

"Let me think, now," Miss Sarah said. "I don't have a copy of it, but I believe the exact words were 'the wedding is off.' "

"The wedding is off," Julie repeated. "That

doesn't sound a lot like 'I'm leaving town' to me. Why did people think it meant she was leaving?"

"I suppose they just naturally drew that conclusion because Karen Willard was never seen again."

"I suppose." A change in rhythm and tone. "Well, this has been fascinating, Miss Sarah. You sure did take me by surprise with that old yearbook. Took me back to an unhappy time in my life. Could you let me borrow it? Trade you for the handwriting books?"

"No, I don't think so, Julie. Doris trusted me with this book, and it's precious to her," Miss Sarah said. "I couldn't let you have it without asking her first. I'm sorry."

"All right, then."

Julie rose and turned to go. When she caught sight of me, she looked startled, then she turned angrily back toward Miss Sarah. "What are you trying to do?"

Miss Sarah's false look of innocence was quickly replaced by fear as Julie advanced on her. Miss Sarah grabbed on to the armrests of her chair, dodging as best she could when Julie snatched the yearbook away from her and swung it wildly.

"Julie! Stop!" I yelled. "What are you doing?"

Julie abandoned her attack on Miss Sarah and turned to me, the wild look in her eye matching her wild movements. Like a trapped animal, she seemed bent only on getting past me. She threw the book at me and grabbed up a reading lamp from the nearby table, brandishing it overhead.

"Julie, wait!" I yelled. "Calm down! Stop!"

But she didn't wait, calm down, or stop. She charged. I had instinctively raised my arm, my left arm, to protect myself from the lamp, so it was my poor vulnerable left wrist that took the blow. Of course it would be my left wrist. Of course it would be a lamp. Julie ran.

The commotion had attracted the attention of one of the nurses, who stood wide-eyed and paralyzed as Julie ran past her and Miss Sarah and I yelled. Finally, Miss Sarah shushed me and calmly, but authoritatively, instructed the nurse to call an ambulance. When she nodded dumbly and went to do that, I fumbled out my cell phone and called Hen.

They took me to the hospital emergency room in an ambulance. Miss Sarah summoned the full force of her personality and managed to convince them that my welfare depended on her accompanying me. That was probably the truth. The whole time my wrist was being re–x-rayed and re-set I amused myself by giving Miss Sarah Kennedy a piece of my mind. It gave me something to think about besides the pain.

She took it pretty well, no doubt making allowances for my injured status and her own certain knowledge that she'd been foolish and in the wrong.

"I wouldn't have kept on pushing her if I hadn't known you were right there," she said, sucking up as much as she was ever likely to.

I groaned and covered my eyes with my good arm.

"She did write that note, Trudy. You don't have to be an expert to tell that the capital T and those distinctive double-d's are the same in her signature in the yearbook as they are in the note."

I groaned again.

"You're pouting."

"Am not."

"Then what are you doing?"

"Okay, maybe I am pouting. I had realized that if Julie killed her, everything made sense. I'm jealous that you came up with evidence before I did."

We kept that up the whole time the medical staff were tending to me. I think they piddle around, not hurrying, to make sure you aren't going to pass out or anything before they let you leave, so it was probably close to two hours before they started talking about letting me leave, and then we had to discuss whether I could drive myself or should wait for somebody to give me a ride. That debate was brought to an end by the appearance of Hen, who knocked me for my second loop of the day.

"What are you doing here?" I asked.

"Came over with Julie Todd," he said.

"That's nice of both of you, but if she thinks

an apology will get her out of trouble, she's got another think coming. Hen, it was Julie . . ."

He shook his head and held up a hand like a traffic cop, to make me stop.

"I know," he said. "She's left another note."

"What?"

"She's down the hall in a room of her own. By the time I caught up with her at her house, she had emptied her medicine cabinet down her throat."

Chapter 26

One of the best times in my life as a police officer is usually immediately after closing a case, especially a challenging case, which this one surely was. As with completing any task, there's a sense of achievement. Particularly, for me, in this case, there was a sense of validation in my decision to be a police officer, an assurance that it's something I do well. Even when the outcome isn't necessarily happy, I have to believe it's better to know the truth about things.

Julie Todd never recovered from the lethal combination of drugs she ingested (technically something like "cardiac toxicity brought on by an overdose of the tricyclic antidepressants amitryptiline, desipramine, and nortryptiline") after her confrontation with Miss Sarah and me, and the looming revelation of the secret she'd lived with all those years. She died at the hospital only a few hours after she was brought in.

True to the code of the Pittmans, the *Beacon* handled the news in a way that balanced the public's right to know with the individual's right to privacy, treating Julie's death not as a news item or a lurid solution to an old crime but in a brief obituary:

Juliette Taylor Todd, 51, only child of the late Wilbur and Wilette March Todd, died at Cowart Memorial Hospital June 28. Miss Todd, a lifelong resident of Ogeechee, was a graduate of Ogeechee High School and Georgia Southern College and a valued supporter of the Ogeechee library. There are no surviving family members. Funeral services will be held Sunday at 2 P.M. at the First Baptist Church of Ogeechee, the Rev. Randall Tarver officiating. Burial will be with her parents at the Sandy Oak Cemetery.

With the closure of the Karen Willard-Julie Todd case, Hen was free to join his family in Florida. He left me (okay, me and Dwight) in charge of law and order. He was so eager to leave he didn't even pretend to worry about leaving the town in my hands, or "hand," even though he couldn't resist making that feeble joke.

Crime-fighting immediately snapped back to what passes for normal in Ogeechee.

Hen can't have been far across the state line when Dwight got to go break up a fight at the Jive Joint and I took a call about a bank robber wearing a black plastic trash bag for a disguise. The tiny eighty-five-year-old woman who committed the crime — so tiny that the trash bag did cover her completely — was pitifully easy to catch since I had a pretty good description to go on and she was on foot. I caught up with her while she was stuffing the trash bag into her purse with the money and the water pistol she'd used in the hold-up. She chattily, and without any sign of embarrassment or remorse, confessed on the spot that it had seemed like a good way to supplement her "so-sha-curity" and it always looked so easy on television. I had to arrest her and get in touch with social services and her family, and I managed to do it with one hand.

Aunt Lulu had come back home when Hen joined Teri and Delcie, and she and Miss Sarah got right down to comparing notes about the Willard case. I had given Miss Sarah a copy of the "Karen Willard" note for a souvenir, and the two of them, helped along with the library books Julie Todd had delivered, started delving into handwriting analysis. Aunt Lulu didn't even try to conceal her chagrin at having let Miss Sarah get ahead of her on the police work.

I was trying to get into a Hen-like state and imagine how I could make a funny story out of the trash bag bandit, instead of the truly heartbreaking story it was, when I got a call from the Claxton officer I had talked to early in the investigation in an attempt to identify our corpse.

His news was that when they looked into it, they found out that Loyce Lewis had married and come back to Claxton under the name of Loyce Oglesby, so she couldn't be who I was looking for but thanks for asking since it helped them close a case. I felt good about that for Loyce's sake as well as my own. And then I started wondering if I should have alerted the other towns I'd queried that I had identified my corpse and they could quit checking their old cases. And then I decided to leave them alone and let them keep on working on them. If they were working on them. I figured it was too much to hope that there would be other happy endings like Loyce's, but you can never tell.

Alvin Burkhalter had recovered enough that he was home. Miss Sarah Kennedy was home and walking better every time I saw her. Doris Burkhalter seemed to be relaxed in a way I'd never known her. Those were happy things, but seemed more like beginnings than endings.

Oddly, the upshot of all that had been going on was that instead of feeling satisfied and like I'd done good work (which I undeniably had; even Hen said so), I felt melancholy. That's the only word for it.

I went home and scooped up a couple of cats and sat on the kitchen stoop. Wide awake but trance-like, I watched the white moonlight shine and shift, making mysterious patterns out of the familiar landscape of my yard, my trees, my bushes, my woods. Even my fingers, my feet, my cats, looked unfamiliar.

In a city, or a suburb of a city, you're never alone, never quiet. Behind my house, at the end of a short street on the edge of a small town, I could be alone, and quiet.

The moon, we learn in school, has no light of its own. It merely seems to shine because it reflects the light of the sun. As the ghostly moon-light played tricks with my topographical landscape, making strange forms out of the familiar, so the events of the past few days worked on my emotional landscape. I saw things, myself included, in light reflected by the people and relationships I'd been so wrapped up in.

I couldn't see myself marrying Phil Pittman, even though, like Julie Todd, I found myself the object of family expectations — both his family and mine, apparently. Since Phil and I hadn't been torn by passion, had in fact become friends because of propinquity, I felt sure we'd be able to remain friends. My brief marriage had brought me passion and then great pain. I wondered if it had worked like an inoculation, keeping me from feeling that kind of passion or that kind of pain again. Did I need passion? Did Phil?

Without Phil, though, would I wind up like Dinah Willard, or Marie Burkhalter? Or Julie Todd? Marie, at least, seemed to have some self-respect and enjoyed life.

I had some serious thinking to do about my life and where it was going, and no one to talk to about it — not Miss Sarah, not Aunt Lulu. Not Phil. Certainly not Hen. Laughing at myself as I cuddled a reluctant cat, I wept passionate tears at the idea that I felt no passion in my life. This is where being an eccentric old lady starts, Trudy, sitting alone and cuddling your cat. I hoped I'd turn out more like Marie Burkhalter than Julie Todd. I wondered how much control I would have over that.

Was it sheer contrariness (as Hen would have said) or something more admirable (as I'd like to believe) that made me decide to attend the services for both Julie Todd and Karen Willard? I certainly didn't expect either to cheer me up.

Chapter 27

My reasons for doing anything are often complex, not to say confused. So my reasons for deciding to attend the services for Julie Todd and Karen Willard weren't entirely straightforward or clear, even to me.

Without being able to say why, I knew I'd been instrumental in Julie Todd's death and somehow felt implicated. Too, she was intimately bound to Karen Willard, whom I had never known as a living person, but in whom I had become very interested. So the two services were, in some complicated ways, linked to each other in my mind.

Julie Todd's service was much as I'd expected — gloomy, predictable, and fairly depressing. Even though the *Beacon* had been discreet, most people who knew Julie knew something of the circumstances of her death, and that alone would have been enough to cast an additional pall over what is never a truly joyous occasion.

The service was reasonably well attended, however. Julie's parents, not that long gone from community life, had been generous supporters of the church, and Julie herself had been well known, even if she was generally an object of curiosity instead of affection. Some people may have come hoping to learn more details about Julie's death than the *Beacon* had told them.

The pastor was experienced enough to be able to put together a funeral service for a controversial figure who had died in controversial circumstances. It was brief, neutral, efficient.

Calling on surprising reservoirs of compassion and physical strength, Alvin and Doris Burkhalter showed up. Kenneth and Marie were there, too. They'd been Julie's high school friends, after all.

Aunt Lulu and Miss Sarah came together, but since I was feeling uncharacteristically unchatty, I barely even spoke to either of them. Without any kind of reception afterwards for family, we all just drifted away. Perhaps everybody else was mulling over the recent upheavals, as I was. The effect was depressing.

Naturally, I found comparisons and contrasts with the Willard service, which took place just two days later.

Cremation isn't the usual route in our part of the country, where a lot of people believe in the literal resurrection of the body on Judgment Day and don't want to take the responsibility for sending anybody into eternity without all the body parts. In spite of that, in the case of Karen Willard, cremation was the obvious choice. Dinah had arranged for Karen's remains to be placed near her parents, near where Dinah herself would someday rest.

"Considering how long Karen was gone, I thought about keeping the ashes in an urn at home, sort of a homecoming," Dinah told me when she called with the details about the service, "but this is better. Mama would have liked it better. And Darrell pointed out I'd be likely to lose her again if I had her at home. That kid's growing on me."

There was a smaller crowd at the memorial service for Karen Willard than there had been at Julie Todd's service. It had been a long time since Karen had been a part of anybody's life, and Dinah was not a very active community member, either. Besides a scattering of people who had known Karen and Dinah's parents, only the Methodist minister, Dinah, Darrell and his parents, and I gathered to pay our respects, to Dinah, if not to Karen.

The young minister, Reverend Tucker, was doing his best, but it seemed obvious to me that this occasion was unprecedented in his experience and he was having to figure things out as he went along. Even the minister at Julie Todd's service had had an easier time of it. It seemed to me that Reverend Tucker clutched the United Methodist Book of Worship as much for security as for the outline of the service and the scriptures he'd use.

Dinah had gone to Reverend Tucker mostly out of a reversion to her early training, because the family had been Methodist, although she herself had long since given up church for the society of the Internet, and she told me he'd been kind and thoughtful about trying to do what she wanted. He'd asked about the circumstances and about her sister, and done his best to find appropriate things to say. His reading of the thirteenth chapter from the book of First Corinthians, "Though I speak with the tongues of men and of angels, and have not love, I am become as sounding brass or a tinkling cymbal," may be conventional, but it took on special overtones in this case, considering that it was love — misguided and proprietary — that led to Karen's death. On second thought, maybe I was underrating the minister. Maybe he knew what he was doing — or had divine guidance in his choice of scriptures. If Julie Todd had understood the kind of love he was reading about, Karen Willard wouldn't have wound up in a refrigerator.

When Reverend Tucker moved on to "Let not your heart be troubled," I threw a glance in Dinah's direction. She was solemn, and appeared to be thoughtful, but not troubled. Her breathing was deep and even. I got the feeling that although her grief was well under control she wasn't necessarily buying in to what the pastor was selling.

The reverend gave us a mercifully brief and carefully worded message, designed to comfort without raising troubling issues of whether the deceased or her family had ever professed a Christian faith. When he began reading the twenty-third Psalm, "The Lord is my shepherd," I drew a breath of relief. The whole thing, all fifteen minutes of it, had been well done.

Dinah had wanted to have a small gathering after the graveside service to add a little more to the ceremony of finally saying goodbye to her sister, so we adjourned to the Willard home for light refreshments — pretty little pimiento and cheese sandwiches, Bisquick-sausage balls, and sugared pecans — which the United Methodist Women had prepared and young Mrs. Reverend Tucker had arranged on cut glass platters.

"The service was very nice," I said to Dinah, who sat in an armchair that hadn't even been visible under the stack of books the last time I'd been in the room, safely out of the way of the milling guests. Keeping the oxygen apparatus safe from others, and keeping others safe from it, would be a real social challenge. No wonder she'd turned to the Internet.

I had been looking forward to going to Dinah's house again and being reminded that I might not have clear title to the Messiest Housekeeper in the Universe crown, but I was disappointed. I took a chair between Dinah and the refreshment table, so I could have a solid place to set my cup since my reintroduction to a cast had increased my clumsiness quotient all over again.

"It was just right," she said. "The poor preacher was under more stress than anybody else, but he did just fine, don't you think?"

"Just fine," I agreed.

"You're probably wondering why I even bothered with it."

"No," I said. "I think the psychologists would say you needed closure."

"That's one way to put it, I guess. Somehow or other I felt like I owed it to Karen because we'd thought so poorly of her all this time. And I know Mama and Daddy would have liked it."

"That's two good reasons," I said. "I meant it when I said it was nice."

"I know you did. I thought so, too. I don't know as I believe it makes any difference to Karen, but it has made a difference to me. It feels like closing a door on unfinished business and opening a new door. Maybe that's what the shrinks mean when they say closure, after all. It may sound funny, but all this uproar over Karen, finding out she was murdered and you catching her killer, after all this time, has had some pretty good fallout for me."

"Such as?"

"Getting the place cleaned up feels good. Hadn't wanted to waste what energy I have on cleaning house." She smiled. "But I'm learning to ask for help."

"Did you go to all this trouble just so you could have this little party here?" I asked, looking through the clean front window to the tidy front yard and trying to match her mood.

"One thing led to another," Dinah said, looking around with a satisfied smile. "Sort of a reverse domino effect, things coming up right instead of falling over. When Darrell and I started looking for Karen's things we did a lot of cleaning and rearranging at the same time. We found a lot of trash, so we trashed it. That made a big difference, made it a lot easier for me to get around in the house with the Loch Ness monster, here" — she gave a shake to the plastic breathing tube — "without all that clutter. I'm not up for any homemaking award, mind you, and the mess'll probably all come back, but it does look nice right now, doesn't it?"

"It sure does. I didn't want to mention it, but I hardly recognized the place. It made a big difference just to be able to see out of the windows."

"This is more like Mama kept it," Dinah continued. "When you've got four people living in a place, you can't let it go the way I did. Living by yourself, you just don't notice."

"I know what you mean," I said.

"And then, once we started looking at all that stuff, I realized it wasn't all trash. Darrell and me, we had us a good time figuring out what to do with the stuff that still had some good in it. His mama works for social services and she knows of people who need things, so we gave away a lot of clothes and furniture that way. Old stuff, but if you're hard up you don't care. And we sneaked some of the magazines into libraries and nursing homes and clinics, any public place where there's a waiting room." She grinned at me. "We didn't ask if they wanted 'em, and we made sure none of 'em had my name and address on 'em, just took for granted people in the waitin' rooms would like to see something different. Gave some books to the library. I tell you what, Trudy, we got an education about how many kinds of places and people can find something to do with old second-hand goods."

I felt like I should be taking notes.

I looked over to where Darrell appeared to be teaching Reverend Tucker some flourish on the Internet. His parents were quietly talking with an older couple near the punchbowl, which held a nauseating punch made out of lime sherbet, some kind of fruit juice, and ginger ale. Thank goodness Mrs. Tucker and the UMW had provided coffee.

From my strategically-placed chair, I reached my good right hand out for a pimiento-cheese sandwich.

"Turns out I'm not as hard up as you might think to look at me," Dinah said.

"Umm?" I asked encouragingly around a bite of pimiento-cheese.

"I'd never thought about it much, never needed much, but our rootin' around in these old chests and boxes turned up some valuables."

"Really? Antiques?"

"Matter of fact, yes. Sold a desk of Daddy's and some of Mama's jewelry to an antique dealer and next week we're going to go to that big flea market in Savannah and try our luck with some other stuff."

"You're branching out all over the place. Better watch out or it'll cut into your Internet time." I'd finished my sandwich, and Mrs. Tucker, who had been circulating with the coffee, refilled my coffee cup.

"Well, yes. That. I'd been using Nessie here as an excuse to stay at home, but now with Darrell willing to help me, it looks like I'm finding excuses to get out. He may not look like an angel, Trudy, but he is. I can't tell you what a difference he's made in my enjoyment of life."

Darrell didn't look angelic, there at the computer, one hand pointing to something on the screen while the other manipulated a mouse, but maybe I'm not clear on what an angel looks like.

"I've talked things over with Darrell and his parents, and we're going to kind of adopt each other," Dinah said. "Like I'm some kind of an aunt or godmother or something. They aren't hard up, Darrell's folks. I mean they can afford all that computer stuff, but they aren't what you'd call rich, either, and since I don't have any people of my own left, they're going to let me team up with them and see what we can do for him."

"Dinah, I'm impressed." I took my eyes from Darrell and smiled at Dinah. "What a generous idea."

"Oh, no! I'm getting, not giving. Darrell's going to get responsibilities out of the deal. He's got to keep his grades up. But if he does that and gets into a college, I'll cover it. Besides, he's earned it, helping me clean up and all. I found some stock certificates I never even knew I had." She shook her head in wonderment.

"Sounds like a pretty good deal."

"For both of us, it is. Part of the deal is that he'll keep an eye on the cemetery plot after I'm gone. I've done the legal stuff so they won't try to talk anybody into believing what I'd want is an expensive casket and all that garbage. I'll be cremated and go next to Karen."

"You aren't going any time soon, are you?" I asked.

"Not if I can help it. Truth is, Trudy, I'm getting more of a kick out of life now than I have in I don't know when."

"Good for you."

"Good for Darrell. Havin' him around has shown me there's more to life than a computer terminal. He's a good boy. I'll want to stick around and see what kind of a difference I can make to him."

So, my trip to Bristol wasn't depressing. In fact, it seemed to have turned me around. As I drove back home, I was thinking, oddly, that Karen Willard's memorial service had provided some closure for me as well as for Dinah, some healing. My wrist had had a setback, but the doctors didn't foresee any complications beyond the double stint in a cast, so I felt even that was healing. And I felt like I was putting some things to rest and was ready to look ahead. Like Dinah, I could say I felt like I could close a door on old business and open a door to new.

Chapter 28

I had decided I wanted to cook supper for Phil when he finally got home, so we could have a long talk, but the difficulties of using a can opener and the challenge of cooking while keeping my cast dry convinced me to let Kathi do the cooking instead. I didn't want to eat in a public place, though, in case our conversation took a turn I didn't want the whole town to be in on. Kathi doesn't normally do take-out, but I'm a good customer and when I brought my own containers for her to put the food in — for convenience, not because I thought I could fool Phil — we worked it out.

I set the table for two, in the dining room, not on the porch over the dry well. I used Grandma's good china and silverware, and I lit the candles I had stuck in two of Grandma's tarnished silver candlesticks, but of course it was the food Phil noticed.

"Mmm, pot roast!" he said. I'd picked pot roast because Kathi comes nearer getting it like Grandma used to than I've ever been able to do. It's one of my favorite things. With rice, plenty of dark brown gravy, green beans, and okra (you always get two vegetables at Kathi's), it was the ideal homecoming meal. Pecan pie would come later. "Road food is good for a while," he said, "but there is no way you can beat home cookin'."

"That's what I always say," I said.

As soon as we'd filled our plates, naturally, he wanted the inside story on Karen Willard.

"I won't ask you to start at the beginning. I've got a lot of that already. What I want to know is how you knew it was Julie Todd who killed her."

"What was it Sherlock Holmes said about the curious incident of the dog in the night?" I returned, feeling very smug.

"Was it something about how the curious part was that the dog hadn't done anything?"

"Quite so, my dear Watson, or at least almost quite so. The point for Sherlock was that something that should have happened hadn't happened. And what finally clicked for me was that something that should have been with Karen Willard's body wasn't."

Phil dug into his pot roast instead of begging me to explain. Somewhat miffed, I took my time awkwardly cutting my meat, tender though it was, before I explained anyway.

"I was a young woman once," I said. "And I had an engagement ring. The engagement ring was the most precious thing I owned. In that respect, I think I was a perfectly normal young woman. Karen Willard was planning a wedding and had just had a wedding shower. Her engagement ring should have been on her finger. Since it wasn't, there had to be an explanation.

It wasn't on the body or with the things Doris Burkhalter returned to the Willards. Where was it? Actually, the better question was why she wasn't wearing it."

"Why couldn't she have taken it off to wash her hands?" I was pleased to see that Phil could quit eating long enough to ask.

"She could have, but then it would have been around somewhere. I realized that if Julie Todd had killed Karen, it would explain everything. The way I piece it together, Julie was trashing the shower gifts when Karen unexpectedly came in on her and she lashed out with whatever was at hand, like she did at me at the hospital. Karen fell. Julie took the ring she thought should have been hers, and left."

"Well, yes. Daddy says she always was quick tempered."

"The community was surprisingly understanding of that quick temper. She must have been unstable all her life. She even left town for a while after Donnie's death. She went to a treatment facility."

"What was she treated for? Quick temper?"

"What they used to call a nervous breakdown. Which could have looked like a fondness for throwing hissy fits. They gave her medication and calmed her down and sent her back home. She'd been taking medication ever since then — maybe even before."

"And that's what she used to kill herself?"

"Yes. When she left me and Miss Sarah at the

hospital, she went home and swallowed everything in her medicine cabinet. She left a note — another note — in that same unmistakable handwriting that hadn't changed much in thirty years."

"Belated remorse? You'd think she'd have come to terms with what she did a long time ago."

"No, not remorse exactly. The note said she hadn't known Karen was dead. Remember, Donnie died that day, so Julie managed to believe that Karen just left, maybe that she'd scared her off. And now, learning that she was a killer, and knowing it was all going to come out probably pushed her over the edge. She probably stayed pretty close to the edge all the time, even with medication, and then when a body turned up in that old refrigerator and we put Karen's name to it, Julie must have started losing her shaky grasp on reality. As far as I can tell, she died not knowing how it got there."

"How did it get there?"

"It's a tangled web. Alvin Burkhalter bundled up the body and cleaned up the house. He admitted that to me after Julie died and he could quit thinking Donnie had killed her. Then, Kenneth Burkhalter disposed of the body, thinking his daddy had killed her and stashed the body in the truck till he could get rid of it. Think of the strain they've all been under all this time!"

"Serves 'em right for trying to cover things up."

"Maybe."

"So you're satisfied it's all straightened out and you've got to the bottom of it?" Phil had managed to clean up his plate around questioning me, and he began loading up on seconds.

"As much as I can be. Alvin and Kenneth had already confessed to their part, remember. It just didn't make sense without the main part, Julie's part. And once we knew what to look for, the experts confirmed Julie's handwriting on that original note. Even better, they found her fingerprints on it. Now, those teenagers that came to the Burkhalter house after that football game could have handled the note, but Julie wasn't with them. The only way her fingerprints could have been on it was if she had written it."

"That's pretty strong, but still circumstantial," Phil said.

"Yes. But the ring was the clincher. She still had that ring. She made things easy for us by setting it out on her bedside table with all the empty pill bottles. As close as she would come to a confession."

"No kidding!" Phil was so amazed he forgot to chew. "How'd you know it was the ring?"

I had to swallow, even though there was nothing to swallow. "It had been engraved. It had said 'Donnie and Karen.' Very traditional. But Julie had scratched out Karen's name."

Phil returned most of his attention to finishing off his second helpings, but he watched me as he ate. "She had a sad life, didn't she?"

"Julie? Uh huh. In a lot of ways, I guess she

did. Seems like she could have gotten over Donnie, but you never know about people, do you?"

He shook his head in agreement, swallowed, and leaned back. "Just for instance, I never knew you were such a good cook."

"Thanks, but I'm not. I'll come clean. It's from Kathi's."

"I should have known. Not that you weren't a good cook. But that Kathi is. You know."

"I know. It'll help you look forward to dessert. I got a whole pie, and unless you want your piece wrecked, maybe you'd better come help me get it out of the pie plate."

By the time we'd dished up pie and poured out coffee, and settled down again, there being very few questions remaining about Karen Willard and Julie Todd, our conversation took a different turn.

"When you go off to these newspaper conventions," I asked, "are there newspaperwomen as well as men?"

Phil paused, fork halfway to open mouth. "Are you on one of your feminist kicks? Yes, there are. I won't say they're represented in numbers proportionate to the general population, but there are newspaperwomen. They used to call them newshens. To balance the newshawks, I guess. Don't start."

"No, that's not why I asked. I was just wondering."

"Where is this conversation going? It doesn't

sound like you're jealous." Was he trying to sound wistful?

"No. Not jealous. But I was thinking it must be great to be able to talk to people — men and women — who can get excited about what you're excited about. Passionate."

"Yes." There was a cautious note in his voice. "There's always an atmosphere of excitement and a special kind of camaraderie at things like that. That's why there are so many jokes about convention-goers. The rules are off! Nobody here knows me! Whoopee! Are you sure you aren't jealous?"

"Maybe I am. Jealous of that kind of camaraderie."

"Oh. Not of the hypothetical women?"

"Maybe it just comes down to the fact that Vidalia Onions and Boiled Peanuts don't mix," I said.

That stopped him. He actually put his fork back on his plate with a piece of pie still on it. "I'm not understanding much of this conversation."

"Not a thing?"

"Not much after the newshens and the newshawks, to tell the truth, and since I said that, it probably doesn't count."

"Maybe I'm talking in code."

"You gonna translate for me?" He picked up the fork again, tentatively, I thought.

"I would if I could. Vidalia Onions are known for their adaptability, and because of this people sometimes expect too much of them." For some reason, Phil still looked confused. I tried to clarify. "Like onion ice cream."

He put his fork down and straightened his glasses, no doubt hoping that what I was saying would come into focus. "I hope you realize that you aren't making a lot of sense."

"Oh, Phil, I'm just miserable, that's all. My arm hurts and this cast is driving me crazy and I'm . . ."

"Let me see if I can help."

He took my arm and began running his fingernails back and forth across my cast. You wouldn't think it would be possible to feel something like that, through the cotton padding and hard acrylic cast, but you'd be wrong. The vibration of his touch somehow reached and eased my pain through that hard shell.

I began to tell him about the horrorscopes. He laughed at Hen's Catfish and Mrs. Riggs's Sugar Cane. He nodded intelligently when I explained how I'd decided it was Julie Todd and not Dinah Willard who must be Kudzu. Kudzu is known to be undisciplined, but what appears to be random behavior masks a deep-rooted instinct for survival and a need to dominate the landscape. Everybody knows kudzu is wild and totally uncontrollable.

"So the idea is that you're a Vidalia Onion," he said when I'd finished my list, still making my arm vibrate.

"That's right."

"And I'm a Boiled Peanut?"

"Uh huh. That feels good."

"Good. Do you know of any Vidalia onion-boiled peanut recipes?" he asked.

"Uh uh."

"Well, then, I guess we'll have to make some up."

We discussed some of the possibilities. Boiled peanut butter and onion sandwiches? Pureed boiled peanut and onion dip? Peanut and onion sauce for . . .

It turned out to be a very nice evening, and I was glad we weren't at Kathi's. I even began to re-think some of my ideas about passion. Vidalia Onions are nothing if not adaptable.

About the Author

Linda Berry's roots on both sides of her family are firmly planted in small-town Georgia, so it isn't surprising that she calls on that heritage in developing the Trudy Roundtree mysteries, making liberal use of family quirks, family stories, and family storytellers — especially a police-officer cousin.

Her father worked for an oil company when she was growing up and the family moved frequently. The best guess (compiled during a family storytelling session) is that Linda lived in 64 different places in 41 towns and attended 21 schools before graduating from high school in Thornton, Colorado.

She attended the University of Colorado on a Boettcher Scholarship and earned a B.A. in French and English with a minor in Education. She later earned a Master of Humanities degree with an emphasis in theater and English literature.

She worked for several years at the California Law Revision Commission in Stanford, California, and later as editor of a newspaper for the Colorado and Intermountain Tennis Associations. Freelance publication credits include short fiction for children and adults, poetry, plays, craft articles, church curriculum, and a newspaper entertainment column.

She is married to Jerry Berry and they have two sons, Jeffery and Michael.